SECRETS OF THE GREEK
REVIVAL

The Mystery House Series, Book One

Eva Pohler

Green Press

This book is a work of fiction. The characters, happenings, and dialogue came from the author's imagination and are not real.

SECRETS OF THE GREEK REVIVAL: THE MYSTERY HOUSE, BOOK ONE. Copyright 2015 by Eva Pohler.
All rights reserved.
Cover Design by Keri Knutson

FIRST EDITION

Library of Congress Cataloging-in-Publication has been applied for

ISBN-13: 978-1522734994
ISBN-10: 1522734996

Chapter One: First Impressions

Ellen pulled up to the curb and took a deep breath. The September sun set behind the old house, framing it with a halo. Although the grass, the vines, and the one tree big tree out front were dead, there was something picturesque about the dilapidated building with its peeling yellow paint. Maybe it was Ellen's vision of what it once was—or of what it could, one day, be.

"So, what do you think?" she asked her two best friends. " Isn't it amazing?"

"Well, it looks a little more like a ruin than a fixer upper," Sue said from behind the driver's seat.

"That's why we can afford it." Ellen's stomach tightened as she turned to Tanya, who was sitting up front. She hadn't expected this outright rejection from Sue. "What do you think? Too much work?"

"I don't know, maybe," Tanya said in a lyrical voice that meant she was considering it. "I need to see the inside before I can get a good feel for it."

Although her best friends were opposites in every way— where Tanya was tall, thin, blonde, and blue-eyed, Sue was short, plump, brunette, and brown-eyed; where Tanya slanted toward liberalism, Sue slanted toward conservatism—if one wanted to do something, the other always, invariably, climbed on board.

Okay, maybe not *always, invariably*, but often.

Ellen, being in the middle of her two friends in size, color, *and* politics, was usually the odd woman out, but if she could get one of them on her side, there'd be a chance.

"Then let's go look inside." She stepped onto the street in the still hot air and gazed at the house as she waited for her friends.

Sue cracked open her car door but didn't get up. "Aren't we waiting on Paul?"

"He had to show another house at the last minute." Ellen dangled the key her husband had given her. "Come on. This will be fun."

Ellen hid her frustration with Sue as they made their way up the cracked sidewalk of the dilapidated two-story Greek revival, with its broken window and rotted siding. Of the three friends, Sue had been the one pushing the idea of doing something like this. For six months, *she'd* been the one saying they needed an adventure, now that they were all empty nesters. And if the adventure could make them extra money for more vacations (Sue was addicted to Disney cruises), all the better. So why was she frowning?

"You've got to admit that this house is a lot better than the one you showed us last month," Ellen said to Sue. "I mean, this one has *major* potential. Since it's right here on the edge of the historic King William district, it would make the perfect bed and breakfast. Downtown San Antonio is just a few blocks away. The river is right over there. It backs up to a wooded green belt and is on a much bigger lot than most of the other homes in this area. This is the perfect spot."

"So now we're running a bed and breakfast?" Sue's tone was laced with sarcasm.

"*Selling* a bed and breakfast," Ellen explained. "If that's what we want."

"I think it could be fun to run a bed and breakfast," Tanya said as they carefully took the rickety steps up to the front porch between what were once amazing columns now strangled with dead vines.

Ellen didn't want a long-term commitment, but she wanted to keep Tanya's support. "I'm open to that." She put the key into the lock. "I mean, we can at least consider it."

Sue looked up at the ceiling of the portico. "Are you sure this is safe? It looks like it could all come crashing down on top of us."

The columns were rotten, as were most of the boards beneath their feet. "The state of Texas wouldn't be showing it if it wasn't safe." Ellen looked up and saw three big holes.

"I think there's a bird living in there," Tanya said.

"The state of Texas?" Sue asked. "What do you mean?"

"The state owns it," Ellen said. "It's been pretty much vacant since the last owner died in 1994."

3

"Well, I can certainly see why," Sue said.

Tanya giggled. "Oh, come on. Give it a chance."

"Apparently the last owner had no one to leave it to and the mortgage had been paid," Ellen added. "And there was no will."

"That's strange," Sue said.

Ellen's heart ramped up as she opened the door. She'd been admiring this one for a few weeks on her way home from work and had been anxious to see the inside. Having already developed a strange attachment to this house, she hoped it wasn't going to be disappointing.

Why did she already care so much about this damn house?

Maybe it was because she had become desperate for a change. She longed for something new to fill the void that was now her life.

Oh, stop being so melodramatic, she told herself.

They entered a foyer with stairs to the second floor. Her heart felt tight, like it was going to burst, and she felt like she was floating outside of her body looking down from the ceiling at them. The three of them together made her think of a Fruit-of-the-Loom commercial. Tanya was the banana. Sue was the bunch of grapes. Ellen was the apple. Why was she thinking of this now? What was happening to her? This whole experience of going in together to buy a fixer-upper was surreal. Up until a few months ago, it had been nothing but talk. Were they really going to do this? Ellen felt a weight pushing her down until she was back inside her own body. Instead of relief, she found herself dizzy and unable to breathe.

She gulped in air and steadied her head with one hand.

"Are you okay?" Sue asked.

Ellen nodded and was finally able to take note of her surroundings. After blinking several more times, she was relieved to see the interior framing intact and most of the plaster still on the walls. It wasn't as bad as she had thought it would be. Her mind began to imagine the place restored and fully decorated—the eighties' wall paper and shiny brass fixtures replaced with paint and chrome.

"This is actually pretty nice in here," Tanya said. "I wonder why it hasn't sold yet."

"Well, now don't freak out," Ellen said. "The house has a reputation for being haunted."

Tanya and Sue gawked at one another.

"What do you mean *a reputation*?" Tanya asked. "Has something evil happened here? Was someone murdered here?"

"Now hold on, Tanya," Sue said. "Don't assume it's an evil ghost. It might be friendly." She turned to Ellen. "Tell us what you heard."

Ellen was pleased to see Sue's interest in the house piqued by the mention of a haunting. "The state realtor told Paul that every time they got close to selling this property, the owners bailed within three days after closing."

Sue's face lit up. "Did Paul get any more details? Did the buyers say what made them suspect a ghost was haunting this space?"

Ellen shook her head, though she was tempted to make something up, just to keep Sue on the hook. "They all thought they heard or saw something in the attic. Should we look around?"

"We might as well," Sue said. "If we do make this into a bed and breakfast, a ghost could attract more tourists. The Crocket Hotel does really well with its history of ghosts."

Ellen beamed. Sue was practically pulling out her wallet to buy, and she hadn't even seen the whole place. But now Tanya was the one frowning.

"What's wrong, Tanya?" Ellen asked.

"I'm not getting a good vibe," she said. "Did Paul say how many different buyers bailed? That concerns me."

Ellen had hoped neither would ask that question. "Um, six."

Tanya's eyes widened and her mouth fell open. "Six different buyers? And they all bailed within three days of closing?"

Ellen sucked in her lips and nodded. "But come on, guys. There's got to be a logical explanation. Paul says there's probably a draft in the attic that makes noises when the wind blows. He was supposed to be here today to check it out for us,

6

but he's really close to selling another property and had to meet the client for a second showing."

Tanya folded her arms. "Oh, come on. A draft wouldn't fool *six people*. That's odd. That's really odd."

Sue had already started the tour without them. She called to them from the front room. "Come check this out. The fireplace seems in excellent condition."

Ellen stepped into the living room and was pleased with what she saw. "The hardwood floors and crown molding are in good shape, too."

The room was empty except for a single painting over the mantle that had the look of a Victorian portrait. The subject of the painting was a beautiful young woman with dark eyes and dark curly hair and pale skin. She wore a red brocade jacket over a white dress, and one of her breasts was nearly exposed. The painting was both sensual and enigmatic, for the woman's expression was difficult to read.

"*You're* an art teacher, Ellen," Sue said. "Do you recognize that painter?"

"Just because I teach college art—part-time, mind you, as an adjunct—doesn't mean I'm aware of every painter who ever lived."

"I was just asking," Sue said. "Sounds like you might have a complex."

The truth was, Ellen's memory was failing her. She used to be able to name off all the great painters of the Renaissance, the Enlightenment, the Romantic Period, the Modern Period, the Post-Modern-Period, and so forth, but somewhere along the way, between the ages of forty-nine and fifty-five, only a few of her favorites remained accessible in her mind.

Tanya giggled, and Ellen ignored them as she continued to look around.

Beyond the living room through a pair of columns was a dining room with an old wooden table and four chairs. It led through to the kitchen at the back of the house, attached to a laundry and mud room. The cabinetry was falling apart and would have to be gutted, but the bones were good. She also found a half bath beneath the stairs and another full bath shared by two bedrooms. Although both bedrooms were vacant, there was an old trunk in the bathroom. Ellen lifted the lid to find it full of dust and cobwebs, but nothing else. Except for the crack in the mirror above the sink, the bathroom was in decent condition.

"Well, I'm pleasantly surprised," Sue said at the bottom of the stairs. "It looks a lot better on the inside than on the outside, that's for sure."

"What do you think so far, Tanya?" Ellen asked.

"I don't know. It's nice, but I'm still not happy about the six buyers and the ghost."

"There are no such things as ghosts!" Ellen said, forgetting that she needed the ghost card to keep Sue interested.

"Let's go upstairs," Sue said. "You go first, Tanya, since you're the skinny one, just in case these stairs lose their integrity."

"Oh, it's okay for me to risk *my* life?" Tanya teased.

"It'll just be easier to carry the dead body out of here." Sue chuckled. "If I broke the stairs and my neck along with them, the state would just decide to leave me here and burn the whole place down."

"Oh, stop," Tanya said.

"I'll go." Ellen tested the first step. "So far so good."

They made their way up the creaky stairs and were surprised to find that the second story had a completely different look from the first. Where the downstairs had eighties' floral wallpaper, along with shiny brass fixtures still intact, the upstairs looked as though it hadn't been updated since the house was built in 1860. The much older wallpaper was peeling off the walls in many places, and the floors were badly scratched. The second floor looked as dilapidated as the exterior of the house.

"Well this is disappointing," Sue said.

They entered the first bedroom to find it had its own bath. Both the sink and toilet looked ancient, and the tub was badly stained.

"It stinks up here." Tanya covered her mouth and nose. "It's making me nauseated."

The second bedroom looked exactly the same, along with another horrid bathroom.

"It's very rare to have so many bathrooms in an old house like this," Ellen said. "I wonder if it might have been turned into a bed and breakfast by the previous owner."

"The floorplan is conducive to that," Sue agreed. "Back in the late 1800's, it would have been called an inn."

"It had to be later than that," Tanya said. "Weren't they still using outhouses in the late 1800's?"

"Good point." Ellen followed the others back to the hall. "I think in the thirties and forties a lot of these historic homes were turned into apartments."

"What is with these windows?" Tanya asked as she entered the third bedroom. "I noticed them in the other rooms, too."

Ellen crossed the floor to see what Tanya was looking at. There were strange holes in the window frame on both the bottom and the top. They were evenly spaced and perfectly round.

"Burglar bars, maybe?" Ellen offered.

"But those would be on the outside, not on the inside," Sue said as she walked into another room. "Oh, wow. Look at this."

Ellen and Tanya followed Sue into the last of the four bedrooms.

"Bars on the *inside*?" Tanya asked. "But why?"

"Maybe this was a storm room or something," Ellen said.

"And look at this," Sue pointed to the bed. The other rooms were vacant, but this room had a bed with an iron frame. "The frame is bolted to the floor. Try to lift it."

Ellen and Tanya both attempted to lift the iron footboard. It wouldn't budge.

"Someone was a prisoner in this room," Sue said. "And maybe that person is the ghost that haunts this place."

Ellen turned her back to Sue and rolled her eyes.

"I saw that," Sue said. "I saw your reflection in the window."

"I'm sorry. I just don't believe in ghosts."

"We know that," Tanya said. "But just because you don't believe in them doesn't mean they don't exist. I told you about that experience with Dave and his mother's spirit. Do you think I made that up?"

Ellen sighed. She didn't want to have this conversation. "No, I don't think you made it up. But sometimes people see what they want to see."

"You never did come up with an explanation for the story *I* told you," Sue accused.

A few months ago, Sue had told Ellen and Tanya that she had been awakened in the middle of the night several times by the sound of someone whispering her name. Her husband had been out of town, and her youngest had already moved into his college dorm. She had convinced herself that it had been her imagination—that maybe a tree had been rubbing against the

11

window, making a sound like a whisper. But then her mother called her in the morning and said she hadn't been able to sleep either, and when Sue had asked her mother why, her mother had said, "Because all night long, I kept hearing someone whisper my name."

Even Ellen had to admit that Sue's story was pretty freaky. And she didn't think Sue would make it up just to "prove" Ellen wrong about the nonexistence of anything spiritual in the universe. "You're right. I have no explanation. But why is the default explanation always ghosts with you people?"

She followed Sue and Tanya out of the bedroom to the hallway across from the stairs. There was a door they hadn't opened. Because there were bedrooms with baths on either side of it, Ellen thought the only thing it could be was a closet. When she opened it, though, she found stairs leading up to the attic. At the top of the stairs was another door, and it was closed.

"I dare you to go up there alone," Sue said to Ellen.

"Fine. What are we, twelve?" It was dark, because the electricity hadn't been turned on, and there was a door at the top of the stairs, blocking any light that might come through the attic.

Even though she wasn't afraid of ghosts, she *was* afraid of mice, rats, spiders, and rotting boards that caved in. Ellen tried not to show this fear because she had something to prove.

When she reached the door at the top of the stairs, she found it locked from the other side. She pulled the key from her pocket and gave it a try.

Chapter Two: The History File

Ellen woke up from the same bad dream she'd had the night before, and the night before that. She'd had it too many times to count. In the dream, she'd been at one of her husband's work parties or high school reunions—someplace where she didn't know many people. And Paul had been there, too, having a grand time talking to everyone but her. In every dream, she would walk up to him, and he seemed unable to see her. She always woke up at the moment in the dream when she'd finally realized she was invisible.

She'd shared the dream with her two best friends, and both Tanya and Sue had agreed that it was one more sign that they needed an adventure. They were all feeling invisible, now that their children had moved out.

Tanya, who'd worked in civil service at Immigration for ten years before she'd quit to become a stay-at-home mom, had even discussed going back to school to start a new career. Ellen had to admit she was getting bored with the same part-time teaching job she'd had for twenty-five years at the same university, but she told her friends she'd rather sell her body for sex than start a new career.

And Sue, who'd quit her job as an accountant to raise her family, had said, "You won't make much money at that. You don't even have sex with your husband."

14

Which wasn't entirely true, but the way things were going, Ellen believed it wouldn't be long before it was.

It was strange to Ellen, how different her husband was when her kids came home to visit. Nolan, their oldest at twenty-nine, was in medical school in Oklahoma, so they didn't see him much anymore. Their second son, Lane, was in graduate school in Austin, and their daughter, Alison, was in her second year of undergraduate work at the same university as Lane. Ellen had thought she would at least see the younger two more regularly, but their lives had become busy, and it was hard for them to get home.

But when they did, Paul transformed back to the man she'd married. He laughed and told jokes—reminding her of why she'd fallen in love with him in the first place. His sense of humor never failed. But when it was just the two of them, he'd come home from his office, or from showing a house, or from playing golf, or wherever it was he went all day long, and he'd walk in and sometimes not even say hello. Some evenings she'd be in the front room reading, and it wasn't until she'd gotten up to get something from the fridge that she'd notice him in his recliner in the family room half asleep in front of the television.

Maybe she *was* invisible.

She went down the hall to the master bedroom, looking for him. They'd been sleeping in separate rooms for years because she couldn't take his snoring. Some nights, she tried to sleep in the bed with him, but since he never crossed over to her side to stroke her cheek or rub her back anymore, there didn't seem to be a point. If anything ever happened between them, it was up to her to initiate. He'd told her years ago that he wanted intimacy more frequently than she did, and he was tired of being rejected. It was up to her to let him know when she was interested.

Yep. It was pretty romantic.

A tear slipped down her cheek, and she quickly wiped it away.

When she reached their room, she found it empty. She walked through the living room to the kitchen, and then poked her head into the family room. Through the window overlooking the driveway, she noticed his pickup was already gone.

Well, damn. She needed to ask him about a key to the attic. She'd mentioned it to him the night before, and he'd promised to call the state realtor today.

Thank goodness he answered his cell phone. Lately, it was more of a one in four chance that he would.

"There is no attic key," he told her. "Ronnie said the key I gave you is the only one they have."

Ronnie was the realtor representing the state. "Where are you?"

She half expected him to say, "Don't you know I'm with my mistress?"

"Golf course. I gotta go."

It was where he went every Saturday morning these days—at least, that's where she hoped he was going.

Disappointed, she was about to hang up when he asked, "Did you find the file I left on your dresser?"

"What? No." She hurried down the hall to their room. "Yes. I see it. What is it?"

She opened it to find a fax cover page, along with several documents.

"It's everything the state has on the history of the house."

Just when she thought he didn't care. "Thank you, honey! Thank you so much!"

"Sorry there wasn't an attic key. Ronnie said he could have a locksmith there on Monday."

"That's awesome! Thank you so much for taking care of that for me."

"I gotta go now."

"Bye."

She called Tanya right away to tell her about the history file, but, when Tanya answered, her voice was hoarse and shaky, as if she'd been crying.

"What's wrong?" Ellen plopped onto an armchair in her living room and opened the file in her lap, leafing through as she listened to Tanya talk about her mother. When Tanya said her mother hadn't recognized her again, Ellen closed the file and said, "I'm so sorry."

"It's just so hard," Tanya said. "It's like, if your own mother doesn't know you…"

"Deep down, she knows you."

"She thought I was one of her cousins. It's like I don't even exist."

"Your mother doesn't have to recognize you for you to exist. I know who you are, and you're an amazing person."

"Well, thank you, but I don't feel amazing. I feel terrible. The woman who used to hold me and cuddle me and take care of me has no freaking clue who I am."

Ellen wasn't sure what to say. "I have something that might take your mind off of it for a little while."

Ellen picked up Tanya and met Sue at Panera Bread with the history file. Once they had ordered their meals and were seated but hadn't yet received their food, Ellen opened the file. "I thought it would be more fun if we found out about the history of this house together."

"Did we decide to buy?" Tanya asked. "I didn't think we'd made a decision yet."

"No. No decision," Sue said. "But I would like to hear the house's history. What's in the file?"

"I have to see the attic before I can commit," Tanya said before sipping her water. "And you have to agree to let me bring in that psychic I was telling you about."

"How much will that cost?" Sue asked. "Because I've always been told I have the gift."

"Did you sense something yesterday, when we were there?" Ellen asked.

"Yes, as a matter of fact, I did."

"I'll pay her fee," Tanya said. "She's really done a lot for me since Dave's mother passed. She's been able to tell us things that no one but Dave and his mother could know."

"We won't be able to get into the attic until Monday," Ellen said. "So while we're waiting, let's dig into this history file."

Their food was brought to the table, and after everything was settled, Ellen ate a spoonful of broccoli cheese soup and began to read.

The document was an abstract of the house's ownership, consisting of several pages. Ellen scanned through all of the legalese about the plot number and the county and builder information to get the gist of it. "German immigrants Theodore and Alma Gold, along with Alma's sister Inger Bohrmann, had the house built in February, 1860."

"It says that Inger Bohrmann was an invalid," Tanya pointed out. "I didn't know the records included details like that."

"Maybe that's our ghost," Sue said.

Ellen continued, "In 1881, Theodore left the house to Marcia Gold, his only living descendant. Why would it say 'only living'?"

"It must mean he had other children who were deceased," Tanya said. "And maybe…"

"Maybe they're the ones haunting the house," Sue piped in.

"In 1930," Ellen read on, "Marcia sold the house to Dr. Jonathon Piers." She scanned through two more pages about changes in the property—this was when the bathrooms were added. "In 1972, Jonathon Piers left the house to his son, Jonathon 'Johnny' Piers, Jr., who lived in the house until he died in 1994, with no heirs. The state of Texas took possession of the property in 1996 after being unable to locate any surviving relatives or beneficiaries."

"Maybe the ghost is Johnny Piers," Sue said. "Did the realtor say whether people thought it was male or female?"

Ellen shook her head, biting her lip to keep from smiling. Tanya and Sue were taking this ghost thing way too seriously. Ellen just wanted to use her HGTV and DIY knowledge to rehabilitate the old house into something spectacular.

There were a few more pages in the file about the six buyers who had closed on the house but had pulled out during the cooling off period.

"I wonder if we could interview some of the neighbors," Tanya said. "We could pretend to be writing a magazine article or something."

"That's a good idea," Ellen said as she finished up her soup. "We really could write an article about our findings. A little publicity could help us fetch a better price when we sell."

"If we decide to get the house," Tanya reminded her. "We haven't decided yet."

Sue wiggled in her chair, like an excited schoolgirl. "I think we should go there tonight and have a séance. Then we could find out what kind of ghost we're dealing with."

Ellen closed her eyes because she'd been about to roll them. "I don't know."

"Sounds scary but fun," Tanya said. "Why not? Dave's out of town, so I'm home alone tonight."

"Tom's going to be glued to the football game," Sue said. "So I'm free. What about you, Ellen?"

"Seriously? A séance? Doesn't that frighten you? If I believed in ghosts, I'd be too scared."

"But you don't, so what's the harm?" Sue challenged. "Besides, if it gets out of hand, we can break the circle."

"Huh?" Ellen had no idea what her friend was talking about.

"You hold hands to create a circle," Tanya explained. "That's how you summon the spirit. You have to have at least three people and three candles."

"Once you break the circle, the séance ends," Sue added.

Ellen wondered how people who believed in the paranormal came up with their rules and rituals. If there really were such things as ghosts, why would breaking the circle stop them from harming you?

"We don't know what's in the attic," she said. "Maybe a vagrant is living up there."

Sue flapped her hand through the air. "I doubt some homeless person will attack us, but I'll bring my pistol, just in case he takes one look at me and decides to rape me."

Tanya giggled. "I'll bring the candles."

"And I'll make that dip you both like," Sue added. "Do either of you have a box of crackers to go with it?"

Great, Ellen thought. They were going to a strange house, purported to be haunted, at night, armed with a pistol, candles, a box of crackers, and Sue's famous dip.

Chapter Three: The Séance

Later that evening, Sue picked up Ellen and Tanya and headed for the King William district. Ellen sat in the passenger seat holding the stainless steel bowl covered in foil and containing the dip Sue had made. Tanya sat in back with a pitcher of frozen margaritas in one hand and a re-usable grocery bag filled with candles, crackers, and who knew what else in the other.

Somewhere—probably in her purse—Sue packed her pistol.

To Ellen, this seemed like a dangerous combination, but she went along with it because she was out-voted and because she really wanted her friends to buy this house with her.

Sue pulled up to the curb. Daylight savings hadn't yet begun, so, although dusk was near, it was still light enough outside to clearly see the house.

It looked creepy to Ellen, now that they were about to summon a supposed ghost.

"I'm having second thoughts about this," Tanya said. "Maybe this wasn't such a good idea."

"Oh, come on," Sue said. "You're this way about everything."

Tanya blanched. "I am not."

"You said that very thing last month as we were headed to the craft fair," Sue pointed out. "And if I remember correctly, you said the same thing about the trip we took to Dallas last spring. I was literally in the car on the way to pick you up when…"

"But Mikey was getting sick," Tanya insisted.

"It was the common cold, and he's twenty-four," Sue said with a laugh.

"Fine," Tanya said. "But it's probably hot in there. We could go back to my place instead. Ellen, what do you think?"

Ellen wasn't sure what she thought. On the one hand, she was afraid of the neighbors wondering what a car was doing parked in front of a vacant property this late in the evening. She was also afraid of the possibility of a homeless man—or group of them—living in the attic. Her gut feeling was that all the supposed episodes with the buyers during the cooling off period had been caused by someone wanting to keep the house from selling.

On the other hand, she really wanted to buy this property, even if it did look a little creepy right now. Her gut was saying leave, but her heart was in love with this house—with what it could one day be—and she wanted to spend time with it.

"It won't be hot for long with the sun going down," Ellen finally said.

Sue turned off the car. "Then it's settled. Come on."

After Ellen put the key in the door and opened it, she paused on the threshold, waiting for whoever might be living there to clear out. She glanced back at Sue, who gave her a reassuring nod, and then she led the way inside, holding the door open for her friends before closing and locking it behind them.

It was dark inside.

"I almost had to cancel tonight," Sue said as she made her way to the old dining room table, where she sat the bowl of dip. "My mom called about thirty minutes before I needed to leave to pick you up."

"We could have canceled," Tanya said.

"I know, but that's not the point," Sue said, pulling out a chair and testing it before putting her weight all the way onto it. "I hope I don't break this thing."

"They seem sturdy enough," Ellen said of the chairs, taking one across from Sue.

Behind Ellen, the kitchen was the brightest room in the house because it faced the west. The living room in front of her, on the other hand, appeared dark and eerie.

Tanya stood near the end of the table pulling things from her re-usable grocery bag: a plastic tumbler for each of them, a box of crackers, three large pillar candles, three paper plates, and a box of matches.

"So why did you almost have to cancel?" Tanya asked Sue. "Is your mom okay?" She poured the pitcher of margaritas into each of the three cups.

Sue took a sip of hers and said, "Mmm," before saying, "You know my mom. Her whole life revolves around me. I can't take a dump without her knowing about it."

"So nothing's wrong?" Ellen asked.

"Well, if you were to ask *her*, she'd say the world was coming to an end because I made plans without her. I really need to find that woman some friends."

"Surely she understands that you have a life," Ellen said before taking a sip of her margarita. "Mmm. This is good, Tanya. Thank you."

Tanya sat at the end of the table between Sue and Ellen with her back to the foyer and staircase. Her eyes narrowed at the window across from her. "What's that?"

Ellen and Sue turned to the window.

"What?" Ellen asked.

"Never mind," Tanya said. "I thought I saw something. It was nothing. Can you pass me that box of crackers? I'm starving."

Ellen handed over the crackers while Sue removed the foil from the dip.

"I forgot a spoon," Sue said.

"That's okay." Tanya took a cracker and used it to scoop dip onto her plate. "Can one of you light the candles? I didn't eat dinner tonight, so I think I'll pig out first."

"Just save some food for the spirits," Sue said.

Ellen frowned. "The spirits?"

"You're supposed to have a food offering, along with the light, to lure them to you," Tanya explained.

Ellen grabbed the box of matches, trying not to laugh. "So how does this work, exactly?" She struck a match and put the flame to one of the wicks.

All three faces turned toward the ceiling when they heard a creak overhead.

"What was that?" Sue asked.

Ellen's stomach dropped. "Do you think someone could be living up there?"

"Maybe we should go," Tanya suggested.

"Old houses creak," Sue said. "I'm sure it was nothing. And if someone is living up there, I doubt he'll come down and risk exposing himself. Anyway, it could be the ghost. Let's get started."

Ellen struck another match and lit the other two candles.

"We can't break the circle, once we hold hands," Sue said. "So let me finish this margarita real quick." She cocked back her head and emptied her cup.

Tanya laughed at Sue. "Do you want some of mine?"

"No, I'm good. Finish eating so we can hold hands."

"So what is your mom doing tonight?" Ellen asked Sue. "Is she mad at you?"

"She said she's not mad, but I know better."

"Did you have plans with her before we made ours?" Tanya asked.

"No. That's the thing. We usually talk on the phone each evening, but we didn't have plans. I guess she's upset that I couldn't chat on the phone. I told her I'd call her when I got home, but she said not to bother."

"I suppose you could have invited her along," Ellen said.

Sue rolled her eyes. "It crossed my mind, but, really, Ellen, she needs her own friends. Besides, she would have tried to take over the séance. You think *I'm* a believer, but you should see *her*. She'd probably start talking in tongues before we even held hands."

They all three laughed.

Then Sue said, "Maybe I should have asked her to come along. She would have really enjoyed this."

Ellen realized then that Sue must have all the confidence in the world that they were dealing with a ghost and not a vagrant, or she never would have considered inviting her seventy-something-year-old mother. Ellen bit her tongue, though, rather than point out her feeling that the odds were much greater that the sound above them came from a squatter than a spirit.

The idea of someone in the house with them was making her nervous. Why had she locked the front door behind them? She'd been thinking about keeping nosy neighbors from walking in on them, but she should have been thinking about an escape plan.

"Let's get this show on the road," Ellen said. "Before it gets dark outside."

"Scared, are we?" Tanya teased.

"Not of ghosts," Ellen said.

Tanya stuffed her last dip-covered cracker into her mouth and swallowed it down with margarita before taking the hands of her friends. "Ready."

Sue reached across the table and took Ellen's hand. "Remember, don't break the circle until I tell you it's okay."

Ellen nodded, feeling a lump form in her throat as something Tanya had said sent a shiver down her spine: *Just because you don't believe in ghosts doesn't mean they don't exist.*

The statement had been true. Ellen hadn't believed one of her children would ever do drugs, and he had. She hadn't believed her marriage could ever fall apart, and it had. She hadn't believed she'd ever partake in a séance, and here she was.

"Spirits of the past who dwell here," Sue said with her eyes closed. "Move among us. Be guided by the light of our world and by the aroma of our food. Tell us who you are."

Ellen took a deep breath and waited. Nearly a minute went by, and nothing happened. "How long is this supposed to last?"

"Sshh," Tanya hushed her.

"Spirits of the past who dwell in this house," Sue said again. "Follow the light of our world, and the aroma of our food, and come to us. Make yourself known to us. Is anyone here? If so, please rap twice."

They waited quietly for another minute. Ellen kept her eyes wide open, unlike Sue and Tanya. The living room behind Sue was almost in complete darkness now. Very little light came in from the windows in the kitchen. A shrub covered most of the dining room window, where Tanya thought she might have seen something.

As Ellen looked at that window now, she too, thought she saw something: a face. "Holy shit," she muttered, her heartrate accelerating.

Tanya and Sue opened their eyes and looked at her.

Whispering, Ellen said, "There's someone out there. I saw a face. A man, I think."

"Don't break the circle," Sue warned. "It's probably just a neighbor wondering why we're here."

Ellen took a deep breath and tried to bring her heartrate back down to normal again.

"Spirits of the past who dwell here," Sue said again, gazing into the candlelight. "Rap two times if you can hear me."

Ellen froze: Two unmistakable knocks resounded on the ceiling above them.

Sue and Tanya smiled as Ellen wondered what the hell was going on. She refused to believe a spirit had actually replied to their summoning.

"Oh, thank you, spirit from the past," Sue said. "We would like to ask you some questions. If we have your permission to proceed, please rap once. If you don't want us to speak with you further, rap twice."

Again, unmistakably, a single knock to the ceiling.

Sue and Tanya smiled again. Ellen wanted to leave. The vagrant was toying with them. It was the only explanation.

"My first question," Sue said. "Are you female? Please rap once for yes and twice for no."

A single rap.

Ellen broke out in a sweat. "We should leave," she whispered.

"Sshhh." Tanya glared at her and shook her head.

"Do you live in this house?" Sue asked next. "Please rap once for yes and twice for no."

A single rap.

Followed by loud pounding.

"What the hell?" Ellen whispered, looking from one friend to the other.

More pounding. It was the front door.

"Don't break the circle," Sue said. "Let me ask one more question."

Before Sue could ask it, they heard a loud creak, like the sound of a door opening, followed by a slam.

"That sounded like the attic door," Tanya whispered, craning to look behind her without breaking the circle.

The ceiling above them shuddered, as though someone were walking on the second floor.

"Oh, spirit," Sue said desperately. "Are you a friendly spirit? If so, please rap once for yes and twice for no."

A single rap, but not from the ceiling. This time, it came from the stairwell behind Tanya.

"She's friendly," Sue whispered.

"Unless she's a liar," Ellen said.

Now someone was pounding on the back door.

"It's got to be the neighbor that was looking in the window," Sue said.

"I think we better answer," Tanya said. "We should break the circle."

They heard another creak on the stairs behind Tanya. They all three turned in time to see a thin figure with white hair and a white dress run across the foyer toward the back door.

"The ghost!" Sue cried in a mixture between a whisper and a squeal.

"I saw her!" Tanya said, holding tight to Ellen's hand. "Did you see her, Ellen?"

"I saw something," Ellen admitted.

They heard more creaking and footsteps at the back of the house.

"Don't break the circle!" Sue warned again. "Wait and see if she speaks again." Then more loudly she said, "Oh, spirit, please come to the light. If you like dwelling among the living, please rap once for yes…"

Sue hadn't finished speaking when the floorboards of the bottom floor shuddered with loud, quick, heavy footsteps.

"That's not the same spirit," Tanya whispered.

Sue's mouth dropped open as she gazed at something behind Ellen's back.

Ellen turned to see a man with an axe in his hands. Ellen screamed and scrambled to her feet, shaking all over as she backed away from the man.

"What the hell's going on in here?" the man asked sternly, glaring at each of the women. "If you don't vacate these premises immediately, I'll call the cops."

"Who are you?" Sue asked.

"I might ask you the same question," he said.

"We're the new owners of this place," Sue said.

"The hell you are," the man said. "I'd know if this house sold. I know the realtor."

"Ronnie?" Ellen asked. "You know Ronnie?"

"That's right," the man said less sternly. He lowered the axe to his side. "You know him?"

Ellen nodded as she caught her breath. She put a hand to her heart. "Man, you scared the heck out of me."

"How do you think *I* feel?" the old man, probably mid-seventies, said as he rubbed the gray whiskers along his jawline. "For a minute, I thought you were the three witches of Eastwick."

33

Chapter Four: The Man with the Axe

"Would you like some crackers and dip?" Sue offered the man with the axe.

"No, thank you." He scratched his head. "So have you already closed on the house, then?"

"Not yet," Ellen said. "My friends wanted to see if the rumors were true—the rumors about this place being haunted."

"Oh, they're true alright. My wife and I have both seen her. You should have a chat with my wife before you buy this place."

"Come have a seat and tell us what you know," Sue suggested.

Tanya seemed to have swallowed her tongue. She was almost as pale as the ghost girl, or whatever it was Ellen had seen dart through the foyer.

The man with the axe took the chair where Ellen had been sitting. Ellen continued to catch her breath near the wall with the window.

She'd been so freaked out that she may have even peed a little.

"We just saw the spirit," Sue said. "She ran toward the back of the house. Did you see her when you came in?"

The old man's face turned as white as Tanya's as he shook his head. "No. I didn't see her."

"So she just vanished?" Tanya spoke for the first time.

"I guess so," the man said. "It wouldn't be the first time. Like I said, you need to have a conversation with my wife."

"Who do you think the ghost is?" Sue asked. "A former resident of this house?"

"Probably," the man said.

"I'm Sue, by the way. It's nice to meet you, Mr...."

"Forrester," he said. "The name's Bud Forrester."

"I'm Ellen." Ellen took the chair on the other end of the table across from Tanya. She was not about to put her back to any of the rooms in the house. "And this is Tanya."

Tanya gave the old man a silent nod.

"It's a pleasure to meet you," Bud Forrester said without shaking anyone's hand. "Like I said, the rumors are real. What are you doing here, having one of those what-do-you-call-'em's, with the Ouija Board or something?"

"Séance," Sue replied. "We were communicating with the spirit until right before you came in."

"What do you mean, *communicating*?" he asked with narrowed eyes.

Sue explained, "We would ask a question and then ask her to rap once for yes and twice for no."

"And the ghost answered?" he asked.

All three women nodded.

He rubbed the scalp beneath his gray hair. "What questions did you ask?"

35

"If she dwelled here, if she was female, if she was friendly," Sue said. "We didn't get very far, unfortunately."

"Well, I tell you what. You women have a lot of guts coming into this haunted house hoping to communicate with ghosts, that's for sure," Bud Forrester said. "But this here house is dangerous. You could have been hurt. You wouldn't believe what we've seen."

"Like what?" Sue asked.

"Gives me the creeps to talk about it," Bud Forrester said enigmatically. "I tell you what. My wife and I would surely benefit if this house ever sold. It's brought down our property values something fierce to have this disaster next door to us. But I wouldn't wish this place on anyone. This here is a piece of hell, is what I think."

"Why haven't you moved?" Ellen asked.

"Oh, that's out of the question," Bud Forrester said, shaking his head. "My home has been in our family for generations. My wife's mother grew up there and lives with us still."

Ellen sat up in her chair. "How old is she, if you don't mind my asking?"

"Ninety-five in October," Bud Forrester said.

"If you think this place is a piece of hell," Sue asked, "why are you sitting here so calmly? I would think you'd be begging us to leave with you, to save our lives."

36

"I thought about it," the man said. "But I was afraid you'd think I was a crazy lunatic. We really should get out of here, as soon as possible. Can I help you ladies out?"

Tanya frowned. "We can manage, thank you."

They all four stood up.

Something suddenly occurred to Ellen. "The back door was locked, wasn't it?"

"Yes, ma'am. I picked it," Bud Forrester said. "I saw you through the window and was worried about you."

"That's why you brought your axe?" Sue asked. "Because you were worried about us?"

"I brought it for protection," Bud Forrester said. "Like I said, this place here is something you don't want to mess with. It was nice meeting you. Be sure and come by and chat with my wife before you close on this place."

"Would tomorrow afternoon work for you?" Ellen asked.

"Yes," Bud Forrester said as he headed toward the back door. "Come at three. I'll tell my wife to expect you."

As Tanya and Ellen started packing things back into Tanya's re-usable grocery bag, Sue said, "Let's try to contact the spirit once more, now that the old man is gone."

"What?" Tanya shook her head. "I say we get out of here."

"I agree," Ellen said.

"But maybe she'll come back and tell us who she is," Sue said.

"I think I'd like to get my psychic to come out here," Tanya said. "She can find out what we need to know without the séance. I'm a little spooked after seeing that apparition. Aren't you?"

Ellen nodded. She was more than spooked. Her whole belief system had been upturned. Although she wasn't completely convinced that she'd just seen a spirit, she also didn't think the girl looked like a real person. She was as thin as a skeleton and as white, too. The white dress hung down to her ankles. She hadn't been wearing shoes. And how could a young woman manage to live in the attic all these years? Maybe she wasn't alone. Memories of a novel she'd read as a girl made her shudder. It was called *Flowers in the Attic* and was about a mother who imprisoned her children in the attic, where they had to grow up and fend for themselves. The brother and sister eventually fell in love because they had no one else.

"But it was exactly what we were hoping for, wasn't it?" Sue said, bringing Ellen from her reverie. "I really want to buy this house now more than ever. Now that I know the spirit is female, friendly, and willing to talk to us, I'm excited. Aren't y'all?"

Ellen still wanted the house, even if she wasn't excited about its resident. "I'm still interested. What about you, Tanya?"

"If you two agree to let me bring my psychic to interrogate the spirit, then I'll be more inclined. I just want to make sure no one was murdered here and that there's nothing evil haunting this place."

"How soon can she come?" Sue asked as she put her arm through the strap of her purse and picked up the bowl of dip.

"I'll give her a call. Maybe she can stop by Monday while the locksmith is here. I'll see."

"Do you guys want me to pick you up around 2:30 tomorrow?" Ellen offered.

"That sounds good," Sue said, leading them to the front door. "I'm anxious to hear what Mrs. Forrester has to say."

"I didn't much care for Mr. Forrester," Tanya said. "He gave me the creeps."

"Me, too," Ellen agreed.

They hadn't yet stepped out of the house when they heard a flurry of footsteps inside.

Tanya hastened outside and into the front yard faster than Ellen realized her friend could run.

Sue stood on the threshold as though she might go back inside.

"Come on, Sue," Ellen said, pushing her out the front door. "Let's go."

Chapter Five: Mrs. Forrester

That evening, Ellen arrived home to find Paul had fallen asleep to the television. She took a shower, and by the time she got out, she saw the familiar lump of his body beneath the sheet on his side of the bed and heard the buzz-saw sound of his snoring.

She'd wanted to tell him about the ghost girl.

Disappointed, she found her Kindle and went down the hall to Nolan's old room, where she'd slept for the past five years. As she tried to get into the new mystery she'd started a few days ago, her mind kept wandering back to the séance, to Bud Forrester, and to the slim white figure that may or may not have been an apparition.

The girl had to have been a living, breathing person. There were no such things as ghosts.

Ellen heard a creak in the attic above her and for a moment worried that the spirit may have followed her all the way home to prove she existed.

It was the wind, of course. It was nothing.

So if the girl was a living, breathing person, what would she be doing in that dilapidated old house? Maybe she'd been abducted and made a prisoner. Maybe Bud Forrester was her captor. Maybe that's why he didn't want anyone in the house!

Ellen sat up in the bed and glanced at the digital clock on her son's dresser. It was just after ten. It was definitely too late to call Tanya, but Sue might be up. Ellen teetered with indecision.

No. It could wait. Besides, if the girl was Bud Forrester's prisoner, how would she have been able to run freely in the house? Wouldn't she have made her escape after Bud entered through the backdoor?

Ellen lay back down on the bed.

If the girl had been a prisoner, she would have cried out for help.

And, if she were a living, breathing person, then someone would have found her out by now. Six different buyers wouldn't have been so easily fooled.

Could it have been the margarita?

Ellen sighed and closed her eyes. The questions spun round and round in her head, making it almost impossible to fall asleep. She couldn't wait to talk with Mrs. Forrester the next afternoon, and she was equally anxious to have the locksmith come on Monday after work to open the attic door.

The next morning, Tanya called.

"I'm just not up to going to that creepy man's house," Tanya said. "You two are going to have to go on without me."

"Come on. Don't be a wimp."

"Sorry. I'm tired and don't want to get dressed today. I just want to lounge around and do nothing."

"Are you still planning to meet me tomorrow to see the attic?"

"What time?"

"I still don't know yet."

"I'll see how I feel. I may try to get in touch with my psychic."

"Call her today, Tanya. Please. I'll split the fee with you."

"I knew that if you ever had an experience like Sue and I've had, you'd believe."

"I'm not saying I believe."

"Sure you're not."

After Ellen hung up, she called Sue.

"Do you mind if my mom comes along?" Sue asked. "I'll drive."

"I don't mind. Tanya's bailing anyway."

"What a shocker."

Ellen was waiting by the curb when Sue pulled up. Since her mother, Jan, was already in the passenger's seat, Ellen climbed in back.

"Hello, Jan," Ellen said. "How are you?"

"I'm just fine, but I'm worried about Sue."

"Mother…"

"What's wrong with Sue?" Ellen asked.

"Well," Jan started. "All I said is did she remember to put on deodorant this morning, and I got an earful. I bet you don't talk that way to your mother, Ellen."

"I've said a lot worse, believe me."

"Well, that's too bad," Sue's mother said.

In the rearview mirror, Sue smiled at Ellen.

Ellen was always surprised by how Sue allowed her mother to bully her. Sue barely said two words the whole way to the historic district.

Jan, on the other hand, had plenty to say, and she spoke as though her daughter wasn't even in the car with them. Ellen wondered if Sue felt invisible, too.

Ellen sucked in her lips and held back tears. Tears seemed to come too easily these days. A commercial with kittens and babies would get her faucets pouring in no time. This time of her life was so different from any other. Was the natural course to recede into the realm of death slowly, starting with invisibility? Maybe Jan resisted by holding on to her role as Sue's mother with an iron grip. Ellen and her two best friends needed to hold on to something, too. They needed this house project. They needed this adventure to keep them from fading into the darkness.

Sue parked in front of the old Greek revival and pointed it out to her mother.

"You've got to be kidding me," her mother said. "It's a good thing you're an only child."

"What does that have to do with anything?" Sue asked.

"Because you're going to need every dime I leave you if you invest your money in that pile of wood."

"You haven't seen the inside," Ellen said. "This place has amazing potential. We plan to restore it to its original grandeur."

"Well, hopefully I won't be around much longer," Jan said. "For your sake, Sue."

Sue gave Ellen a look in the rearview mirror that said *if she only knew.*

They walked up the sidewalk to the Forrester's light-blue two-story Victorian. It had a wide front porch framed by two enormous oak trees. Ellen's throat felt suddenly dry and tight at the thought of seeing the man with the axe again. Maybe Tanya had been right to bail.

When Bud Forrester answered the door, he was friendlier this time, though that wouldn't require much, considering his behavior the evening before. The fact that he was no longer brandishing an axe did wonders for his new and improved disposition.

He welcomed them in and led them through a foyer to an old-fashioned living room, where Mrs. Forrester was waiting in a wheelchair—at least, some of her was. She was so large that the majority of her was not actually in the wheelchair.

Sue didn't have to say her thoughts for Ellen to know what they were: *For once I'm not the biggest girl in the room.*

"Goodness gracious," Jan muttered as they entered.

Sue and Ellen exchanged glances of sheer and utter embarrassment. They shouldn't have brought Sue's mother.

Ellen smiled at the woman in the wheelchair, who pretended not to have heard Jan. Ellen extended her hand as Mr. Forrester introduced them all. Sue introduced her mother, too.

Amelia Forrester asked to be called Millie, and then she offered everyone iced tea or lemonade. Everyone wanted iced tea, so Bud left the room to get it.

When Millie Forrester smiled, she was quite pretty in the face. Her nails were also nicely manicured, and she wore tasteful, dainty jewelry on her fingers, ears, and very large wrists. She spoke with a mixture of southern drawl and German accent, which reminded Ellen of Paul's parents in New Braunfels.

"Please sit down and tell me what you want to know about the Gold House ghost," she said sweetly.

"We want to know everything." Sue sat in one of two beige armchairs as her mother took the other.

"Keep in mind that the house next door isn't the only haunting in this area," Millie said. "I was just talking with the Robertsons, who live in the Victorian on the other side of the Gold House, and they could tell you some things that will keep you awake at night, that's for darn sure."

"Do you call it the Gold House because of its color?" Ellen wondered if maybe it was once a deeper yellow than it was now in ruins.

"Oh, no," Millie flapped a hand in the air. "The Golds were the original owners. It's been the Gold House for as long as I can remember."

Ellen recalled the names in the file: Theodore and Alma Gold.

"There's also an old legend," Millie added. "It's just an old story, but they say that Theodore brought German gold to this country and buried it somewhere on the property. So I guess the name may have a double meaning for some folks." Millie laughed.

"You don't think the legend is true?" Jan asked. "Has anyone looked into it?"

"Oh, sure. For decades." Millie said. "Even Bud has gone over with his metal detector hoping to find something. He's spent hours over there. Other neighbors, too, especially old Mitchell Clark. I'm telling you, if there was gold, they'd 've found it by now."

To Ellen, the legend made the house even more interesting. She smiled at the idea of her and Sue and Tanya digging every square inch of the grounds. This really could be an exciting adventure.

"Let's get back to the ghost girl," Sue said.

"Where should I begin?" Millie asked.

"Why don't you start with the very first time you saw or sensed her," Sue suggested.

"I thought you said she was a young woman," Jan said. "Or was she a child?"

"She's a very young woman, I think," Millie said. "Perhaps a teen. We don't know for sure. We don't know much about what she must have been like alive. We've found no records for her whatsoever. We have researched all the hauntings in this area, and this and that, but haven't quite figured out the one next door. So I can only tell you what I've learned about her since her death."

"Please go on," Ellen prompted.

Millie looked up toward her ceiling, retrieving the memories. "The first time I ever saw her was a couple of years after the Gold House went on the market—1998, I believe. I had just had my final back surgery a few weeks before. I remember because I was feeling very hopeful that I might walk again after nearly thirty years—I was in a car accident in my twenties, not long after we were married."

"Oh, I'm terribly sorry to hear that," Jan interjected.

"Thank you," Millie said. "So on that particular spring morning in '98, I was out in my garden—I used to have a beautiful rose garden, and this and that, and it's still there, but overgrown with weeds and not as productive as it once was."

"My garden is overgrown now, too," Jan said. "I used to love to work in the front beds, but it's gotten harder over the years."

Ellen wished Jan wouldn't interrupt. "Please, go on, Millie."

"Anyway, Bud had wheeled me out to the garden on the side of our house, next to the abandoned one next door. I had a pair of pruners and was pruning and just a talking away. Talking is good for plants, you know."

"I talk to my plants, too," Jan said with a satisfied smile.

Ellen sat forward. "So then what happened?"

"Well, Bud was mowing the front yard, and wasn't there to see it, but I saw something dart across my backyard. We didn't have fences back then, either. It was all open just as you see it now. A creek used to flow behind the houses, but it's all dried up. Anyway, I turned and saw a girl with white hair and a white dress and just as thin as a skeleton disappear into the abandoned house."

"Are you sure she was a ghost?" Sue asked, with a glance toward Ellen. "How do you know she wasn't just some kid messing around?"

"That's what I thought she was, at first," Millie admitted. "Even though she was ghostly pale and thin, and this and that, I assumed she was alive."

"What changed your mind?" Ellen asked.

"I was leaning over the roses, and this and that, when I felt a tap on my shoulder that made the hair on my neck stand on end. I turned to see her gaunt, pale figure looking down at me. The sun was just behind her head, shining right in my face, but I could see her well enough, and I felt a coldness overcome me. She narrowed her eyes with the oddest expression and said, 'You ain't ever getting out of there.' It made me shiver."

"What did she mean?" Jan asked.

"Before I could ask, she ran off," Millie said. "But later, when I found out that my back surgery was a failure and I would never walk again, I came to believe the ghost was telling me that I would never get out of this chair. And she was right."

"What did your husband think?" Ellen asked.

"As soon as I heard the mower turn off, I hollered out to him. He came running, all sweaty and exhausted. I told him about the girl, but he thought I was imagining things."

"He didn't believe you?" Sue asked.

Bud returned with a tray of glasses filled with iced tea and set it on the coffee table between them. He handed a glass to Jan. "She was on a bunch of meds from her surgery. I thought she was hallucinating." He handed a glass to Sue.

"Thank you." Sue took the glass.

"When was the first time *you* saw the ghost?" Ellen asked Bud as she accepted a glass from him.

He tapped his chin. "Was it after the third or fourth visit?"

"Third, I think," Millie said.

"So the girl came back?" Sue took a drink of her tea. "Here, to your house?"

"She's been back many times," Millie said.

49

"How recently?" Sue asked.

"About two weeks ago, I was on the phone with Ida Robertson and saw the girl as clear as day pass down my hallway to the stairs," Millie said. "I had just been telling Ida what I'd heard about the twins down the street—those two high school dropouts that everyone suspects are in a gang, and this and that."

"Did you see her, too?" Sue asked Bud.

"Not that time."

"He didn't believe me years ago, when I first saw the ghost," Millie said. "It took a few weeks for him to finally see her."

He turned to his wife. "That time she came to your bedroom."

"That was bizarre," Millie said shaking her head. "One night, I was already sound asleep in my bed. I felt someone tap my shoulder, and when I opened my eyes, she was leaning over me. I felt a cold shiver travel down my back. I even felt a tingle in my toes and had the strangest feeling that I could move my legs, and this and that, but, of course, I couldn't."

"Did she say anything?" Jan asked.

Millie nodded. "She said, 'Where's Momma?'"

"Did you get a better look at her?" Sue asked.

"It was dark in the room." Millie took a sip of her tea before continuing. "There was a light on in the hallway—we always keep it on. Still do. So she made a kind of silhouette in her white dress. I got the feeling from her voice and from the way she spoke, and this and that, that she was young—maybe a teenager."

"Did you say anything?" Ellen asked.

"I asked her who her momma was, and she said Cynthia. I told her I would look for her. Then when I asked the girl what *her* name was, she ran away. I wanted so badly to follow her."

"Why didn't *you* follow her?" Sue asked Bud. "Or did you sleep through all of that?"

Bud's face turned red.

"It's hard for me to sleep in the same bed with Bud," Millie said quickly. "He wasn't there when the ghost appeared."

"I sleep upstairs," he added. "So, yes, I did sleep through the whole thing, apparently."

Millie reached out and took her husband's hand. "He still hadn't seen her yet and was getting worried about me, weren't you, Bud?"

"I thought she was losing her mind," he said. "I thought maybe the medicine she was taking, or maybe the depression…I didn't know what to think."

"But then you finally saw her, too," Millie said, smiling.

Bud nodded with his lips pressed together. "Indeed."

"He was in the shower," Millie said. "Shampooing his hair, eyes full of soap, and this and that, and next thing you know, he sees her standing outside the glass doors."

"I couldn't breathe," Bud said. "I knew it couldn't be Millie or her mother."

51

"My mother was already bed-ridden at the time," Millie explained.

"What did you do?" Jan asked.

"I hollered, 'Get the hell out of here!' and she disappeared."

Sue's eyes widened. "Into thin air?"

"Hell, I don't know," Bud said. "The room was full of steam. I got out and threw on a robe to look for her, but she was gone."

Ellen still wasn't convinced they were talking about a ghost. Couldn't this have been a neighborhood kid playing tricks on them?

"Did you ever have the Gold House cleansed?" Sue asked.

"You mean like with a priest?" Bud asked. "*We* haven't, but I think I heard about someone else doing it a few years back. Not sure."

"Every time that house comes close to selling, she shows up *here*," Millie said. "Then, when the buyers leave, the ghost returns home."

"Sounds like you've gotten used to her presence," Jan said. "Do you think of her as a friendly spirit then?"

Both Forresters shook their heads.

"I don't trust her," Bud said. "One night, I saw her run across the back lawn toward the creek bed. Blood dripped down her arms and splattered her white dress. It gave me the chills.

The next morning, one of our neighbors found her cat dead—decapitated."

"You think the ghost did it?" Ellen asked.

"You tell me," Bud said. "It's a strange coincidence if she didn't."

Sue met Ellen's eyes. They were probably thinking the same thing: Tanya wouldn't like hearing that. Maybe Ellen would ask Sue to keep that detail between the two of them. Ellen still wanted the house.

"And she killed my dog," Millie added. "About twelve years ago. Pedro was the sweetest little lap dog you'd ever seen. It was cruel of the ghost to kill him."

"How do you know she did it?" Ellen asked.

"Bud saw her," Millie said.

"I didn't see her do it, but I saw her with him," Bud explained. "And the very next day, we found him dead."

A chilling moan sounded from somewhere in the house.

"What was that?" Sue asked, jumping nearly six inches out of her seat.

Ellen had also been startled, though Jan seemed not to have heard.

"My mother," Millie explained. "Bud?"

Bud nodded and climbed to his feet. He gently kissed his wife's cheek before excusing himself from the room.

Ellen guessed a man who took care of two invalids for most of his life couldn't be that bad, could he?

"The girl whose ghost has been haunting this area was most likely insane," Millie said as her husband left the room. "For many years, that house was a rest home for the mentally handicapped. You did know that, didn't you?"

Ellen felt her jaw drop open, and her expression was mirrored by Sue.

"No, we didn't," Ellen said.

Chapter Six: The Attic

After they left the Forresters' blue Victorian, Ellen and Sue led Jan across the yard to the house next door to show her the yellow Greek revival—the Gold House. As they stepped beneath the portico between the vine-strangled and decrepit columns, Ellen said, "We're going to have to tell Tanya the truth, aren't we? We can't keep it from her—the fact that this place was an asylum, or rest home, or what have you."

"We have to tell her," Sue said. "But if she wants out, I'll still go in with you. I'm fascinated by this place."

Ellen frowned. "I'm not sure I can afford half." Plus, this adventure was something the three of them were going to do together. She didn't want to buy the house without Tanya.

"You girls are crazy," Jan said. "I guess the inside must be amazing."

"Mother, try to use your imagination to envision what it *will* be when we're finished with it."

"I'll have to use my imagination, all right."

Ellen unlocked the front door, pausing once again on the threshold and listening for any signs of a presence. Then she opened the door for the other two and followed them inside.

"Of course, if you find gold, it'll be worth it," Jan added.

"As soon as I get home tonight, I'll do some research on the internet," Ellen said as they showed Jan the front rooms. "Millie said the doctor's name was Jonathan Piers, isn't that right? The same name we read about in the abstract from the realtor?"

"There was no internet in 1930," Jan said.

"Mother, have you ever heard of archives? It's worth a Google search, anyway."

"This house reminds me of your Aunt Mary's," Jan said. "I never did care for gold fixtures."

"What happened to using your imagination?" Sue asked sarcastically.

"I think this wallpaper might be sabotaging it," Jan retorted.

"It is pretty bad," Ellen agreed. "I can't wait to peel it off."

They finished touring the bottom floor and headed for the stairs, but as Ellen started to ascend, Sue grabbed her hand. "The last thing you should do is scream if you see her, okay? We want her to feel comfortable around us, if we're going to share the same space for a while."

Ellen could think of nothing to say, so she nodded and continued her climb.

The first thing she did after reaching the second floor was to have a peek up the attic stairs. A cold chill shuddered down her spine, and she lost the air in her lungs.

"What's wrong?" Sue asked.

Ellen's mouth was as dry as sandpaper. "The attic door. It's ajar."

Sue's face turned white.

"So what?" Jan asked. "Is it not supposed to be?"

"It was locked the last time we came," Sue explained.

"Should we investigate?" Ellen asked, her stomach in knots. She wasn't sure she was brave enough to go up there.

"I'm so curious," Sue said. "I won't be able to sleep tonight if I don't go up there and check it out."

"I'm scared," Ellen admitted. "Should we go get Bud first?"

"Oh, you girls." Jan brushed past them and headed up the stairs, though not very quickly. She held on to the rail and pulled.

"I'm more scared of Bud than I am of the ghost," Sue said. "Come on. We'll stay together, all right?"

Ellen nodded and followed Sue and Jan up the steps. The whole, miserable way, Ellen was tempted to ask Sue to get out her gun, just in case, but she was afraid that might make the situation worse.

The smell reached them before they made it to the top. Ellen worried they would find a dead body.

"There's no one here," Jan said. "Unless I'm detecting an otherworldly presence. Do you feel that, Sue?"

"I can barely breathe," Sue said, tucking her nose and chin beneath the neckline of her blouse. "What's that smell?"

Ellen covered her nose and mouth with her hand as she glanced around the large room. Eight very old hospital beds

57

lined the perimeter—two against each wall. All but one of them was cluttered with what appeared to be medical equipment.

"Maybe the patients of the asylum were kept up here," Sue speculated.

"That would explain the restraints but not the external orthopedic apparatuses," Jan's mother, who was a nurse for thirty years before she retired, said. "Or those bassinets."

In one corner, three bassinets covered in cobwebs were crowded together.

Ellen stepped over a litter of paper and books as she crossed the attic floor to one of the beds with a pile of metal apparatuses. "What are those things used for?"

"Repairing bone fractures," Jan said. "They have quite a collection up here."

"Maybe the patients were susceptible to falls?" Sue wondered. "Maybe they broke a lot of bones."

"That machine over there in the corner is called a Bergonic chair," Jan said. "It was used in the thirties and forties for treating psych patients with shock therapy. We had an old one at the state hospital, though it was never used while I was there."

Ellen shuddered. "I wonder why all this stuff is still here."

"I guess if you buy this place, you get the antiquated equipment, too," Jan said with a laugh. "Not sure what you'd do with it though."

"Maybe a museum would buy it," Ellen offered.

"We might be able to salvage the bassinets," Sue said.

Ellen crossed her arms. "No way would I let any baby in one of those. They look about to disintegrate."

"Not to mention the bugs," Jan added.

"Mother, do you know what that machine is over there?" Sue asked, pointing to the far left corner.

"I think that was used to measure brain waves back in the day," Jan said, bending over one of the beds. "Oh, and I can't believe they have one of these." She held up a rubber tube that was attached to a squat machine. "They used to force-feed patients through the rectum with these."

"Oh, God." Ellen wrinkled her nose. "What was the purpose of that?"

"They thought body fat was the cure to mental health, because so many people who suffered from nervous disorders were extremely thin."

"I guess we would have been pretty safe back then and considered rather sane. Don't you think, Mother?" Sue laughed.

"Right up until they heard us talk," Jan said.

They all three laughed.

"And I think I've figured out where the smell is coming from," Jan said, bending over one of the beds.

Ellen peered over Jan's shoulder to see a shoebox filled with fur and blood. "Oh, God. What is that?"

"Dead rats," Jan said. "Four of them, looks like."

Just then, the hair stood up on Ellen's arms and neck as she heard a flutter behind her, like papers blowing in the wind. She was chilled to the bone, and as she turned, she felt like she was doing so in slow motion.

Jan cried out in surprise as something white scurried across the floor and down the attic steps. It wasn't the girl. It was smaller and on all fours.

"Was that a cat?" Ellen asked, clutching her heart.

"A ghost cat," Sue said. "It was as white as the girl and as ethereal."

"That's what it was, all right," Jan said, catching her breath. "Maybe it's what killed these rats and placed them together in this box."

Ellen felt dizzy, chilled, and faint. She struggled to slow down her breathing.

"Are you okay?" Sue asked her.

Ellen didn't answer right away.

"Close your mouth," Jan said, placing her hand on Ellen's belly. "You're hyperventilating and need to take deeper, slower breaths. Look at me. Breathe with me. Hold it. Come on, Ellen, hold it. And now out. Nice and slow. Use your belly to push away my hand. That's it."

Later that evening, with a plate of grilled steak and potatoes Paul had cooked, Ellen sat in front of a football game—

she had no idea who was playing and didn't care—and told Paul about the attic.

"I guess I can cancel the locksmith then, huh?" Paul had paused the TV during the commercials and was now fast-forwarding to the game.

Ellen wiped her chin with her napkin. "Won't Ronnie want a key made anyway?"

"Yeah, I guess so." He found the game and hit play. "Are you still interested in the place? I mean, I wouldn't let a bunch of old hospital equipment and ghost stories stop you from following your dream."

Ellen's mouth dropped open for the second time that day. She hadn't told him that she'd personally seen what might be a ghost or a vagrant because she was worried he'd try to stop her from pursuing the house. Now she wondered if she should give him more credit. Maybe he did care about her dreams.

"Well, there's a little more to it," she admitted before telling him everything. It felt amazing to have a real conversation with him again. Although he stared at the television, she could tell he was listening to her. "What do you think I should do?"

"Well, if the girl was a vagrant, I'd think the neighbors would have caught on to her by now, don't you? And if she's an apparition, maybe she just needs closure. And maybe you're the one to give to her."

Ellen had to bite her tongue to keep her mouth from falling open a third time. She also had to close her eyes to keep the tears back as she was reminded of the man she'd married, the man she loved. Why didn't she see him more often? Was he invisible, too?

"That's a good point," she managed to say after clearing her throat. "Thank you, honey. That's good advice."

Ellen felt more determined than ever to uncover the real story behind the old house. Maybe she and her friends wouldn't buy it, but she would definitely investigate it. She wanted to see if she could find out about the patients who lived there. Maybe there had been a young girl among them, and maybe that girl had owned a cat.

After clearing away the supper dishes and wiping down the kitchen counters, Ellen sat in the front room in her favorite reading chair with her feet propped up on an ottoman and ran a Google search on Dr. Jonathan Piers using her laptop. As she waited for the page to download, she cleaned her reading glasses and was reminded that her last eye visit had got her a recommendation for progressive lenses. She hoped to put that off a little while longer, however.

With reading glasses perched on her nose, she read over the first page of her search results. Only the top result was for "Piers." The rest of the page was full of Jonathan Pierce. So she clicked on the one link, hoping it would lead her somewhere, and before she had a chance to find out, Paul entered the room.

She was so unused to him coming into that room, that she was at first startled, giving a small cry similar to the sound Jan had made when the ghost cat had run across the attic floor.

Paul laughed. "What was *that*?"

"You scared me." She laughed, too. "All this talk of ghosts, I guess."

"Are you staying up?" he asked. "I'm thinking about turning in."

Ellen hesitated, caught off guard by this subtle but clear invitation for intimacy. If she refused, she would probably not get another for several months; if she accepted, her research would have to wait.

Would she be able to relax and enjoy herself with her curiosity so intensely piqued?

She should accept. She should accept. "Well…"

"Good night," he said. "The Cowboys won, in case you were interested."

Before she could think of what to say, he turned and walked away.

She sat there in her chair, stunned, and unsure how to respond. Should she chase after him? Had she misread him? Maybe he hadn't extended an invitation after all. Had he mistaken her indecision for disinterest? Maybe he'd been afraid to wait too long for the rejection he must have come to expect from her.

She decided she would read this one page about Dr. Jonathan Piers, and then she would follow Paul to his bedroom. She would wait to research the gold legend another time.

Dr. Jonathan Piers, 1900-1972, was a popular and controversial doctor who practiced the highly criticized "rest cure" developed by Dr. Silas Weir Mitchell in Philadelphia during the Civil War. Piers operated a rest home for "hysterical and nervous" women on an inconspicuous estate in San Antonio from 1930 until his death. He treated such famous persons as actress Willa Von Kempf and author Virginia Mason. Although the rest cure has been praised by some patients and their families, it has been heavily criticized by both feminists and professionals in the medical community for its oppressive treatment of women. It required months of bed rest, shock therapy, force-feeding, and isolation.

Piers's rest home was one of the last of its kind, officially closing to new patients in the wake of the doctor's death in 1972. Although the cause of the doctor's death is inconclusive, suspicions of suicide dominated public opinion.

Ellen closed her laptop and flattened her hand over her pounding heart. This house was calling to her—she could feel it. Injustice happened there, and the ghosts of its residents needed closure. She jumped from her chair and practically skated in her stockinged feet toward her husband's room, anxious to relay what she'd learned.

Through his closed door, she heard the buzz-saw sound of his snoring.

She was too late.

Chapter Seven: The Psychic and the Locksmith

As Ellen drove toward the King William district on Monday from the university where she taught, a phrase from Thomas Merton's *No Man Is an Island* played over and over in her mind: "Art enables us to find ourselves and lose ourselves at the same time." She had just been discussing the meaning of art with her students, offering them multiple perspectives and inviting them to share their own, and this quote from Merton was her favorite. To find and to lose oneself in the most positive ways, she had explained, was what had attracted her to art. She found herself by connecting with her creative spirit and allowing it to breathe through what she painted. And when she lost herself, it wasn't a feeling of *loss* but of transcendence from everyday routine to something extraordinary.

And yet, except for her standard demonstrations for her students, she hadn't painted in years.

In a strange way, her desire to rehabilitate the Greek revival stemmed from this deep and urgent need to find herself and to lose herself. And now that there were other women—victims of an archaic and oppressive "rest cure" whose voices had been stifled—her need to resurrect the house was more compelling than ever. She wanted to find out as much as she could about the women who had lived there, and she wanted to give those women a voice.

But she dreaded showing Tanya what she and Sue had discovered in the attic.

If only Sue could be there, too. Unfortunately Jan had guilted her daughter into going with her to a doctor's appointment, even though it was a regular checkup and nothing out of the ordinary. Sue would not be able to meet them at the house this evening. It was up to Ellen to convince Tanya that this was the house they should buy.

When Ellen pulled up to the curb in front of the Gold House, she saw Tanya already sitting in her car waiting. Ellen climbed from her vehicle and gazed at the old Greek revival, imagining how it must have looked back in 1860, when it was newly built and before it had been turned into a place of torture. Suddenly, she could clearly see the prominent columns along the front portico, joining the arches between them. The yellow paint trimmed in white was crisp against a yard of green grass and vibrant foliage. The wisteria came to life, and its purple blooms hung like chandeliers from the portico. The porch itself was cleanly swept and lined with pots of colorful flowers. Two rocking chairs flanked one of the front windows, framed with clean white shutters and matching those on the story above.

Tanya said hello and pulled Ellen from her vision.

"You okay?" Tanya asked.

Ellen caught her breath and blinked, and it was then that she noticed that Tanya's eyes were red-rimmed. "I'm okay. What about you?"

Tanya swiped at tears with the back of her hands. "I honestly don't know."

"Is it your mom?"

Tanya nodded.

"I'm sorry. Has something else happened?"

"I went by there on the way over here, and my dad is just so overwhelmed and depressed. It's really hard on him, you know?"

"I can imagine."

"And Dave and I have begged them to move in with us, but Dad wants his own space, wants to stay in his own home."

"Have you thought about moving in with them, just temporarily?" Ellen asked.

"Yes, but Dad insists he can handle it." She broke down into more tears. "But I don't think he can."

Ellen put her arm around Tanya and tried to comfort her. "I guess you'll have to trust him to tell you when he can't."

"If she doesn't kill them both first," she said. "He had to put out a fire yesterday in the kitchen. I can't believe he didn't call me."

Ellen wasn't sure what to say. "Maybe he was embarrassed. Or maybe he didn't want to worry you."

"I tried to talk to my mom, too. And, for a second, I thought she knew who I was again. She seemed to recognize me, but she called me Vivian again. That was her cousin. She passed away last year." Tanya covered her face. "My mom's forgotten all about me. Her own daughter."

"Somewhere deep inside, there's a part of her who senses you and loves you."

"How can you know that?" Tanya asked.

"I choose to believe it."

Tanya nodded but didn't look convinced.

"Ready to see the attic?" Ellen asked. "It will definitely get your mind off of your parents."

Tanya followed Ellen up the cracked sidewalk. "Sue warned me about the medical equipment and the dead rats—oh, and the cat ghost! Sounds creepy. Are you sure you're still interested in this place?"

Ellen stopped to face Tanya. "More than ever. Look, I don't know if that girl is a ghost or just some vagrant who is pretending to be a ghost, but regardless, this house has a history that needs to be brought out into the open. The women who were imprisoned here need their stories to be told, don't you think?"

"We don't have to buy the house to research its past residents."

They continued toward the front door. "True. But wouldn't it be something to give the original house its dignity back? After all it's been through?"

Tanya smiled. "Yes. Yes, it would."

As Ellen opened the front door, the locksmith pulled up behind her car, and she and Tanya waited for him to catch up with them before entering. He carried a toolbox and wore a cap and coveralls. His brown face was sweaty beneath the cap, and he looked tired. After introducing himself as Miguel, he asked to see the lock that needed to be rekeyed.

Miguel followed Ellen and Tanya up the steps to the second floor. Ellen's heart raced as they reached the door to the attic steps, because she was anxious about seeing the girl or the cat again. When she opened the door to the dark stairwell, she did get a shock, but it wasn't ethereal.

The attic door, which had been left ajar, was closed.

"How is it closed?" Ellen whispered.

"Are you sure you left it open?" Tanya asked.

Ellen nodded, clasping her trembling hands together.

"Maybe someone else has viewed the house," Tanya offered.

"Maybe." Ellen climbed the stairs in spite of her fear and tried the knob. "It's locked."

Tanya glanced at Miguel before whispering, "You think the ghost may have locked it?"

Ellen shrugged. She didn't know what to believe anymore.

"Ghost?" the locksmith asked.

"The house has a reputation," Ellen explained. "The neighbors say it's haunted. I just know I left this door open yesterday, but it's locked now, so I guess you'll have to pick it before you can rekey it."

"That's no trouble, Miss," he said. "I have to take it all apart anyway. I'll go ahead and get started."

He took out a flashlight and shined it on the knob.

As Ellen and Tanya headed downstairs to wait, there was a knock at the front door.

"I bet that's Jeanine," Tanya said.

Ellen took a deep breath before opening the door to let the psychic inside.

The psychic wasn't at all what Ellen was expecting. Jeanine was short, petite, probably in her late thirties, with shoulder-length, frizzy brown hair, pale skin, and big spectacles. In her old-fashioned high-buttoned blouse, she looked more like a librarian than a woman skilled in the paranormal.

"Hey, Jeanine," Tanya said. "Come on in. This is my friend, Ellen."

"Nice to meet you," Ellen said as she shook the psychic's hand.

Jeanine held onto Ellen's hand and gave it a squeeze. "I sense you're nervous. Don't worry. I've done this before, okay?"

Ellen fought the blush spreading across her face and failed. "Of course."

Jeanine entered the foyer and stood at the base of the stairs to the second floor with her eyes closed. "I sense a great deal of energy in this house."

"Can you sense anything in particular?" Tanya asked anxiously. "I need to know if there's evil here. Can you tell?"

Jeanine opened her eyes and frowned. "I see someone beside you, Tanya. Someone who knows you. She followed you here."

"Who is she?" Tanya glanced nervously at Ellen.

"Dorian? Marian?"

"Vivian?" Tanya asked. "My mother had a cousin named Vivian."

"That's it," Jeanine said. "She's here to tell you that you need to let your mother go. Your mother's spirit is ready to leave, but she's holding onto a frail body with a faulty brain because she's worried about you."

Tears flowed from Tanya's eyes as she patted her chest and fanned her face. "How sure are you that it's Vivian and that she's speaking about my mother?"

Ellen wrapped an arm around Tanya's waist, worried her friend was going to lose her balance and falter to the floor.

"I'm so sorry, hon. I'm so, so, sorry. Vivian is leaving. She said what she needed to say. She's gone now. I'm so sorry. I'm very sure."

"Maybe my mom wasn't calling *me* Vivian," Tanya said in a breathless voice as she continued to stagger against Ellen. "Maybe she *saw* Vivian next to me. Do you think that was it?"

"It could be," Jeanine said.

Ellen didn't know what to believe. She held her friend but looked at Jeanine with skepticism. This woman knew Tanya, but Ellen wasn't sure how well. Could the psychic have made up the whole thing? Most of Tanya's friends knew about the struggle she was going through with her mother. Was the psychic just trying to give her good advice? Or had she really seen the spirit of Vivian?

At that moment, all three women were startled by the locksmith crying out, "Ahh! Ahh!"

Ellen climbed the stairs to the second floor with the other two women at her heels. When she reached the landing, she rushed over to the attic steps and peered up the stairwell. "Miguel?"

He bolted down the dark stairs toward her, his tools jangling around in his tool box. He exited the attic stairwell, dropped his toolbox on the floor, and flattened his back against a wall. "Jesus."

"What's wrong?" Ellen followed him into the hallway. "What happened?"

"Jesus, Mary, and Joseph, I saw the ghost," he said in between quick breaths. "Oh my Jesus, I saw her."

The three women gawked at one another in stunned silence.

"Was she a full-bodied apparition?" Jeanine asked. "Or was she more like a hazy, transparent aura."

"Full bodied," Miguel said, still breathing heavily. "Very thin, though, and freakishly white. Scary as hell."

"What was scary about her?" Tanya asked.

"She threw a book at me," he said. "And she told me to get out. She growled it, like a dog."

"Then what happened?" Jeanine asked.

"I didn't hang around to find out."

"If she's an evil spirit, I'm out of here," Tanya said. "I can't take this right now, Ellen. I hope you understand."

Ellen did understand. "It's okay."

"Wait," Jeanine said. "Don't give up so easily. We can perform a cleansing ritual. Let me get my sage smudge stick out of the car. I'll be right back."

"Hurry," Tanya said.

"Let's wait for her downstairs," Miguel said.

"Good idea." Tanya followed the locksmith down.

"Are you sure you want to stay for this?" Ellen asked Miguel. She hoped he would. There was safety in numbers.

"I left half my tools up there," he said. "I don't want to have to replace them."

They met Jeanine at the front door. In one hand, she held a bunch of dried sage bound together with twine. It looked like a hand-held broom. In the other hand, she carried a beautiful shell bowl with a box of matches in the bottom of it.

"Do we have running water in this house?" Jeanine asked.

"I'm afraid not," Ellen said.

"Hmm. Okay. Can you help me open all the windows on both floors before we get started? That way the spirits can flee along with the smoke."

"Wait, you aren't going to light that thing, are you?" Ellen asked. All they needed was to accidentally burn the place down.

"That's how she gets the evil out," Tanya said. "And it's the only way I'll even consider buying this place."

They opened the windows in each of the rooms on the bottom floor before going upstairs to the bedrooms.

"What about the attic?" Miguel asked. "Do we need to open the window up there, too?"

"We'll save that for last," Jeanine said.

Ellen touched Tanya's shoulder. "I think Sue will be disappointed if we do this. She was excited about this place being haunted." Ellen could hardly believe what she was saying. Had she decided to believe in ghosts? Had she decided to give this cleansing ritual any credibility?

"I'm only forcing the impure, negative, and evil spirits to leave," Jeanine said. "I sense so much energy in this place. I think you'll continue to have visitors here."

"Just not evil ones," Tanya said. "Right?"

"That's right," Jeanine said.

Ellen wondered how the psychic could guarantee such a thing. What would prevent other evil spirits from coming here after the ritual? Or what if the same ones came back? She

75

decided not to bring this up in front of Tanya. She needed her friend to believe in Jeanine's abilities and reassurance.

The bedroom windows were difficult to budge. There were two that even Miguel couldn't open.

"No worries," Jeanine said. "We've given them enough escape routes. Let's begin downstairs."

They followed Jeanine to the bottom floor and watched her light the end of her sage stick. Once it made a decent flame, she blew it out until only burning embers were left at the end of the stick. Then she held the sage over the abalone bowl to catch the ashes. "Ready?"

They nodded. Ellen felt a lump in her throat and wondered what the hell she'd gotten herself into.

"Before I cleanse this place, I need you to bathe yourselves in the smoke, as a protection." Jeanine showed them how to use their hands to pull the smoke over their faces and bodies. "This will prevent any of the spirits from attempting to possess you."

Tanya giggled nervously. Ellen gave her friend a smile but was holding back from muttering, *You've got to be kidding me.*

The locksmith didn't seem a bit phased. He was a true believer.

Once they had fully bathed in the smoke, Jeanine went to the living room, waved the smoking stick throughout the room, and said, "I cleanse this room of all impurities, negativity, and evil. Fly away, never to return."

Ellen watched the smoke swirl throughout the room until it found its way to the open window. Jeanine repeated this step in every room on the bottom floor, including the bathrooms, pantry, and closets.

When they reached the base of the stairs to the second story, something flew past Ellen's ear.

"What the hell was that?" she asked, clutching her chest.

"One of my picks," Miguel said, finding it on the old wooden floorboards.

Another flew down and grazed Tanya's elbow. "Ow! That hurt!"

"Get behind me," Jeanine said. "We have a fighter."

"Shit. I may need to pay you more money for this," Tanya said, gasping. "Has this ever happened before?"

"A long time ago," the psychic whispered. "When I was first getting started." Then out loud, she said, "I cleanse this house of all impurities, negativity, and evil. Be gone! Never to return!"

The floor above them creaked and shuddered. It sounded like a herd of buffalo frolicking around up there. Then it stopped.

Jeanine reached the top of the stairs. "I cleanse this house of all impurities, negativity, and evil. Fly away, impure spirits, never to return."

They went through each of the rooms on the second floor without another incident.

Now it was time to go to the attic.

Chapter Eight: The Doctor's Ledger

"**I** think I'll wait down here," Miguel said. "Maybe she'll like you ladies better."

Ellen would rather the locksmith go up with them, but she supposed doing so was a little outside of the scope of his job description, so she nodded and followed the other two up. Her heart was beating hard and fast, and she could feel it all the way up in her throat. Whether this was an apparition or a real person, it seemed as though anything could happen, and Ellen was terrified.

Jeanine entered the attic first, followed by Tanya. As Ellen crossed the threshold, she gazed about the room but saw no sign of the ghost girl.

"Could one of you open that window?" Jeanine asked.

There was one window on the center front exterior wall, shaped like a clamshell. Ellen went to it and found a handle for cranking the window open. It was really hard to turn and only opened the window about six inches. "Is that good?"

Jeanine nodded as she stepped over the litter of papers and books on the floor to wave the sage smudge stick around the room. "I cleanse this house once and for all of all impurities, negativity, and evil. Leave this place never to return, but guardian angels and all positivity are welcome. Be gone, evil! Be gone, impurities! Fly away! Fly away, never to return."

They all three watched as the smoke curled around the room and made its way through the clam-shaped window. Jeanine batted it in that direction with the smoking stick. Ellen was worried an ember would fall on the litter of paper and books on the floor and start a raging fire, but Jeanine was careful with her bowl and put Ellen at ease after a few minutes.

"Is it working?" Tanya asked.

"Yes," Jeanine said. "I can feel the negativity leaving us."

Ellen thought this was as good a time as any to put on the latex gloves she had in her shoulder bag and bring out the Ziplock bags.

Tanya stopped fanning the smoke toward the window and gave Ellen a quizzical look. "What are you doing?"

"Collecting evidence." She found a book on the floor—some kind of medical book—and popped into the bag, sealing it shut. "I found a lab online that will check for prints and DNA and match them up against a bunch of different databases. Maybe we can identify our ghost and help her find closure, if that's what she needs."

"Wouldn't it be easier to ask Jeanine?" Tanya continued to bat the smoke toward the window. "Jeanine, can you sense anything about the ghost girl?"

"I can sense her energy, but I don't see her," Jeanine said. "I think she's a very troubled spirit—not evil, just troubled. What is all this stuff?"

"Old medical equipment," Ellen said as she took the pillow case from the one empty bed and stuffed it into another bag before sealing it shut. Before she moved on to gather another piece of evidence, something shocking caught her attention. It was a long hair, a human hair, as white as cotton, lying on the bed. Ellen picked it up in her gloved hand and put it in one of her bags. "I wonder how old this hair is." She held up the bag to show it to them. "I think it's from our ghost. Maybe the lab can identify her from it."

All fear left Ellen as her excitement over solving the mystery of the house built up inside of her. The website had said it would take thirty to sixty days for them to analyze any samples she shipped to them, and it was not cheap, but she felt it would bring her peace of mind. She didn't say it out loud to the others, but it would answer the question once and for all of whether their ghostly girl was dead or alive.

"Whoever she is, she has unfinished business here," Jeanine said. "The house is clean of impurities, but I still sense the girl's presence. I think she's very attached to this house. Something happened to her here that she hasn't yet recovered from. She's looking for answers. I think it has something to do with her mother."

Ellen's mouth dropped open.

"What's wrong?" Tanya asked.

"That's what Millie Forrester said the ghost asked her. This was years ago, I think. The ghost appeared to Millie in her

81

bedroom and asked where her mother was." Goose bumps tingled all up and down Ellen's arms. "And when Millie asked the ghost who her mother was, the ghost said 'Cynthia.'"

"If you can discover what happened to the girl's mother, maybe the ghost will finally be at peace," Jeanine said.

They heard someone coming up the attic steps. The hair raised on the back of Ellen's neck.

"Everything okay up here?" It was Miguel.

Ellen had forgotten about him. She sighed with relief and almost laughed at herself. "We haven't seen any sign of the ghost."

"Oh, thank you, Jesus," Miguel said. "If I can just get these tools back, I can finish my work downstairs." He knelt on the floor and picked up a small case. "Man, these pins are expensive. I'm glad I won't have to replace them. It looks like the ghost kept one of my picks, though."

"Maybe it will show up somewhere here in the house," Jeanine said. "Ghosts will often move things around like that."

"This is the book she threw at me." He held up a thick, black, leather-bound notebook. "It's a ledger book, I think. It looks really old."

He knelt on the floor flipping through the pages.

"Can I see that?" Ellen asked.

Miguel gave her the book. On the very first page, she saw a table with the headings *Client, Patient, Age, Diagnosis, Treatment, Paid,* and *Month.* The first line was filled in with

Marcia Gold, Marcia Gold, 70, severe melancholy, BR/FF/OS/MT, Mortgage Credit/March '30.

"Marcia Gold?" Ellen said out loud. "Wasn't she the daughter of the original owner?"

"I think so," Tanya said. "The paperwork on the house said 'only living descendant,' remember?"

Ellen nodded. "She paid with mortgage credit? Do you think Marcia gave Dr. Piers the house in exchange for treatment?"

Tanya shrugged. "Maybe."

According to the ledger, Marcia was the doctor's only patient for the first six months of his practice. Then in September, another patient was listed: Hilary Turner. The client was James Turner. According to the entry, Hilary was seventeen years old and diagnosed with "neurasthenia and grave insomnia." In the "Treatments" column were the acronyms BR/FF/OS/MT/ST. The ledger indicated the monthly payment was $125.

"One of his patients was only seventeen years old," Ellen muttered.

Tanya peered over Ellen's shoulder. "Are you serious?"

"Yes. And check this out," Ellen said. "This doctor was making good money—a hundred and twenty-five dollars a month in 1930 from each patient. Wow."

"That was a lot of money during the Depression," Jeanine commented.

83

As Ellen scanned down the list she saw other names added over the next pages, and an entry in December of 1931 marked Marcia Gold "deceased" at age 71. A notation was made as to her cause of death: "Died in childbirth."

At age seventy-one?

"Look at this." Ellen pointed the notation out to Tanya.

"That's got to be a mistake," Tanya said.

"I'll just go downstairs to finish rekeying the lock." Miguel climbed up from the floor and collected his case of pins.

As he went downstairs, Tanya asked Jeanine, "Should we close the windows now?"

"Let me put out this stick, first," she said. "We need to make sure all the smoke has left the house."

The three went downstairs. Ellen sat at the old wooden table in the dining room looking over the doctor's ledger as the other two handled the smoke. Miguel sat at the opposite end working on the lock. She felt a little guilty for not helping with the windows but was now more interested in learning about the house's patients than she was in ridding it of impure spirits. She held the book up in the diminishing light pouring in from the kitchen. It wouldn't be long before dusk came, so she eagerly combed through the book as quickly as she could. She was hoping to find out if Marcia really had given birth at age seventy-one, and, if so, what had happened to the baby.

On the inside back cover, she found a key:

BR = Bed Rest

FF = Force Feeding

OS = Organ Stimulation

MT = Massage Therapy

ST = Shock Therapy

DT = Drug Therapy

SJT- Straight-Jacket Therapy

Ellen shuddered.

The ledger showed Hilary Turner as the only patient until April of 1931, when Victoria Schmidt joined her. The client was Karl Schmidt, and the diagnosis was hysteria. Every acronym, including the one for straight-jacket therapy, was listed in the "Treatments" column.

In the fall of 1932, two more patients were added in the ledger, and the monthly cost went up to $140. Over the next ten years, all the names changed except for Hilary Turner. Then, in 1945, the name Regina Piers was listed in the "Patient" column, and her age was recorded as fourteen. The name listed in the "Client" column was Jonathan Piers. A zero value was written in the "Paid" column.

"He treated his own daughter?" Ellen murmured to herself. And where was the mother? *Who* was the mother?

Then it hit her. Fourteen years before, Marcia Gold had died in childbirth. Regina Piers could very well have been Marcia's baby.

Ellen flipped through the few hundred pages remaining in the thick, dusty book. Although ink smears made some names difficult to discern in some rows, they were repeated often enough where she could make out what they were. All the names varied throughout the rest of the pages, with patients typically being treated for six months to one year before being released. Only Hilary Turner and Regina Piers remain listed through the duration of the years.

Then in 1970, there was another listing that gave Ellen a shock: Cynthia Piers, age fourteen. Cynthia was the name the ghost had given Millie.

Could this have been the ghost girl's mother?

Chapter Nine: Mothers

Over the next two weeks, all efforts at making a decision over whether to buy the Gold House were stalled when Tanya's mother unexpectedly passed away.

Tanya told the story to Ellen and Sue: She had taken a pan of lasagna to her parents the day after the cleansing with the psychic. As they were eating at the table together, she and her parents had a pleasant time, even though Tanya's mom kept asking her if she and her people were from the hills. Tanya just nodded instead of explaining. She had taken to heart what Jeanine had said: her mother's soul was depending on a frail body and faulty brain, but the soul knew Tanya.

Tanya's mom also told her the same story about the new carpet three times, but instead of saying, "I know, Mom," like she had in the past, she pretended like it was the first time she was hearing it. Each time her mother told the story, Tanya pretended, and it made the whole dinner together so much more pleasant.

After they had finished eating, after her Dad had insisted on putting away the dishes and cleaning up, Tanya, sitting alone at the table with her mother, took her mother's hand, and said, "You can let go, Mom. I'll be okay."

Tanya said that her mother had a flash of recognition— she could see it in her eyes. Her mother said, "Don't cry, sweetie. It'll be all right."

Even though her mother didn't mention Tanya's name, Tanya felt sure her mother knew to whom she was speaking.

That night, Tanya's mother passed in her sleep.

The service was beautiful and well-attended, and, although Tanya was devastated over losing her mother, she said again and again that she was relieved for her father and relieved that her mother was finally at rest.

The whole ordeal had a profound effect on Ellen. Her belief that the supernatural was just something willing believers embraced because it was easier than accepting a final death had now been officially shaken. Had Vivian's spirit really come to tell Tanya to let her mother go? Normally, Ellen would say, no; it was a coincidence. But Ellen was no longer sure of her answer.

Tanya's mother's loss also took a toll on Sue. Over lunch one day when it was just the two of them, Sue told Ellen that she knew she needed boundaries between her and her mother, but she feared it was too late to draw them.

"This is my fault," Sue said. "I should have done something about it in the early years of my marriage, but the truth is I get lonely, unlike you, who can go days without talking to a soul and with your head in a book. So it was convenient that my mother was always there."

"I can understand that," Ellen said before taking a sip of tea.

"So I think I have to pay the price of that convenience now, when I don't feel like I need her as much." Then she added, "And the truth is, maybe I need her more than I realize."

Although she understood Sue's predicament, Ellen had one of her own, and it was the exact opposite of Sue's. Ellen only spoke to her mother about once a month. And she only saw her a few times a year. This wouldn't sound so bad if it weren't for the fact that they lived in the same town.

As much as Ellen teased Sue about her mother's constant interference, Ellen had to admit she was jealous. The only time Ellen spoke to or saw her mother was when Ellen initiated it. Maybe it was time to go see her again.

"So I guess we're dropping the idea of buying the house?" Sue asked after a few minutes had passed.

"Not dropping it. Just putting it on hold. It's not like there are people knocking down doors to get to that place. It will still be there when Tanya's ready to talk about it again."

"I didn't find a single shred of information about the gold legend, by the way," Sue said. "Did you?"

"Nothing." Ellen had done both an internet and library search and had come up empty.

"Well, it doesn't matter," Sue said. "I really want that house."

"So do I."

That weekend, Ellen drove in the pouring rain to the other side of San Antonio, past the King William district, to her childhood home, where her mother lived. Her father had died of a heart attack ten years ago, and since then, her mother only left her home to go the grocery store. Although Ellen had a younger brother, he'd moved to Kentucky, to live near his wife's family, and they only saw one another at Thanksgiving and Christmas.

Sometimes Ellen would be sitting at home in her reading chair after having just finished a book, and an overwhelming need to see her brother would seize her. Tears would flood her eyes, and she'd feel panicky, like if she didn't see him, and tell him that she loved him, she would lose him forever. Over the years, she saw her brother in her sons. Little things they said and did—like a facial expression or a laugh—would remind her of him. Growing up, she had been more of a mother to Jody than their mother had, and she supposed it was a mother's love for a son that she often felt for him. Maybe that panicky feeling was a fear that she had lost a son, her first son, and hadn't been a proper "mother" by not staying in better touch with him as adults.

"Oh, Jody," she whispered now beneath the rhythmic beat of the windshield wipers. "I wonder how you're doing these days."

He'd only been five that day they'd walked in on their mother and found her putting a razor blade to her wrist. Ellen had been ten years old, and she and Jody had come in from playing kickball with the neighbor kids on a hot summer day. Their dad was still at work. They'd come in hungry and thirsty and hoping for lunch when they found their mother in the bathroom sitting in front of her vanity with a cigarette propped between two shaky fingers and a razor blade between her thumb and ring finger. She held the blade against the skin beneath her left wrist. Their mother rarely smoked and never drank, but there were empty beer cans lining the vanity. She was wearing more makeup than usual—though mascara was streaming down her cheeks—and a silky robe Ellen had never seen. The radio was blasting, and it wasn't even music—just some commercials.

Ellen could remember the scene so vividly because her mother looked like a completely different person. She'd almost asked, "Who are you?" before finally recognizing that this shaking, sobbing, smoking woman was her very own mother.

"Get out!" her mother hollered at them as soon as she had noticed them. "I'm busy right now!"

"But we're hungry!" Jody complained, too young to realize that something was terribly wrong.

"Can't you two open a can of raviolis? You need to start acting like big kids. You aren't babies anymore." Their mother burst into full-blown sobs.

"Mama?" Ellen said gently. "What's going on?"

"Can't I smoke a cigarette in peace? Just get out! Both of you go!"

Her mother didn't speak about the incident again until six months later.

It was after school before their father had come home from work. Because Jody was in kindergarten, and the lower grades were dismissed from school an hour earlier than the upper, he'd gotten home on the bus before Ellen, who was in fifth grade. She arrived to find her mother and brother sitting side by side in the front room on the sofa.

"Come sit with me, Ellen," her mother said as soon as Ellen had entered. "I need to talk to you."

Even at the age of ten, Ellen knew something was wrong. This wasn't going to be a love fest. Her mother wasn't that kind of person. This was going to be bad news.

"Did someone die?" Ellen asked.

Her mother smiled, "No sweetheart. Just sit down."

Ellen sat stiffly beside her mother, waiting for the ball to drop.

"Do you remember that day last summer when you and Jody came into the bathroom and found me smoking and drinking? Remember how hard I was crying?"

Ellen nodded.

"It's because I need to leave this world."

"Huh?" Ellen and Jody spoke at the same time.

"Just listen. Some people don't get along as well in this world as they do in the next. I'm one of those people. I had my babies and I got you this far, and although I love you both very much, I'm a terrible mother, I know I am, and you'd be better off without me."

Ellen couldn't breathe.

"I'm just not meant for this world. It's too painful for me. You want your mama to be happy, don't you?"

"Where are you going?" Jody asked.

"To heaven," their mother replied. "And I'll be waiting for you there."

Ellen couldn't speak.

"No, Mama, I don't want you to go!" Jody broke into tears. "Don't leave us, Mama!"

Their mother started crying, too. "I can take you with me, baby. Would you like to go to heaven?"

Jody nodded.

Ellen snapped to attention. "No!" She jumped to her feet and tugged Jody away, even though Jody kicked at her and screamed at her to leave him alone. Ellen managed to get him in her arms and out of the house. She ran next door and asked for help.

To Ellen's knowledge, nothing had ever been done about her mother's suicidal tendencies. Maybe her parents kept things private, but that horrible day was never mentioned in front of her again. Ellen wasn't sure if Jody even remembered it.

But from that day on, Ellen would never leave Jody alone with their mother. And as she got older, she took him with her everywhere she went. Where her friends looked for every opportunity to get away from their younger siblings, Ellen did the opposite. She didn't trust her mother. Not one bit.

Her mother's married name was Ima Frost. Every time Ellen overheard her mother introduce herself, Ellen had thought, "Yes, you are, Mother. You're cold as ice."

The rain had stopped by the time Ellen arrived at her mother's house. Ima greeted her at the door and invited her to come sit in the back room, where the television was always on, whether her mother was watching it or not. Ellen supposed her mother needed to be surrounded by noise.

Ima turned down the volume on the television and offered Ellen something to drink. "I've got tea, milk, and water."

"No, thanks," Ellen said.

Her mother looked thinner and older since the last time Ellen had seen her, three months ago. The uncontrollable tremor in her head had gotten a little worse, too.

"So how've you been?" Ellen asked sitting on the edge of the sofa, near her mother's recliner.

"I'm fine. How are you and Paul? And those grandkids of mine? Tell me what's going on with Nolan, Lane, and Alison."

"Everyone's fine."

Ellen told her a little about each of her kids and what they were up to—realizing that she hadn't spoken to her own children in some time. A pang of nostalgia swept over her as she glanced at a framed collage of her babies on her mother's entertainment center. Ellen had put it together for her mother years ago as a Christmas gift. "They're all fine," Ellen said again.

And then she told her about Tanya's mother.

"I'm sorry to hear that," her mother said. "I guess I'm not too far behind her."

"Please don't talk like that."

Her mother laughed. "Well, it's true."

Ellen changed the subject by telling her about the adventure she hoped to go on with her friends, about buying and flipping a house. She told her about the Gold House.

"A doctor by the name of Jonathan Piers used to practice the rest cure on female patients," Ellen explained. "It all sounds so awful."

"Oh, I know about that place," her mother said. "In the King William district?"

"What? What do you know?"

"Well, I went there once."

"As a patient?" Ellen's eyes nearly popped from their sockets. Surely she would have recognized her mother's name in the doctor's ledger.

"No, but I wanted to. Your father and I just went and toured the place and talked to the doctor during a free consultation. I really wanted to be admitted, but we couldn't afford it."

Ellen covered her gaping mouth.

"You were probably too young to remember this, but I had a nervous breakdown when I was in my thirties. It was a hard time."

Ellen didn't say anything. She wasn't sure what to say.

"I needed help and a neighbor recommended Dr. Piers."

"How did the neighbor hear about him?" Ellen asked.

"She'd read about him in the paper. A famous actress had just been admitted—Willa Von Kempf. I think your dad was hoping he'd have a chance to see her. I think that's why he was *all for* getting the free consultation." Her mother laughed.

"What was it like?"

"It was really nice and fancy," she said. "Brand new furnishings and finishes. The upstairs was kind of plain, but the doctor said it was to keep the patients from getting overstimulated by their surroundings. They were kept in a dark, quiet room, on strict bed rest. They weren't even allowed to turn themselves."

"What?"

"That's right. Two nurses had to go around several times a day and turn the patients, so they wouldn't get bed sores."

Ellen wondered if she should tell her mom about the force-feeding through the rectum but decided not to.

"I would have loved to escape to that place," her mother said. "I was so overwhelmed with life, with everything. I needed to be a vegetable for a while."

"What was it that overwhelmed you?" Ellen asked bravely.

"Oh, you don't want to know," her mother said. "And it was so long ago. It won't do either one of us any good to talk about it."

Ellen dropped it, not wanting to make her mother uncomfortable, but her curiosity was piqued. She wondered if she should ask Jody if he knew anything. No, he was too young. Maybe Ellen's Aunt Mary knew something.

"And I guess it's a good thing we couldn't afford that place," her mother added. "Because apparently, that doctor was having sex with his patients."

Ellen gaped again. "How do you know?"

"The actress, Willa Von Kempf, exposed him. It was the late sixties, maybe early seventies. The actress got pregnant and brought criminal charges against the doctor."

"Was he indicted?"

Her mother shook her head. "He committed suicide before he could be tried."

Chapter Ten: Murphy's Law

Two weeks after Tanya's mother's funeral, Tanya joined Ellen and Sue for lunch at Panera and surprised them by saying she wanted to buy the Gold House.

"Are you serious?" Ellen covered her heart, not sure if she should let hope for the house bloom there again. She had just begun to come to terms with not moving forward on the purchase. It had been a gloomy two weeks because of it.

"I need a distraction," Tanya said.

Ellen couldn't stop the smile from spreading across her face. She turned to Sue. "What about you? Still interested?"

"Absolutely," Sue said. "A day hasn't gone by that I haven't thought about that house."

"Me, too," Ellen admitted. "If you're sure, Tanya..."

Tanya nodded. "It's time for me to move on. I'm sure."

They all three met with Paul at Ellen's house the next day to discuss an offer. Paul recommended that they go in at five thousand below the asking price. They agreed and Paul immediately got on the phone with Ronnie while Ellen opened a bottle of champagne. She hadn't been this excited in ages.

The celebration was cut short by the expression on Paul's face as his conversation with the state's realtor came to an end.

"I'm sorry, ladies," Paul said after ending his call. "According to Ronnie, the San Antonio Conservation Society submitted an offer last week, and the state accepted it. The house is no longer on the market."

Ellen's head spun and her chest felt tight. Had she heard him correctly?

"How can that be?" Sue asked. "Did Ronnie ever mention that there were other interested parties?"

"Not at all," Paul said. "In fact, the offer came to him unexpectedly. He'd tried to get the Conservation Society to buy the house ten years ago, but some kind of legal case prevented the sale."

"Are they beyond the cooling off period?" Tanya asked Paul.

"I'm afraid so," Paul said. "I asked Ronnie why he didn't call me first, but he said, since he hadn't heard from us in two weeks, he didn't think we were interested. He'd been trying to get rid of this property for decades, so he jumped on it."

Ellen couldn't stop the tears from welling in her eyes and dripping down her cheeks. Was this really happening? Had they really lost the house? She couldn't speak.

"I'm sorry," Paul said again.

Tanya covered her face with her hands. "This is my fault."

"Don't say that," Sue said. "Of course it's not your fault. It's no one's fault. Things happen."

That night, Ellen lay in her bed in the dark, unable to fall asleep. She'd tried to read the mystery novel on her bedside table, but couldn't concentrate. She also couldn't get interested in anything on her son's old television. So she lay in bed thinking about the past two weeks. Every day had been the same: She'd have coffee and toast in the morning, teach a few hours of painting at the university, and come home and load the previous night's dinner dishes into the dishwasher after taking out the clean dishes from the night before that. Then she'd cook one of the twenty or so meals that had become a staple of her dinner menus. Then she'd eat, usually alone but occasionally with Paul. Soak the dishes in the sink. Take a shower. Watch a little home and garden television. Read a little mystery. Go to sleep, only to begin again the next day. What was the point of it all?

She thought maybe if her kids ever gave her grandchildren, purpose might be restored to her life, but this interim period between raising her own and waiting for grandkids was making her restless and insecure about her existence. Wasn't she meant for something more than this?

Her tears became sobs as she felt more alone in the universe than she'd ever felt in her whole life. Her children were gone, her father was dead, her mother had never really been there in the first place, her brother was in fucking Kentucky, and her husband was estranged from her under the same roof.

She had her friends, she reminded herself. And they shouldn't give up on this adventure. Maybe they could look at other properties...

The moment she allowed herself to consider that possibility, her stomach filled with bile, and she rushed from the room to the bathroom, where she was sick. She chastised herself for becoming so emotionally attached to this house—but there it was. She loved this house, and she loved the women who'd been victimized in it, and she wanted to be a part of its restoration—of their resurrection. She didn't want the women who had lived there to be invisible to human history.

Then an idea hit her: could she become involved with the Conservation Society? Could she help *them* to restore the house?

She cleaned her face and hands and went to the front room to her laptop to research the San Antonio Conservation Society. After clicking through several pages, she clicked on the most recent newsletter and was surprised to see an article written the day before by the society's president, entitled: "Our New Fourth Vice President Spearheads the Acquisition of the Historic Gold House." The article read:

The second time's a charm. The San Antonio Conservation Society attempted to purchase the historic Gold House on Alta Vista over a decade ago but was unsuccessful due to a claim of ownership that hadn't yet been settled by the courts. That claim was denied two years later, but by then the society had moved on to other projects.

Led by our new fourth vice-president, Mitchell Clark, the historic home has been successfully acquired by the society. While the society has no immediate use for the property, someone else has a vision for it: the San Antonio Zoo is interested in turning the grounds behind the house, which butte up to a greenbelt and dry creek bed, into a petting zoo with the goal of educating elementary-aged students about animals native to Texas. Although improvements to the structure may not happen anytime soon, the society will retain rights to the easement to protect the historical character of the façade. Negotiations with the San Antonio Zoological Society are underway.

Ellen gawked at the glowing screen of her laptop. How could this be? As much as she loved animals and educating children about them, the Gold House was not the place for that. What about its unique history? What about the lives of the women who had suffered through that history? A petting zoo would annihilate everything that old house had to say about human rights and female equality. Ellen had to do something to stop this plan from moving forward.

Although it was almost midnight, she called Sue.

"Did I wake you?" Ellen asked.

"I hadn't yet drifted off. What's up?"

Ellen told her what she'd learned.

"Oh my God," Sue said. "We can't let them do that."

"I agree. What should we do?"

"I guess we can start by emailing the president of the Conservation Society. Do you want to do it, or should I?"

"I'll do it. I can't sleep anyway."

"Neither can I."

"I want this house, Sue."

"Maybe we can convince the society to let us buy it from them," Sue offered.

"We won't be able to get it for the same good deal, though."

"Well, let's not assume the worst just yet. Okay?"

"Okay."

Then, as they were about to hang up, Sue said, "Wait a minute. Mitchell Clark. The new fourth vice-president. Why does that name ring a bell?"

Ellen searched her memory. It sounded familiar to her, too. "I don't know."

"The gold digger," Sue said. "Millie Forrester mentioned him to us. He's the neighbor who believes in the old legend."

Ellen gasped. "Oh my God, you're right."

"I bet he got wind from the Forresters that we were going to buy the property," Sue said.

"Are you suggesting he had the Conservation Society step in to prevent us from making the purchase?"

"I don't know, but this can't be a coincidence. That man must be up to something. Don't you think?"

Ellen's mind spun. Could Mitchell Clark have anything to do with the girl who might or might not be a ghost?

"We can't let this go," Sue said. "Okay?"

"I'm with you, there," Ellen said. "There's no way I'm giving up on this house now."

The next day—a Saturday—Sue drove Ellen across town to the King William district to pay a visit to the Forresters, hoping they would be willing to chat about the recent acquisition of the Gold House by the San Antonio Conservation Society. They had invited Tanya, but she had no desire to be in the presence of Bud Forrester. As Sue pulled up to the curb, Ellen glanced at the Greek revival next door, biting her tongue in an effort to keep the stupid tears from coming again.

Bud answered the door. He didn't look surprised to see them.

"I bet I know why you're here," he said. "Come on in and have a seat. I'll go get Millie."

"Thank you." Ellen was surprised by how welcoming Bud was. For someone who'd initially given her the creeps, he was downright charming.

While they waited, Sue whispered, "I wish we could have called. I feel bad surprising them like this."

"Me, too, but this is urgent."

"To us, it is. Maybe not to them."

"To them, too. Do you think they want a petting zoo right next door to them?"

"I guess not."

"If we can get their support, we might be able to convince the Conservation Society to sell to us instead of the zoo."

"I hope so," Sue said. "I really do."

The two of them sat there, whispering and fretting, for over twenty minutes before Millie finally appeared around the corner in her chair, being pushed by Bud. Ellen was startled by the strong odor that accompanied her, which a mask of perfume only made worse. Millie's face, too, looked washed out, and her hair was oily beneath a colorful scarf.

Ellen tried not to judge. She imagined it must be hard on Bud to bathe Millie regularly, not to mention Millie's mother. Maybe Millie wasn't comfortable hiring strangers, leaving him with all the hard work. And she imagined it must be no easy feat to lift her from her chair into a shower or tub and back into the chair. Maybe it was impossible, she thought as she tried to picture it. Maybe he gave her sponge baths and washed her hair at the sink.

"We're so sorry to barge in on you like this," Sue began. "But we feel this is important. Have you heard the news about the Gold House?"

"We have," Millie said.

"You don't seem upset about it," Ellen said.

"Why should we be?" Millie asked.

Sue raised her brows. "So you won't mind having a petting zoo next door?"

"It'll never happen." Bud took a chair next to Millie. "Not on this street. They could get away with something like that in other parts of King William, but not on this street."

"The Conservation Society published an article in their newsletter," Sue said. "It sounds like it's going to happen. Why do you think it won't?"

"The neighbors on Alta Vista have a few political strings," Bud said.

"This is all Mitchell Clark's doing," Millie added. "He wants to keep looking for his gold. When he heard about you, he lured the San Antonio Zoo in with promises he can never keep. And he used the zoo's interest, and this and that, to get the Conservation Society behind him. He knows the residents on this street will do everything in their power to prevent the sale."

Ellen felt the blood rush to her face. "So you think he set this up so that the house would stay vacant?"

"I'm sure of it," Bud said. "We were just on the phone with him three days ago. He called everyone on the block and told us straight from the horse's mouth."

"And the other neighbors are okay with this?" Sue asked. "They would rather the house stay in ruins than see it restored to its original beauty?"

"Well, they don't want a petting zoo," Millie said. "But I'm not sure they wouldn't prefer a restoration."

"They know it's not safe," Bud said. "They know Mitchell likes to take his chances scouring the property for gold, but I don't think anyone likes the idea of stirring up the ghost in that house. We all know she's likely to come to one, or all, of our houses during the renovations, you see."

"That's true," Millie said. "People are afraid of her, and this and that."

"So far, she's only harmed our pets," Bud said. "But who knows what she'll do if she's displaced?"

"We don't want to displace her," Sue said.

"What do you mean?" Millie asked. "You want that horrid thing to stick around?"

"We don't think she's horrid," Ellen said. "We think she needs closure. It has something to do with her mother. We want to help her. And if she wants to stay, she can stay."

Bud's face turned white. "Well, I guess it doesn't matter anymore what you want. What's done is done."

That night, Ellen dropped off Sue and Tanya in front of the Gold House and then parked a block and a street over before walking the distance to where they were waiting for her at the back of the house. She still had the key Ronnie had loaned out to Paul, but they weren't so sure the house hadn't already been rekeyed. Ellen tried the back door with no luck.

"I'll go around front, just in case it still works," she whispered.

She jogged around the side opposite of the Forresters hoping to avoid detection. She lifted up a prayer in case anyone could hear it, and then she slipped in the key.

The door opened.

Her heart pounded as she paused on the threshold, listening for evidence of a presence. When she heard none, she went inside and closed the door behind her. She used the flashlight on her phone to light her path to the back door, where she let in her friends.

She'd been terrified to be inside the house alone and was grateful to have them join her. But even with them beside her, she found herself trembling.

"Ready?" she whispered.

They both nodded and followed her to the stairs.

The stairs groaned beneath them all the way up. When they finally reached the second floor, they heard something drop in the attic above them—like a book or a box.

"She's up there," Ellen whispered, still not sure whether she referred to a person or a ghost.

"Maybe we should try to talk to her again," Sue whispered.

"But we don't have any candles or food," Tanya said.

"We may not need them," Sue said. "You forget I have the gift."

Tanya gave Ellen a look of skepticism but didn't say anything more as they followed Sue to the base of the attic steps.

"Do you have your gun?" Ellen whispered. "Just in case?"

Sue nodded. "But it won't do much good on something ethereal."

"We still don't know for certain," Ellen said.

Tanya touched Ellen's elbow. "You're the only one who feels that way."

With their phones illuminating the stairwell, they took the creaky steps up to the attic door, which was closed again. When Sue turned the knob, it was locked.

"I'll try to speak to her through the door," Sue whispered. Then, out loud, she said, "Friendly spirit of the past who dwells here, if you can hear me, please rap once for yes."

They were all three trembling and sweating in the heat in the little halos of their phones, waiting nervously. Ellen felt faint.

They heard the floor boards in the attic move beneath the weight of something, and this was followed by footsteps toward the attic door.

Shit! Ellen wanted to run away, but she stood perched on the tiny step behind Sue with Tanya behind her. Tanya grabbed her arm and made her jump.

"Oh, friendly spirit of the past," Sue said with a shaky voice. "If you can hear me, please rap once."

On the door between them and the attic came an unmistakable knock.

Ellen's heart raced a million miles a minute. She found it difficult to breathe.

"Thank you, friendly spirit," Sue said quickly. "We've come here because we want to help you find closure. If you're willing to talk to us, please rap once for yes and twice for no."

Ellen nearly jumped from her shoes when the knock came at the door again.

When a second knock did not follow, Sue sighed with relief and said, "Friendly spirit, are you here because you're looking for your mother? Please rap once for yes and twice for no."

One very loud knock.

"And, friendly spirit, is it true that your mother's name is Cynthia?" Sue asked. "Please rap once for yes and twice for no."

Nothing.

Sue waited for at least thirty more seconds, which is quite a long time when you are standing in the dark in a hot attic stairwell with a possible ghost on the other side of the door. Then she said, "Oh, spirit? We want to help you find your mother. Is her name Cynthia? Please knock once for…"

The attic door began to open.

Tanya rushed to the bottom of the stairs, emitting a shrill cry.

Ellen's feet were glued in place, grounded by fear.

Sue's curiosity seemed greater than her fear. She didn't budge from the top step, even though her whole body was shaking and her breathing was as fast as Ellen's.

The white ghost cat rushed down the steps. Tanya screamed again as it flew past her.

Ellen, who had followed the cat with her eyes, turned back to the attic door to find the ghost girl standing before them. Half in darkness and half in the light of their phones, the girl's white hair and white eyes shone like the moon.

"Help me," the girl said in a voice as shaky as Sue's. "Please help me find my mother."

Tanya tip-toed back up the steps toward them. None of them knew quite what to do next. It seemed the cat had got Sue's tongue. They were all three in awe of the ghost before them.

Ellen cleared her dry, tight throat. "We promise...We'll do everything in our power. First we need to take some pictures of the antique medical equipment up there, so we can stop this place from being turned into a zoo."

Ellen wasn't sure what to expect once she'd finished her speech, but the girl did the last thing Ellen would have guessed: the girl screamed a blood-curdling cry and slipped past them in the narrow stairwell, down the attic stairs. It was too dark to tell, but it was as if she went through Sue. They heard her go to the first floor and out the back door, screaming the entire way.

Tanya shook Ellen from her shock by saying, "Hurry! Let's get this over with before she comes back!"

They entered the attic and, using the flash on their phones, snapped as many photos as they could in the darkness.

Ellen stumbled when her foot hit something near the one empty bed—possibly the thing that had been dropped on the floor when Ellen and her friends had been on the story below. She shined the light of her phone on the floor and discovered a dusty shoebox without a lid.

"I hope it isn't more dead rats," Sue said as she moved beside Ellen.

With trembling hands, Ellen reached down and scooped up the box. She held her phone light up to it and gasped.

"Oh my God," she said. "Photographs. At least fifty, maybe more."

They were mostly black and white portraits of women—none of them smiling.

Tanya looked over Ellen's shoulder. "Do you think those are of the patients?"

"I think so," Ellen said.

"Let's take them," Sue said. "I can scan them and include them in our letter."

Their conversation was interrupted by the sound of the back door slamming shut followed by heavy footsteps—too heavy for the ghost girl.

"What the hell's going on up there?" a man's voice carried up from the first floor.

"That's not Bud, is it?" Tanya whispered.

Ellen shook her head.

"I swear, I'm gonna burn this place down," the man called out again.

"What do we do?" Sue asked.

"Hide," Ellen said. "He wouldn't dare smoke us out."

"Don't move," Sue whispered. "There's no way we won't be heard creaking around on the floorboards. We should stay right where we are."

Once again, the angry man's voice came up to them from the first floor. "I'm getting too fucking old for this, sweetheart! I've got my grandbabies over, and now you have them wanting to sleep in my bed. You need to cool your jets, or I swear I'll burn this place down!"

Ellen held her breath as the man stomped out through the back door. All three of them sighed with relief. Then they hurried down the steps as fast as they could. When they reached the bottom floor, they heard someone on the front porch.

"Just great," Ellen said.

"Out the back," Tanya whispered frantically. "Now!"

Ellen followed Tanya out the back door and down toward the wooded dry creek bed. Sue was just crossing the back stoop when a light flashed around inside of the house. Ellen and Tanya huddled behind the trees with their stomachs in their mouths. Sue was about to get caught by whoever was waving around the flashlight.

As the light neared the back of the house, and Sue was still floundering across the back yard at her turtle's pace, Ellen couldn't take it anymore. She handed the box of photos off to Tanya and raced toward Sue.

"Get down," she whispered when she reached her. She pulled Sue to the ground.

Sue let out a soft cry as she fell on her knees.

"Flatten yourself," Ellen whispered. "And don't move."

The grass was not like carpet grass. It was dry and crackly, but possibly tall enough to hide them from someone not too close.

The light shined across the yard and out toward the woods in back. Ellen could hear someone pacing near the backdoor. Then that person, a man, shouted, "You better not come back here, if you know what's good for you. Stay the hell away!"

Ellen and Sue lay frozen on their bellies in the grass as the back door slammed shut. The voice hadn't sounded like Bud or the man from earlier. She and Sue didn't move for several more minutes.

Then Ellen felt someone walking toward them, and she may have peed a little.

"Let's get out of here." It was Tanya. "He's gone for now, I think."

Tanya helped Ellen up, and then the two of them helped Sue.

114

"God, that was close," Ellen said. "Are you okay, Sue?"

Sue nodded. "I'm not sure who was more dangerous, though—those men, or *you*."

"I'm sorry," Ellen said. "I was afraid you'd get caught."

"And so what if I had?" she asked. "Do you think he would have shot me? What was the worst he could do?"

"I was too afraid to find out," Ellen said. "Are you mad at me?"

"No. Of course not." She brushed dirt off her pants and shirt. "Now, why don't you go get the car while Tanya and I wait here?"

"I think we should wait in the trees," Tanya said. "In case someone else comes around."

"I'll take the box of photos." Ellen reached out for the dusty shoebox and took it from Tanya. "I'll be right back."

She rushed from the back of the house to the street and half-jogged toward her car. Even though she was in terrible shape, the adrenaline rushing through her system must have given her a boost, because she made good time and wasn't out of breath until her butt was in the seat behind the wheel.

As she drove up the street, she saw a man walking away from the Gold House. He glared at her as she passed. She decided not to stop, in case he was watching. Instead, she circled around, pulled over, and texted Sue to let them know she was waiting to come around the block again when the coast was clear.

A text from Sue immediately lit up her screen: *Come now! 911!*

Ellen's heart pounded as she pulled away from the curb and circled back around, going ten miles an hour faster than the speed limit. She hoped there were no patrol cars hidden along the street. All she needed was to get pulled over. What would she say to the police officer? My friends and I broke into a vacant property and something went wrong during our escape?

She saw Sue and Tanya hobbling toward her on the road two houses up from the Gold House. She pulled up beside them and unlocked the doors.

Tanya must have hurt herself, because Sue had to help her climb into the passenger's side. Then Sue climbed in behind Tanya and said, "Get us out of here. *Now.*"

Ellen stepped on it and drove away from the neighborhood. "What happened?"

"It was scary as hell," Tanya said. "I think I twisted my ankle."

"What was scary as hell?" Ellen asked.

"The ghost came back," Sue said. "She was all bloody and was carrying the body and head of her ghost cat."

"What do you mean?" Ellen asked as she turned out of the district toward the highway. "They weren't attached?"

"The cat had been decapitated," Sue said.

"And the ghost was crying and carrying on," Tanya said. "Blood was everywhere."

"She wanted our help," Sue said. "She kept saying, 'No, not again. Help me. He killed my cat again.'"

"She was literally floating around us in a circle," Tanya said. "And she circled closer and closer in on us, until I tripped and fell and she was practically on top of me."

"Oh my God," Ellen said. "Then what happened?"

"You mean you didn't hear?" Sue asked. "I was sure the whole neighborhood had. It may have even awakened the rest of the dead."

"It wasn't that loud," Tanya said.

"Tanya screamed," Sue explained. "Lights came on in both houses adjacent to the Gold House. I thought for sure our goose was cooked."

"Oh my gosh! What about the ghost?" Ellen asked.

"I calmly told her I was sorry about her cat," Sue said. "And then she disappeared into the woods."

"I wouldn't say *calmly*," Tanya said.

"Anyway, that's when one of the men started looking for us again, hollering that he had a gun and he wasn't afraid to use it," Sue said. "I had to practically carry Tanya down the street to avoid being caught."

Ellen didn't know what to say. It was all so bizarre.

"I'm not sure if I'm up for this," Tanya said. "Not after the ghost appeared with the mutilated cat."

"I wonder what she meant when she said, *He killed my cat again*," Sue said. "Who keeps killing her cat?"

117

"She could be reliving a traumatic experience from her life," Tanya suggested.

Ellen turned to Tanya. "I know this was hard on you, but wasn't it also exciting? Yes, it was scary—terrifying, really. I get that. But I have to say, I've never felt more alive."

"You weren't pushed down in the grass and badly bruised," Sue said.

"Or attacked by a bloody ghost until you twisted your ankle," Tanya added.

"You guys can't be serious," Ellen said. "Are we really going to give up now?"

"Not me," Sue said. "I was just teasing you. I want to help the girl more than ever. Come on, Tanya. Don't be a wimp."

"I'm not a wimp."

"It's not like she attacked you," Sue said. "She just wants our help."

"I don't know," Tanya said. "It's so stressful."

Ellen bit her tongue, not wanting to push her friend too hard on the heels of her mother's death.

Tanya folded her arms and hugged herself. "And it is kind of crazy, don't you think?"

Tears sprang to Ellen's eyes. She'd really begun to think that this is what she was meant to do. But since when did she care anything about ghosts finding closure and about preserving mental health history? Maybe this *was* kind of crazy.

"A little crazy," Sue said.

Now, Ellen felt like a fool. She shook her head and muttered, "What are we doing? Are we having a midlife crisis together?"

"Yes," Sue said. "That's exactly what we're doing. And maybe something good can come of it. But we have to put on our big girl panties and not cry every time something goes wrong."

Ellen wiped her tears with the back of her hand.

"I guess this has been an interesting night," Tanya admitted. "I didn't think about my mom being gone until just now."

"Really?" Ellen asked.

Tanya nodded and also wiped tears away.

"That's a good sign." Sue leaned forward from the backseat and glanced at each of them.

"You don't have on your seatbelt?" Ellen asked.

"She never wears one," Tanya said. "Why do you think she prefers the backseat?"

"Great." Ellen focused harder on the road, feeling like she had Sue's life in the palm of her hands.

They were all quiet for many minutes. As Ellen drove further and further away from the house, she felt it pulling at her, as though her destiny and it were bound together. She took a deep breath and said, "Maybe, I don't know, maybe the house *called* to us. Does that make sense?" When neither responded right away, she added, "Maybe the house chose us to solve the mystery and bring it to light. Do you think that's possible?"

"*I* think so," Sue agreed. "What do *you* think, Tanya?"

"I guess so. Maybe."

"If you don't feel comfortable, Tanya," Ellen started.

"No. I want to do this," Tanya said. "I do. I'm just scared."

"That's partly why it's an adventure," Sue said. "What kind of adventure would it be if it weren't a little scary?"

"So we move forward?" Ellen lifted her brows and glanced at Tanya.

"Let's pull over at a Starbuck's and have a late snack while we look at that box of pictures," Sue suggested. "All that running around has given me a craving for a latte and a muffin."

Chapter Eleven: Plan Hatching at the Coffee Shop

Ellen, Sue, and Tanya sat at a small corner table in Starbucks. No one else was dining in, but a few customers stood in line waiting for coffee. Ellen picked up the first photo and read the name written in black ink on the back. "Judith Bailey." Then she handed the photo to Tanya.

"Can someone tell me what the hell just happened back there?" Tanya asked. "I'm sorry, but who were those men? Why were they threatening us? I'm not sure who was more frightening—the ghost and her bloody cat or the men."

Sue took a sip of her latte. "I bet I know who the first man was."

"Who?" Ellen looked up from the box of photos.

"Sam Robertson," Sue said. "He and his wife, Ida, live on the other side of the Gold House from the Forresters."

"How do you know that?" Tanya asked.

"Millie mentioned them, remember? Plus, I did my research. You can look up any house in the county on the Bexar County Appraisal District website. Haven't either of you ever played on it before? I've even looked up your houses."

"So what makes you think it was Sam Robertson?" Ellen asked.

"Well, we know it wasn't Bud, because we know his voice," Sue explained. "And the man said that his grandkids were too afraid to sleep alone, probably because they heard the screaming, so it had to be a nearby neighbor, right?"

"Right," Tanya said. "But why not the neighbor across the street?"

"Because that house is owned by Maddie Jenkins, and she's a widow," Sue said. "The houses on either side of the widow belong to younger couples. So using deductive reasoning, I'm fairly certain the man who threatened to burn down the place was Sam Robertson."

Ellen took a sip of her Frappuccino. "Well, it wouldn't have been Mitchell Clark. He wouldn't burn down a place where he's looking for gold."

"True." Tanya said.

Sue tore her muffin in half and added, "However, Mitchell does live on the other side of the Robertsons, so he may have heard the screaming, but, like you said, Ellen, the gold digger wouldn't want the house burned down."

"So then who was the second man?" Ellen asked.

"The one Ellen nearly killed me to save me from?" Sue asked.

Tanya and Ellen giggled.

"You never know," Ellen said. "Maybe I did save your life."

"I'm not sure who that was," Sue said. "He might have been just some random neighbor that had been out for a walk when he heard the screaming. He was probably harmless." Sue shot a teasing glance Ellen's way. "But I suppose he could have been Mitchell Clark."

"I did see someone walking away from the Gold House past the Robertson's," Ellen pointed out. "I think I would recognize the man if I saw him again. He gave me the meanest look."

"Well, just because you saw him out walking doesn't mean he was the one searching the house with the flashlight," Sue said.

"What about the third man, that came after us in the trees?" Tanya asked. "Any ideas there?"

"I actually think that one may have been Bud," Sue said. "At first, I was so caught up in the ghost and the bloody cat that I couldn't hear straight. But after we were safe in the car again, I thought it might have been Bud. What do you think, Tanya?"

Tanya shrugged. "I was too freaked out. But maybe. I wouldn't rule him out."

"Do you think we should ask him?" Ellen wondered. "Or should we not even bring the whole thing up?"

"I don't trust that man," Tanya said. "I don't think we should ask him anything, or admit to anything about tonight, if we're asked."

"My mom says she likes him," Sue said. "Both of the Forresters. But I'm not sure how I feel."

"Maybe once I get the results from the lab, we'll know more," Ellen added. "It's been thirty days. I should be hearing something any day now."

"Meanwhile, let's figure out how we're going to approach the Conservation Society with these photos," Sue suggested.

Ellen picked up the next photo. A bright-eyed, striking woman stared back at her. "This woman was beautiful." She turned the photo over. "Cynthia Piers. I wonder if this was the ghost girl's mother."

"Let me see." Tanya took the photo and held it close. "It does kind of look like her."

"Can I see it?" Sue had her turn. "Yes. It does."

"And this one's Regina Piers. Look how pale she is. Like Cynthia. They could be sisters."

"Let me see." Tanya took the photo. "Or mother and daughter. It's hard to tell in black and white, but this woman looks albino. Look at her eyes."

Sue took the photo next. "I see what you mean. If our ghost is related, she could have been albino as well."

"Or maybe she's not a ghost," Ellen said. "Maybe being albino makes her look like a ghost."

"I can't believe you can still say that, especially after what happened tonight," Tanya said. "Talk about believing what you want to believe."

That stung, so Ellen turned to the next photo. "And here's Victoria Schmidt." She handed it to Tanya, who passed it on to Sue. "This one isn't labeled. And neither is this one." She passed them both on to Tanya. "Oh, and look here. This one is Hilary Turner, look how young she is. She practically lived her whole life in that house."

"It's so sad." Tanya took the photo and then handed it to Sue.

"She wasn't very attractive," Sue commented. "Poor thing."

"Sue!" Tanya chastised her.

"I'm just sayin'."

They continued to look at the photos, including one of the famous actress, Willa Von Kempf. Ellen thought that photo was probably worth something. Then only one remained in the bottom of the box.

"How many is that?" Ellen asked as she reached in for the last photo.

"Fifty-two, I think," Sue said.

"Oh, look!" Ellen said, holding up the fifty-third photo. "I found Marcia Gold!"

Tanya took it. "She looks like a proper Victorian lady. I wonder what went wrong that she needed to hand over her house in exchange for treatment." Tanya studied it for a moment before passing it over to Sue.

"You should paint these portraits," Sue suddenly said to Ellen. "If we get the house, we could hang the portraits of these women all along the stairwell and hallways, with their names, so people know who they were."

Tears rushed to Ellen's eyes and for a second it was as if she had lost her breath.

"That's such a good idea," Tanya said. "You should do it, Ellen. Even if we don't get the house."

Once the air returned to her lungs, Ellen gathered the photos back into the box, fighting tears. "I haven't painted in so long."

"I'm sure it's like riding a bike," Sue said before popping the last bite of her muffin into her mouth.

"At least think about it," Tanya said.

Ellen nodded, and the feeling of *being called* solidified in her heart. She *should* paint them, but the question was, *Could she?*

Sue scanned the photos on her printer at home and sent an email to the president of the Conservation Society that night, and the following Monday afternoon, after Ellen's classes were over, Ellen met Sue and Tanya at the society's main headquarters, hoping to speak with someone in person. They had a print-out of Sue's email, the original photos, and the copy of the history file Ronnie had faxed over to Paul. The headquarters was located inside a beautifully restored three-story Italianate-style home. It had a square covered porch that boasted an American flag on the left and a Texas flag on the right.

"Do we just walk in?" Ellen wondered.

"I believe so." Sue opened the door for her, and Tanya followed.

The inside was also historical and elegant. They walked through a foyer to a beautiful staircase, in front of which was a large desk with a woman about their own age sitting behind it. Sue took the lead and asked if they could speak with a society member.

"Can I make you an appointment with someone in particular?" the woman asked.

"We can't speak with someone today?" Ellen asked.

"Let me check the schedule and see who might be available," the woman said. After glancing over a document, she said, "I have Mitchell Clark…"

"Is there anyone else?" Tanya asked.

The secretary gave Tanya a look of confusion.

"It's a sensitive issue involving him," Sue explained.

"By any chance, are you here about the Gold House?" the secretary asked. "Is one of you Sue Graham?"

"That would be me," Sue said. "So you got my email?"

"Yes, indeed," the woman replied. "And it's caused quite a stir. I believe Penelope Williams is here, and she will definitely want to speak with you. Why don't you have a seat in there while I get her?"

Relieved they wouldn't be sent away without a chance to express their concerns, Ellen followed Sue and Tanya into the elegant parlor across from the foyer. They each took a seat and immediately began whispering.

"This place is amazing," Ellen said. "I really hope we get to do something like this."

"What will we say if Penelope Williams seems set on selling to the zoo?" Tanya asked.

"We'll ask to speak with someone else," Sue said. "And if we can't find a sympathetic ear in this organization, we try the mayor."

"Oh, that won't be necessary," a woman in her sixties said as she came into the parlor. "I'm your sympathetic ear. I'm Penelope Williams. It's nice to meet you."

Sue turned red as she shook the woman's hand and introduced herself.

Ellen and Tanya did the same.

"Did you read my email then?" Sue asked.

"Yes, I did." Penelope took a seat beside Tanya on the sofa. "Is that the box of photos?"

Ellen suddenly wondered why she had brought them. What if she never got them back? How would she paint portraits without them? In spite of her concerns, she handed the box over. "We found them while viewing the house two weeks ago." She wasn't about to admit that they broke in after the society purchased the house.

"And you stole them from the property," Penelope pointed out.

"To preserve them," Ellen said defensively. "Have you seen the attic? There are important papers and books scattered all over the floor."

"I'm sorry to say I have not personally viewed the estate, but after reading your email I wish I had. I had no knowledge of the home's use as a mental health facility. You see, I'm actually from Pennsylvania, where Weir Mitchell's rest cure originated. I have first-hand experience with that barbaric form of treatment."

"You were a patient?" Sue asked.

"No. But my mother was. And as the current president of this organization, I give you my word that I will do everything in my power to prevent the sale of that property to the San Antonio Zoological Society."

"Fantastic!" Ellen said. "What a relief!"

"Does this mean you'd be willing to sell it to *us*?" Sue asked. "With our promise to honor its history?"

"I'm willing to discuss it," the woman said. "I want to hear about your vision."

Chapter Twelve: Marcia Gold

Within one week, the Conservation Society accepted Ellen, Tanya, and Sue's offer at four thousand over the original asking price. Since they were paying cash, they were able to close quickly, and within another week, the contractor had replaced the broken windows and had begun work to reconstruct the exterior walls and roof. While a crew worked on the outside, Ellen and her friends were able to begin the demolition of the kitchen and bathrooms with the help of their contractor. Standing in the middle of the kitchen sporting her boots and work gloves, Ellen couldn't recall the last time she'd felt so excited. She and Tanya scraped away the backsplash as Ed, their contractor, tackled the heavy cabinets overhead.

Since Sue wasn't as excited about smashing cabinets and ripping down wallpaper as Tanya and Ellen were, she was in charge of taking the photos. She had the best camera and the best skills, so it only made sense. She took photos of every room—including the attic—before the demolition. Their plan was to take some during, and then more after, so they could each make a scrap book documenting their experience. Sue was also in charge of bringing the snacks and drinks and entertaining them with her never ending sense of humor.

So far, they hadn't seen any sign of the ghost.

Every night, Ellen went to bed looking forward to the next day. Every afternoon, she went straight over to the Gold

House from work at two o'clock, changed into her work clothes, and got busy. Tanya was usually already there with Ed. Sometimes Sue was there, too, and sometimes she came a little later, but always with generous snacks and drinks.

On Friday, about four days into the project, Ellen had just begun to work on one of the downstairs bathrooms when she got the idea of salvaging the trunk that had been left behind. Maybe they could reuse it in the house. Sue volunteered to refinish the trunk and make it back into a beautiful piece of art. She hadn't been working on it long, when she discovered a secret compartment in its base, and tucked inside was a diary.

Inscribed on the inside front cover was "Marcia Gold, 1881."

Sue began reading right away, but because all of them were eager to hear what Marcia had to say, and each wanted to be the first to read, they decided no one could read it unless they were all three together. So that night they met at Tanya's house, since her husband Dave was out of town on business. They shared a bottle of wine as Sue read the diary out loud.

June 10, 1881

I am not entirely certain why I have been prevailed upon to care for the woman responsible for ruining my life. Surely my father knows that I am fully aware of the injustice he and this woman have done against my mother and me.

If the boarding school where I am currently employed had not decided to close down for summer renovations, I might have had the means to deny this infernal command of his.

It was quite a shock to walk into this house after living away from it for so many years. I was but a girl of fifteen when my mother finally gave up her spirit and my father, perhaps afraid that I might finally speak the truth, sent me away to my beloved school. And now, six years later, to enter my childhood domain and be struck immediately by that scandalous portrait of her, *of* Inger, *hanging above the mantle where my gentle mother's face once perched, was the most cruel abhorrence committed against me since the day that woman poisoned my mother and the day my father, upon returning from the war two years later, pretended not to notice.*

How could they expect a child of five years not to realize the truth? How could they expect me to believe that Inger was Alma and Alma Inger? I was old enough to know the difference even if those far older than I accepted the deceit.

Everything about this house suffocates me. And everywhere I look, I see memories of my innocent brothers, who were as much victims in their mother's scandal as I and my mother. Poor Robert and Roger! Such untimely deaths! Since my mother was a woman of grace, I am certain she will welcome them into heaven and care for them as her own, unlike my cruel aunt who has surely secured her place in hell.

How ironic, dear Inger—yes, I know that is your name! The rest of the world may believe you are Alma, a name given at birth to my sweet mother, but I have always known the truth! How ironic that you are now under the supervision of the person against whom you have committed the greatest harm, since my mother was never in her right mind after you poisoned her. (Had she been cognizant, she would have surely died of heartbreak to have been deceived by her own sister.) How ironic that my father is never here, and it would be so easy for me to kill you.

Perhaps my father has no idea that I know the truth, since I was too afraid to speak it as a child. Or, perhaps he is aware and hopes that I will kill you, since it is so obvious to me he already fancies another.

Sue paused, and all three women looked at one another with wide eyes.

"So Inger Bohrmann, the invalid, was really Alma Gold? And Inger pretended to be Alma?" Tanya asked.

"That's what Marcia seems to be saying," Sue said.

"But how?" Tanya asked.

"Inger poisoned her own sister while Theodore was fighting in the war," Sue said.

"So Theodore comes back and...what? Goes along with it?" Ellen asked.

"Marcia seems to think so," Tanya said.

"Do you think they were in on it from the beginning?" Ellen asked. "Maybe they were in love and having an affair before he left."

"Well, Marcia answers that question on the next page," Sue said. "But I promise that's as far as I've read."

"Go on, then," Ellen said.

So Sue read on:

June 17, 1881

Inger, it is not my responsibility to free your twisted soul, and you do not have the right to make me your confessor. And yet, I am incapable of preventing you from recounting your sins, because I desperately want to know the truth about my poor mother.

And my poor father!

How I have hated that man for over fifteen years, and now you tell me you manipulated him into going along with your scheme. You wicked, wicked woman. I could explode with the hate I feel for you, and yet, here I am, spoon-feeding you and bathing you as though you were a beloved elder. No existence has ever been as miserable as mine. I have wanted to kill you; now I want to kill myself. The only thing that prevents me is the pain it would cause my father.

"What?" Ellen asked when Sue stopped reading. "What is she saying? What did Inger do?"

"Do you think she threatened to hurt Marcia if Theodore didn't go along with her?" Tanya asked.

"Why wouldn't he just have her arrested and thrown in jail?" Sue pointed out.

"Oh my God, keep reading," Ellen insisted.

June 24, 1881

How I wish I would have left dear Joseph on better terms! I miss him terribly, as I knew I would, but of course it was impossible to allow him to court me. My family's twisted history could never properly be explained without frightening off even the most arduous gentleman. I'm afraid the promise of my father's gold would do little to make up for the sins that have been committed beneath this roof; and yet, I could not allow myself to live a lie by hiding my family's crime from him. To do so would place me nearly on the same low level as my evil Aunt Inger. No, only honesty and purity will guide me, and, because of this, I shall forever live alone.

But I shall always think fondly of my beloved Joseph.

"She mentioned her father's gold!" Tanya interrupted.

"I wonder if she mentions it again." Sue skimmed through the pages.

"No reading ahead," Ellen said. "Let's hear the whole thing. If she mentions the gold, we'll get to it when it comes."

Sue sighed. "All right, if you insist. But I may need another glass of wine."

Tanya got up and brought over the rest of the bottle, and once Sue had her glass refilled, she continued.

June 30, 1881

As Inger's last days draw ever nearer, she is overcome with guilt and terror. If she wishes to win me over before she expires, she is in for a rude awakening; and yet, it is difficult for me to not to feel something for this woman. Tears roll from her swollen eyes at all hours of the day. I am often awakened in the middle of the night by her moans and shrieks when the nightmares take an awful hold of her. Then yesterday, she told me more about her relationship with my mother before they moved here from Germany with my father.

As I listened to her tale, I became vaguely aware that my need to hear it was as urgent and compelling as her need to tell it.

It began with a story I had never heard—about a day on the ice in Bremen, when my mother was nine and Inger eight. They were skating together on the frozen pond not far from their home. According to Inger, my mother shoved her to the ground. Inger admits that my mother meant, not to injure, but to tease. During the fall, Inger broke her ankle, and because it was never properly set, she walked with a limp her entire life. Yesterday she said again that she knew my mother had meant her no ill will, but she felt that every misfortune that befell her could be traced back to that careless shove on the icy pond.

When I asked my aunt why I had never been told the story before, she replied that she did not like to think of it, and she had made my mother swear never to speak of it.

She went on to say that because of her limp, she could no longer keep up with the other children at school. Her friendships suffered, and later, she failed in all her efforts to attract the attention of suitors. She became a burden to her parents. When my wealthy father fell in love with my mother and wanted to bring her with him to America, my mother's parents gave their consent on the condition that he bring Inger, too. They decided that their lame daughter could become his burden because he could better afford it.

Inger said her close proximity to their happiness and their deep love for one another drove her mad with jealousy. She felt trapped—an unwilling and miserable spectator to a wonderful life she would never have. If only Alma hadn't pushed her, she would say to herself again and again. And she would fantasize about switching places with her sister. What if their whole lives could be reversed and Inger could be the happy one, the one doted on by a handsome and wealthy man? What if Inger were the one who would have children and host social events and be admired by the community?

While my father served in the war, the madness infected Inger's ability to think clearly. She told herself that the woman

137

living under the same roof was not her real sister but a monster which had ruined Inger's life. Inger believed that if she had any hope for happiness, she must destroy the monster in the house.

I interrupted my aunt's rantings and ravings to ask the question I had wondered my whole life: "How did you make my mother ill?"

"I fed her rat poison for three months."

I couldn't speak for many moments. I am sure my face must have become as pale as Inger's. As I sat there in stunned silence, she went on with her story. I couldn't hear her first few sentences, but when she mentioned that my mother began to bleed from her nose and ears, and that she bruised from the softest touch, I returned to life. Images from my past flooded into my mind, and I recalled those fearful days when I was but five and my mother was falling apart. At first, I believed my aunt's lies, but I eventually noticed something was not right. Why was my aunt so cheerful? I could sense that she had something to do with my mother's condition, but by the time I tried to warn my mother, the dementia had already set in.

Sue stopped to take a few swallows of wine.

"I still don't understand how Inger managed to get Theodore to go along with her," Ellen said.

"Me, too," Tanya said. "That doesn't make sense."

"Should I go on?" Sue asked.

Ellen crossed one leg over the other. "Is that okay with you, Tanya?"

"Of course. I have nothing better to do."

July 7, 1881

I received a letter today from Joseph! It was addressed to my school and then forwarded to our Alta Vista address. My heart beat very rapidly as I opened the envelope. Tears filled my eyes as they gazed upon his sweet words.

He wrote that he misses me and isn't the same without my company. He wrote that he has been stricken with what must surely be a fatal melancholia, and that if I don't reply soon, I will have his death on my conscience. He compared his heart to talc, saying that I could easily crush it to powder with my indifference.

I immediately took pen to paper to reply, but before I had gotten very far, I ripped the page to shreds. What good would it do either of us for me to respond? I am much too broken and damaged by my past to ever fully love with confidence and enthusiasm. In fact, I am sure I will serve him better with silence.

"That's so sad," Tanya said when Sue paused to turn the page.

"She should have given him a chance." Ellen took a sip of her wine. "Maybe she underestimated his ability to love her."

"I think so, too," Sue said just before she continued.

July 14, 1881

Yesterday Inger finally revealed how she managed to deceive my father. He'd been away for two years, and during that time, she had already managed to convince our friends and neighbors that she was Alma. It hadn't been difficult, because during those first few years here in America, Inger had lived in the shadow of my mother. Inger said she was always ashamed and embarrassed to be the misfortunate sister, dependent on her brother-in-law for every necessity. She tried to earn her keep by cooking and keeping the kitchen tidy, and when my mother entertained in those early years, Inger never came out of the kitchen. There were a few instances when Alma insisted that Inger receive guests, but Inger always made sure to be seated before they arrived, and she remained so until they left. She was self-conscious of her limp and hid it as best as she could.

So when my mother became incoherent, Inger took measures to re-create her identity. She told me that she and my mother had always resembled one another and that if it weren't for her limp people would have difficulty telling them apart. It was for this reason that her lameness became her most defining characteristic back in Bremen: she was the sister who was crippled.

But in America, no one outside of our family knew the details of her condition. They knew only that she had a condition that kept her from social engagements. So after my mother fell ill under the power of the poison, Inger dressed in my mother's clothes and began attending events in her name. She explained her need for a cane with a story of having fallen in the garden. Rather than being shunned by others as she'd been as a child, the community expressed sympathy. For the first time in her life, people doted on her.

Inger told me that when my father returned from the war in 1865, he wasn't the same man. He had witnessed too many deaths of both enemies and friends, and because he'd been new to America, he was never really sure on which side he belonged. He'd been quiet and withdrawn, and while Inger's insistence that she was Alma might have confused him, he didn't have it in him to contradict her. Inger told me that he probably found it easier to accept that she was Alma than the alternative: that his beloved wife was an incoherent, babbling idiot.

Chapter Thirteen: The Hunt for Gold

Sue read several more pages from Marcia's diary detailing Inger's confession, and then Marcia described something unexpected: in mid-August, Theodore Gold suffered a massive heart attack. Marcia wrote about her last day with her father as he lay dying:

August 17, 1881

My father revealed to me that he has known the truth about my mother's identity. He said it took him many years to face it. He said that when he returned from the war, he thought he'd lost his mind, and whenever he questioned Inger, she had an answer ready for him. He said that when my mother fell ill, Inger must have feared she would lose his financial support. To prevent him from taking another wife should my mother have died, she switched places. It didn't occur to him that my aunt might have done something even more devious, and I wondered if he should know the truth. I asked him if he had ever confronted my aunt, and he shook his head. I suppose it was easier to continue with the charade than to face the terrible truth. He told me that when my mother finally died, the enormity of what Inger had done finally hit him. Even though my aunt had given him two sons, he never looked at her with tenderness again.

I decided not to tell him about the rat poison. He was too frail and full of agony. I didn't wish to add to his misery on his final day.

"And there's something else," he said between ragged breaths. "I never told her where I buried my gold. If something were to happen to me, I didn't want her to have it."

Tears streamed down my face. I had no words. I sobbed as he struggled to breathe.

"I want to tell you where it is, Marcia," he rasped. "I want you to have the gold, in case you should ever befall hard times and should need it to survive."

"Oh my God!" Ellen cried. "Does he say where it is?"

"Well, don't interrupt, and we'll find out," Sue said.

Tanya and Ellen leaned in and listened anxiously as Sue read on:

My father told me I should never tell a soul the information he was about to convey to me. He said he brought the gold from Germany as an insurance policy in case his business did not do well in America. Fortunately, his business prospered, and when the country broke out in civil war, he buried the gold to prevent enemies from confiscating it.

Since his business continued to prosper even after the war, he left the gold where it was. Then two years later, when Inger begged him to redecorate the main rooms downstairs, he

143

recorded the location of the gold in permanent ink in several places beneath the wallpaper.

"Beneath the wallpaper?" Tanya said. "That wasn't very smart. The drywall sometimes peels right off with the paper."

"I've already removed the wallpaper in the master bedroom," Ellen said. "I didn't see a map or anything."

"If it wasn't so late, I'd suggest we go look tonight," Sue said. "But I suppose we should wait until tomorrow. Right?"

Ellen was as eager as Sue, but she agreed that going tonight would not be a good idea. There was still no electricity.

"We'll search every inch of every wall tomorrow," Tanya said. "Okay?"

"Okay," Ellen and Sue said simultaneously.

"Now finish the diary," Tanya said. "Are there many pages left?"

"Two more," Sue said before she continued.

August 24, 1881

Now that my dear, sweet father has passed from this world onto the next, Inger is fast on his heels. I fear she has but a few days. As I reread what I have written, I realize that even though I hated my aunt and father for so many years, a part of me also loved them. From the time I was five until the age of fifteen, my aunt did care for me. For my entire childhood, she cooked for me, and when my mother became incoherent and bedridden, my aunt never abused and bullied me but treated me as though I was her own daughter. She did that in spite of my every effort to sabotage her. And even though it pained her beyond belief to lose her sons when I was a girl of twelve, she continued to care for me.

I also realize that I have always loved this house, even though I resented being forced back to it at the beginning of the summer. This has been the only real home I have ever known, and soon it will be mine to take care of. Although I am twisted inside and full of sadness over my mother's treatment, I must try to put those feelings behind me and think of the future. Maybe I should reach out to my beloved Joseph. Maybe his feelings for me are strong enough to help him accept my family's shameful history.

"Thank goodness!" Ellen said. "Her aunt may not have deserved Marcia's forgiveness, but at least she made her peace."

"I wonder if she and Joseph ever got together," Tanya said.

"Well, she must not have married him, or she would have taken his last name," Sue pointed out. "There's one more page. Ready?"

"We're really at the end?" Tanya asked. "I guess we aren't going to get all our answers in one page."

"Let's hear it," Ellen said.

Sue took a sip of wine and read Marcia's final entry.

August 31, 1881

The summer has come to an end, and so must this diary. I must return to my teaching position at St. Mary's Boarding School on Monday. At the beginning of the summer, I could not wait to return to my dear school, but as I board up this old house and cover the furnishings, I do so with tears. My attorney says I should rent the house, but he does not know what I know. If renters were to redecorate, they may inadvertently erase the hidden location of my father's gold, or, worse, discover it and take it for themselves. No, my hope is that I shall make this year of teaching my last and, hopefully, in one year's time, if all goes as planned, I shall return to this sweet house as Mrs. Joseph Clark.

"Clark?" Tanya repeated. "Do you think he's related to Mitchell Clark?"

"It seems too strange to be a coincidence," Sue said. "But I suppose it is a common name."

"Are you sure that's the final entry?" Ellen asked.

Sue gave her the diary. Ellen fingered through the pages. Yes, there were no more.

"I wonder why Marcia and Joseph never married," Tanya said.

"I guess we'll never know," Ellen said sadly.

Ellen couldn't sleep that night. She tossed and turned, thinking about the gold and all the possibilities that could come with finding it. Maybe Marcia had dug it up, and it wasn't even buried anymore. But if she had, she wouldn't have turned over her mortgage to Dr. Piers in exchange for treatment, would she have? Had she forgotten the gold? Given it away? Squandered it?

The best explanation was that Marcia had never found it. Maybe Ellen, Sue, and Tanya would.

What would Ellen do with her share? She would definitely help her children. She and Paul felt fortunate that they could pay for their children's college tuition, but, with the gold, she could buy them each a house of their own, and then maybe she could also pay for her grandchildren's college tuition. She could set up trust funds for them. She would also want to share some with her brother Jody and his family, even though they already lived fairly well in Kentucky. And if there was anything left over, maybe she and Paul could buy a vacation home on the coast somewhere. They would both retire, and he could golf and fish, and she could read on the beach. Sue and Tanya could buy vacation homes in the same area, and they could all go together.

As she finally began to drift off, she suddenly remembered that tomorrow was Halloween, and she still hadn't bought any candy for the trick-or-treaters.

Saturday morning, Ellen picked up Sue and met Tanya at the Gold House. The crew was working on the roof and soon it would be time to choose the exterior paint colors. Ed, their contractor, was already there with an assistant refinishing the antique kitchen furniture Sue had found at a shop in a nearby small town. Sue's research had revealed that the original home didn't have built-in cabinets, so, although they would never be able to replicate the original kitchen, they hoped to have something similar created. Tanya had found a cupboard at a flea market, and Ellen had found a solid wooden table that made an excellent island. Ed had recommended adding overhead shelving and one section of a modern stone countertop, which he had already installed with a deep white porcelain sink.

Ellen and her friends said hello to the workers inside and explained that they were going to get to work removing more of the wallpaper.

"Her, too?" Ed jerked a thumb toward Sue.

"Now don't act so surprised," Sue said. "I've been known to get my hands dirty on occasion."

With trowels, rags, and spray bottles of water, the three made their way to the full bathroom. Before getting started on the wallpaper in there, Ellen showed them the work she had already done in the master bedroom.

"No map in here." She waved her arm toward the bare walls.

"But what's that writing?" Tanya pointed to some numbers in one corner.

"I assumed they were measurements," Ellen said. "I saw writing like that on the walls in my house when I redecorated ten years ago."

Sue crossed the room to study the numbers. "Well, darn. This looks like algebra, not a map."

They got to work stripping the paper from the bathroom wall, anxiously tearing, scraping, shredding. Ellen was sure that at any moment a map would be revealed. They were soon disappointed to find nothing on the walls there, either. After Sue snapped a few photos, they moved to the second bedroom.

"Maybe this time we'll get lucky," Ellen said as she sprayed the wall with water.

"I hope so." Sue followed her. "I haven't worked this hard in years. I really hope it pays off."

"At least we're getting the work done." Tanya carried the step ladder. "It's going a lot faster today."

"I'm not leaving until every bit of wallpaper is down," Sue said.

"Even the upstairs?" Ellen asked.

"Even the upstairs," Sue said.

"But Marcia wrote that the map was written on the downstairs walls," Tanya said. "It would take all night to finish the upstairs, too."

"And it's Halloween," Ellen said. "We have to feed the trick-or-treaters."

"Yeah, I'd hate to starve the poor children in our neighborhood," Sue said. "So malnourished."

"And candy is so good for them," Tanya added.

"Fine," Ellen said, scraping near the baseboards. "I'll tell Paul he's on his own tonight. I'll stay as late as you want."

"There's really no use staying after dark," Sue said. "When did Ed say the electrical work would be done?"

"He didn't," Ellen said. "But we can ask him."

"Plus, I'm not sure this is the place I want to be on Halloween," Tanya admitted as she climbed up the step ladder.

"We could always have another séance." Sue sprayed the wall around the window. "Our last encounter with our ghost wasn't very satisfying. I wouldn't mind getting some answers."

"No more séances for me," Tanya said.

Ellen ripped a huge piece of wallpaper from the wall, where she found more numbers written in black ink. "More algebra." They looked like the same numbers as those on the wall in the master. "Wait a minute."

She climbed to her feet and returned to study the other wall in the adjacent room. The numbers were identical.

"What are you thinking?" Sue asked.

"The numbers are an exact match," Ellen said. "If these were dimensions for the room, the numbers would be different from those in the master, right?"

"Maybe it's some kind of code," Tanya said. "We just have to figure it out."

Sue took out her camera and snapped a photo. "I wonder if we tried to Google the numbers, if that would turn up anything."

"Good idea," Ellen said.

Sue punched in the numbers as Ellen and Tanya held their breath.

"Well, I'm not getting anything that makes a lick of sense," Sue said.

"This has got to be it," Tanya insisted. "Don't you think? We haven't found anything else remotely resembling a map or directions. This must be code."

"Let's keep stripping the paper away," Sue said. "Maybe something else will turn up."

They hadn't gotten very far when they heard someone in the hallway outside of the room.

"Ed? Is that you?" Ellen called.

The man who appeared in the doorway was not Ed, but Bud Forrester.

"Sorry to barge in on you ladies," Bud said with his hands in his blue jean pockets. He wore a sweater from the eighties and a sheepish look on his face.

"Hello, Bud," Sue said. "How are you?"

"Fine, thanks. I can see you're working hard in here. Making a lot of progress."

"We're getting there," Ellen said. "So what's up? Is there something we can do for you?"

Bud traced the toe of his boot along a floor board. "No, ma'am. I just wanted to warn you ladies about something."

Ellen glanced at each of her friends. "Warn us?"

"Every year on Halloween, this place gets trashed," he said. "Usually a bunch of kids getting their kicks. I've tried to scare them off, but, short of shooting off my rifle, it never does any good."

"Maybe we should hire a security guard," Tanya said. "I wouldn't want to lose our investment."

"You don't think they'd break inside, do you?" Sue asked Bud.

"They have before. They've come in, egged and toilet papered the place. One year, they poured ketchup on the floor."

"Shoot. What should we do?" Ellen wondered out loud.

"They might not come this year, but I just thought you should know."

"Thank you," Ellen said, her opinion of him much improved.

"I'll do my best to keep an eye on the place," he added.

"That's awfully kind of you," Sue said.

Bud shuffled the toe of his boot along the floor again. "As a matter of fact, there was something else I wanted to tell you…"

"I've got an idea." Sue snapped her fingers. "I think it might just do the trick."

"What is it?" Tanya asked.

"Let's decorate the front porch," she said. "And we'll dress up as witches. I'll bring that big cauldron I use each year to hand out candy. "

"You think we'll get trick-or-treaters?" Ellen asked.

"We do get a few, but not many," Bud said.

"I could fill it with dry ice instead of candy," Sue said.

"I have a strand of jack-o-lantern lights I could string up across the roof of the portico," Ellen said.

"You two are serious about spending Halloween *here*?" Tanya asked.

"I just think that as long as we're here, no one will vandalize the property," Sue said.

"But we can't stand guard all night," Tanya said.

"Why not?" Sue said. "Ellen and I are night owls. We could stay until four or five, couldn't we? I've seen her on Facebook later than that."

Ellen nodded. Her insomnia often kept her up at night. She knew she could stay awake, but did she want to stay here, at this house?

"I bet Millie would enjoy coming over and joining you for a while," Bud said. "We could bring over some hot chocolate and her homemade pumpkin pie."

Sue's face lit up. Pumpkin pie was her favorite. "That sounds delicious."

"I don't know," Tanya said, looking reluctant. "What if the ghost appears to us? What will we do?"

"Talk to her," Sue said. "I still have a lot of questions."

"She's been hanging around our place ever since you ladies started the renovations," Bud said. "We've seen a lot more of her lately."

"Has she spoken to you?" Sue asked.

Bud scratched his head. "As a matter of fact, I was hoping..."

At that moment, they heard a loud crash coming from the kitchen. Bud rushed toward the sound, and Ellen and her friends followed.

As they entered the kitchen, Ed was helping his assistant from the floor. The six-foot wooden ladder lay on its side. Its fall had been the loud crash they'd heard from the other room.

"Everything okay?" Bud asked.

"We saw the ghost." Ed pointed to the wall in the adjacent laundry room.

Painted on the brand new white cabinets in brown mud were the words, "Get out!"

Chapter Fourteen: Halloween Night

When Ellen arrived home that afternoon, she found Paul out on the back deck, grilling.

She opened the back door. "Hey. I thought you had a golf tournament today?"

"I did. It ended an hour ago. I felt like grilling."

"By any chance, did you buy candy?"

"I almost did, but then you always buy so much." He closed the lid on the grill and followed her inside.

Darn. That meant she still had to run by the store. "How did you play?"

"Good. I won the tournament." He gave her a grin.

"Really? That's great. Congratulations." She pecked his cheek. She was unused to seeing him so happy. He hadn't been in this good of a mood in months.

"You got a letter in the mail today," he said as he headed toward the kitchen to wash his hands. "I put it on the kitchen bar. Did you have some kind of lab work done?"

"What? No." Then she realized it must be the online lab, where she had sent the samples from the Gold House. "Oh my gosh!"

She rushed over to the kitchen bar and opened the envelope.

"What is it?" Paul asked.

"I collected a few things from the attic at the Gold House and sent them to an online lab."

"Wow. I bet that wasn't cheap."

"I'm hoping to learn something about the ghost girl, like if she's really a ghost, you know?"

"I get it."

The first page was the bill for $325.

"What does it say?" Paul asked.

The second page was a letter addressed to her. She read it out loud:

Dear Ellen Mohr,

We have completed our analysis of the samples you sent on September 16th, to the best of our abilities.

We successfully isolated two latent finger prints. We found one on the book using a fluorescent dye stain and an orange alternate light source. After taking a photo of the print, we were unable to find a match in any of our databases.

The second print was taken from the pillowcase using a chemical process involving gold and zinc. We identified the print with a record in the Texas Department of Public Safety database. The record belongs to a seventy-three year-old resident of San Antonio whose name is Robert Forrester. His address is 4327 Alta Vista. His phone number is 210-655-3077. No email address or mobile phone number is provided.

Ellen looked up from the letter. "That must be Bud, that neighbor I told you about."

"His prints were on a pillow case? That's odd. What did he do? Go take a nap there?"

"He probably snooped around just like Sue and her mom and I did." She hadn't ruled out the possibility that Bud Forrester was doing something wrong.

She continued reading:

As you requested, we analyzed the hair sample in multiple ways to yield the maximum information. These were our findings:

The hair lacks any pigmentation, indicating that its host possesses an acute form of albinism. Hormones and proteins present in the shaft indicate that the host is female in her mid-twenties in relatively good health, though slightly deficient in iron and potassium.

Ellen's breath caught. Did this mean their ghost was alive? Or did it just mean that the ghost was in her twenties when she died? Ellen thought back to her encounters with the ghost girl. She'd looked more like a teenager, but she supposed it was possible that her thin frame and very pale skin made her appear to be younger than she really was.

"Does that mean she's not a ghost?" Paul asked.

"I'm not sure."

157

Ellen continued reading.

Please note that pigmentation may have been chemically stripped prior to your collection of the sample, rendering our conclusions incorrect. Given other factors present in the shaft, we estimate our results to be 80%-85% accurate.

The hair sample did not contain the living hair root necessary for DNA testing.

Ellen looked up again.

"Oh, so it *is* a ghost," Paul said.

"I'm still not sure. I don't know what that means."

"Maybe you can call the lab for clarification."

Ellen nodded. "Or maybe I can find out on the Internet."

For now, she continued reading.

However, using an electron microscope, we successfully isolated nuclear DNA preserved in the corneocytes of the hair shaft. The DNA confirms that the host is female.

We were unable to match the sample to any records in our DNA databases. We did, however, find an 86% match with a record in the San Antonio State Hospital database, belonging to a current patient. An 86% match indicates that the patient on record and the host of the hair sample are blood relatives. Unfortunately, patient confidentiality precludes us from relaying information about the patient to you in our report.

Air rushed from Ellen's lungs, and her throat tightened. "The San Antonio State Hospital?"

"Sounds like you'll be heading over there soon." Paul took a bottle of barbecue sauce and a pastry brush with him back out to the deck, leaving Ellen with her thoughts.

Could a living relative of the girl—whether the girl herself was alive or dead—be residing in the state hospital at this very moment? She reread the letter. When she came to the end, she read it was signed:

Cordially,

Carl Fromme, Senior Forensic Anthropologist

Later that evening, Ellen sat between Sue and Tanya on the newly reconstructed front porch. It hadn't yet been painted, but the windows, siding, and floorboards were new, and there were no more holes in the ceiling. They each sat in their witch's hats in their folding-chair-from-a-bag with Sue's big plastic cauldron filled with dry ice in front of them. The steam from the dry ice fogged up the porch and looked appropriately eerie in the orange light cast by the string of jack-o-lantern lights they'd hung from the arches of the portico.

Ellen had brought a bucket of candy, and Tanya had made a pitcher of margaritas. There was just enough of a chill in the air to keep them cold.

As they had strung the lights, carefully hammering in tiny nails in the underside of the newly constructed portico, Ellen had told them about the letter.

Now, as they waited for the trick-or-treaters, they sipped margaritas in the cool night air as they each looked out from the Gold House porch.

After a few minutes, Sue broke the silence. "How much did you have to pay for that report, if you don't mind my asking?"

"Three hundred dollars," Ellen said. "It was worth it, even if it doesn't tell us whether the girl is dead or alive."

"I don't understand how you can still be unsure about that," Tanya said. "Why would any living person behave the way she has?"

Ellen shrugged. "I hope to find out."

"So how soon can we visit the state hospital?" Sue asked.

"We should call them first thing Monday morning to make an appointment." Ellen sipped her margarita.

"Why wait until Monday?" Sue said. "They're open on Sundays. We could go tomorrow. I bet my mom could help us."

"That's right!" Ellen sat up. "Your mom worked there for a while, didn't she?"

"Five or six years, I think," Sue said. "It was toward the end of her career, after she retired from the Methodist Hospital System."

"What are we expecting to find at the state hospital?" Tanya asked. "The ghost's mother?"

"Possibly," Ellen said. "And if the girl *is* a ghost, maybe finding her mother will give her closure. If she's a young woman pretending to be a ghost, well, we help her, too. She may be troubled."

"She'd have to be," Sue said. "Though, it would be nicer if she *were* a living person, especially for her mother."

Ellen found it hard to believe that Sue wasn't hoping to prove Ellen wrong about the existence of ghosts. "Really?"

"Of course," Sue said. "Why wouldn't I? You think I want the girl to be dead?"

"It's just that after all the trouble you've gone through with the séance, and then Tanya and her psychic, well, I thought you'd both be disappointed if we discovered that she's not really a ghost."

"I'd be less freaked out," Tanya said. "Either way, she's pretty creepy."

"Not creepy," Ellen said. "Desperate. Either way, she's desperate. I may not be able to sense spirits, but I can sense that."

"I think it's highly unlikely that she's still alive," Sue said. "But I won't be disappointed if she is."

Just then, they noticed Bud pushing Millie in her wheelchair across the lawn toward them. Millie was holding a plate in each hand and another on her lap. Ellen and her friends waved.

"This ought to be interesting," Sue muttered.

"I wish it could just be the three of us," Tanya said. "Do you think she'll stay long?"

"We're about to find out," Ellen said.

"Oh, look," Sue said cheerfully. "She *did* make that pie."

Bud turned onto the sidewalk and parked his wife in front of the porch beside the steps and bannister. There wasn't a ramp, and there was no way Bud could lift Millie and the chair.

"Well if it isn't the three witches of Eastwick," Bud said smiling.

"Hello, Millie," Sue said. "Bud."

"Hello, ladies," Millie said. "I didn't know I should dress in costume."

"Oh, these old things?" Ellen pulled off her hat. "They're just for fun."

"Don't take it off on my account," Millie said. "You three look cute. What kind of potion are you cooking in your cauldron?"

"It's a love potion," Sue said. "I'm a little bored with my husband."

"I heard it was the other way around," Tanya said.

"*He's* the one who wanted us to make the potion," Ellen said with a smile.

They all laughed.

162

"That's my exit cue," Bud said just before he passed a plate of pie to Ellen and each of her friends. "I'll come back in a half hour, Mill. Sound good?"

Millie nodded. "Thanks, Bud."

Bud headed back to his house.

"Thank you for the pie," Ellen said to Millie.

"It looks delicious," Sue said.

"Would you like a margarita?" Tanya asked. "I brought an extra cup for you."

"Oh, no thank you. I can't drink alcohol with my medication. But thank you. That was nice of you."

"Have you seen much of our ghost girl?" Ellen asked her before taking a bite of the pumpkin pie. "Bud said she was hanging out more at your place."

"Yes, we have. Nearly every day. I really hope she doesn't plan to stay."

"I bet once the construction workers leave, she'll migrate back over here," Sue said. Then she added, "Oh, this pie is really good."

"Thank you" Millie said. "It's my mother's recipe. And you're probably right about the ghost."

"Have you ever wondered if she might not be a ghost?" Ellen asked.

Tanya rolled her eyes, and Sue furled her brows, as if to say Ellen shouldn't have asked the question.

163

"I have," Millie said. "She looks real enough, even if she is white as a ghost and always wearing a white dress, and this and that. I have wondered if she might be a con artist or something. But she doesn't seem to be getting anything out of it, if she's pretending. I don't see a motive. And Bud is convinced she's a ghost, so I suppose that has settled it for me."

Ellen's brows lifted of their own accord, and she gave Sue a knowing look. Maybe Bud knew something and was keeping it from his wife. She recalled one of her first theories—that somehow Bud was holding this girl under his control.

"What do you know about the patients who used to live here?" Tanya asked. "Anything?"

"I don't know much about the *patients*," Millie said. "But one of the *nurses* became good friends with my mother back when I was a teenager. She used to come over and tell us things, and this and that."

Ellen's back straightened. "What things?"

"Well, Barbara used to complain a lot," Millie said. "She wanted to quit, but couldn't afford to, so she put up with the doctor."

"Put up with him?" Tanya asked.

"The doctor wouldn't allow some of his patients to move at all," she explained. "The nurses had to do everything for them—turn them in the night, bring and empty bed pans, and clean each patient several times a day, and this and that."

"I can see how that would get tiresome," Sue said.

"The thing she hated most was what the doctor called *organ stimulation*," Millie said in a softer voice.

"What was that?" Ellen asked.

"Some organs were easier to stimulate than others," Millie explained. "Barbara had to massage their abdomens and their lower backs and this and that."

"Like message therapy?" Tanya asked.

"I suppose, but she said this was different. They did massage therapy on the muscles, but organ stimulation targeted the kidneys, the intestines, the stomach, you know, the organs."

"I see," Ellen said.

"That wasn't the worst part," Millie said softly. "My mother didn't know I was listening, but once I heard Barbara say she had to help the doctor stimulate the patients' *sex organs*, too." Millie didn't *say* "sex organs." She mouthed them.

Ellen's jaw dropped open. So her mother had been right. "Did the doctor have *sex* with them?"

Millie nodded. "According to Barbara."

"That's horrible," Tanya said, gaping.

"What prevented him from getting his patients pregnant?" Sue asked. "They didn't have the pill back then."

"Apparently, the doctor tracked their ovulation cycles, but it seems he made mistakes, and this and that."

"Or he put his urges before his medicine," Sue said.

"Barbara hated it," Millie said. "I don't know how she went on with it."

"Well, we know how the *doctor* went on with it," Tanya said. "Maybe his whole practice was just a way to take advantage of helpless women."

"I don't think so," Millie said. "Barbara gave me the impression that he really cared about curing his patients—that he felt he was doing the right thing."

Ellen wasn't sure what to think, or what to say, but at that moment, two little princesses—Elsa and Anna from *Frozen*—turned up the sidewalk carrying bags of candy. They were followed by a smiling woman in her sixties.

"Hi, there, Ida," Millie said. "Are these your lovely granddaughters?"

"Yes, they are," Ida replied. She pointed to Elsa. "That's Haley." She pointed to Anna. "And this one's Kylie."

"You girls make beautiful princesses," Millie said.

"What do you say, girls?" Ida prompted.

"Thank you," they each said softly.

"Ida, I'd like to introduce you to the new owners of the Gold House," Millie said. "This is Sue, Ellen, and...I'm sorry, what did you say your name was?"

"Tanya," Tanya said as she dropped handfuls of candy into each girl's bag.

"It's nice to meet you," Ida said. "Welcome to the neighborhood."

"Thank you," Ellen and her friends said.

"Can you girls thank them for the candy?" Ida said to her granddaughters.

"Thank you," they said.

"So I heard you ladies are planning to flip this house," Ida said. "Is that right?"

Ellen nodded. "Our plan is to restore it and go from there. We'd like to somehow preserve its history."

"We've thought about operating a bed and breakfast," Tanya said.

Ellen scraped the last of the pie crumbs into a neat little pile at the center of her plate. "I'd rather turn it into a museum about the rest cure, but that's a pipe dream."

"A museum would be lovely," Ida said. "Much better than a zoo."

Sue crossed her arms and rested them on her belly. "We may just make it museum-like. We found photos of the patients who used to live here, and Ellen is going to paint portraits from them."

Ellen blushed. "If I can pull it off."

"She can," Sue said.

"Sounds really wonderful," Ida said. "I've always wondered about this house. When my husband and I moved in fifteen years ago, it was already abandoned."

"I didn't realize the house's history was so important to you," Millie said to Ellen. "You should talk to my mother. She probably knows a lot more than I do, since she lived next door all her life."

"Oh, could we?" Ellen asked. She wondered how coherent Millie's mother was.

"That would really be helpful," Sue said.

"Well, it all sounds marvelous," Ida said. "It was nice meeting you."

"Nice meeting you," Ellen said as the three turned and walked away.

Once they had gone, Ellen turned to Millie and said, "Ida seems nice."

"Yes, she's one of my best friends."

Ellen had wanted to ask more about the Robertsons, but their conversation was interrupted when a black Camaro pulled up in front of the house. Ellen wondered if a car load of trick-or-treaters would pile out. Then the windows were rolled down, revealing people dressed in costumes. They didn't appear to be parking or to be getting out to collect candy. They stared at Ellen and the others, like they were waiting for something.

Ellen stood up to get a better look just as an egg hit the column in front of her. Several more eggs came toward them. Millie, who couldn't move fast enough, cried out as she was slammed with one and then another.

"What?" Sue cried out.

"Oh, my gosh!" Tanya shrieked, jumping up and taking cover behind a column.

"This is ridiculous," Ellen muttered.

Poor Millie. She was covered in raw egg, and her cheeks, visible in the orange Halloween lights, were as red as apples.

"I've got your license plate number!" Ellen shouted to the people in the Camaro. "I'm on the phone with the police." She was bluffing, but they didn't know that.

"Screw you, witch!" one of them—just a kid—hollered back, and the car was filled with laughter.

"Should I call 911?" Ellen asked the others.

"Can you really see their license plate?" Sue asked. "I can't make it out. It's too dark."

"No," Ellen admitted.

"Call the police anyway," Tanya said.

"It won't do any good," Millie said as another egg fell into her lap and broke open.

Just then, from out of nowhere, the ghost girl rushed past Ellen from the front porch toward the black Camaro. Her white hair, skin, and dress were iridescent beneath the nearly full moon. The girl screamed a shrill cry as she charged the vehicle full of teens. She waved her arms and jumped up and down, as though she was about to take flight. The driver shouted something incoherent, drowned out by a car full of terrified shrieks, before pulling away and driving off.

Ellen stood there between her two friends gawking from the front porch. Goosebumps had broken out all along her arms, and the hair tingled at the back of her neck. The figure looked more ghostly than ever. Ellen began to think that maybe the girl *was* a spirit, and if spirits were real, well, Ellen had a lot of thinking to do. If spirits were real, that opened up the door to a host of other things she hadn't been able to believe.

The girl turned and looked up at them before dashing toward the back of the property.

Chapter Fifteen: Mitchell Clark

"Should we follow her?" Ellen whispered.

"No," Tanya said.

"Unless *you* want to," Sue added.

"It was unusual for the ghost to come to our defense." Poor Millie wiped at the raw egg on her blouse and lap. "I wonder why she did it."

"Yeah, that was interesting," Tanya said.

"Maybe she heard us talking," Sue suggested. "Maybe she's grateful that we want to help her."

Millie held up her sticky hands dripping with raw egg. "Well, I'm sorry this happened, ladies. I should head back and get cleaned up, and this and that."

"Do you want me to call Bud?" Ellen offered.

"I guess so," Millie replied.

Tanya collected their empty plates and forks and handed them over to Millie. "Thank you. The pie was delicious."

Before Ellen could get the phone number from Millie, she was distracted by a man coming up the sidewalk toward them. He walked like a man with purpose. He took long, quick strides, and anger seemed to emanate from him.

"What was all that screaming about?" he asked as he neared them. "Everything okay?"

Ellen squinted in the dark night. When he reached the illumination of their orange jack-o-lantern lights, she recognized

171

him. He'd been the man walking away from the Gold House the night she and her friends had taken the box of photos—the night she'd pulled Sue down in the grass and Tanya had turned her ankle. Had he been the one in the house with the flashlight telling them to stay away?

"Hello, Mitchell," Millie said.

Mitchell Clark, Ellen thought. He had dark curly hair and a raggedy, graying beard in need of a trim. His flannel shirt hung over an old pair of jeans. If it weren't for the furtive, angry look on his face, he might be handsome. He looked to be in his fifties, about their age.

Instead of returning Millie's greeting, he repeated his question. "I could hear it down at my house and thought I'd come see what the problem was."

"Just kids messing around on Halloween night," Millie said. "They egged the place, as usual."

"Everyone's okay then?" he asked, glancing from Ellen's face to Sue's and then Tanya's.

"Fine," Sue said. "Thanks for checking on us. I'm Sue, by the way."

Sue stood up from her chair beside Ellen, who, along with Tanya, was already standing. Sue extended a hand.

Mitchell didn't take it. He just waved and said, "Nice to meet you," before turning and walking away.

"Well, isn't he friendly," Sue said with sarcasm as they watched him walk toward the street.

172

Ellen stood between her friends and wondered about his story. Why was he so obsessed with finding Theodore's gold? What made him think it was still here? And was he related to Marcia's Joseph? And if he was a descendant of Marcia's Joseph, did he have any knowledge about why they never married?

Just then, the ghost girl appeared from the side of the house and rushed toward the receding figure of Mitchell Clark.

"Stay away!" she screamed frantically, waving her arms maniacally, as she had done to the black Camaro. She stood about five yards in front of him—she on the sidewalk and he on the curb near the street. "Stay away! I mean it! You've no right!"

Ellen could tell by the light of the moon that Mitchell had pulled out a revolver and was pointing it at the white figure dancing hysterically before him. Even in the darkness, Ellen could tell his hand was far from steady.

"Keep away from me," he warned the girl.

"You keep away from *me*!" the girl screamed. Her voice was so loud that it echoed down the empty streets.

"You don't belong in this world!" He said through gritted teeth. "There's nothing here for you!"

"Quit killing my cats!" she cried.

"Those strays don't belong to you! Nothing belongs to you!"

"This is *my* house!" the ghost girl screamed. "This is *my* house!"

Ellen glanced nervously at Tanya, whom she imagined was having major doubts now about their plans to resell the house.

"Why shoot a ghost with a gun?" Sue shouted. "You're more likely to hurt one of us!"

"Mitchell!" Mille shouted. "Put that gun away before you get one of us killed!"

"Maybe the sound will scare her off," he growled.

The ghost girl ran around the lawn, waving her arms, like an angry spectral in a horror film. She moved closer toward the front porch and looked directly at Ellen. Ellen stared back, dumbfounded. It was if the ghost could see directly into Ellen's mind. A chill ran down Ellen's back.

"Help!" the girl said before she dashed behind the house again, disappearing from their view.

Mitchell waved his gun in the air and said angrily, "This is *your* fault. You three witches. You have no right coming in here where you don't belong and stirring up trouble."

"What is he talking about?" Sue whispered.

"You've stirred her up and made things worse!" he shouted. "You need to go back to wherever you came from and leave well enough alone!"

Ellen couldn't think of a thing to say as Mitchell turned on his heel and hastened down the road toward his house. Had he just threatened them? Another chill crept down her spine.

"Oh, thank God," Millie said. "Here comes Bud."

"What happened?" he cried as he ran across the lawn toward them. "Was anyone hurt?"

The four women all talked at once.

"The ghost appeared."

"Mitchell Clark threatened to shoot her."

"The ghost ran off."

"Mitchell threatened us, said it was our fault."

"What do you mean he threatened to shoot her?" Bud asked with wide eyes.

"He pulled out a gun and waved it around like a mad man," Sue clarified.

Bud scanned the yard. "And the ghost?"

"She disappeared," Tanya said.

"Back toward the greenbelt, I think," Ellen added.

Bud took off running.

"What does he expect to find?" Sue wondered out loud.

"Should we go see?" Ellen asked.

"You go," Sue said. "I'll stay here with Mille and Tanya."

Ellen looked from one face to another. They all seemed to think she should follow him.

"All right then," she said. "If I'm not back in a few minutes, though, promise you'll come look for me."

"I'll go with you," Tanya said.

"No, that's okay." Ellen knew Tanya didn't really want to go. "I'll just peek around the back of the house."

Ellen used the flashlight app on her phone to guide her across the back lawn toward the woods. "Bud?"

She was sure he went this way, but right now it appeared she was utterly alone. "Bud, are you out here?"

She wondered if she should turn back. She hadn't meant to come out this far—just to peek around the back and call for Bud. What the hell was she thinking coming all the way out to the woods alone at night? Hadn't she rolled her eyes at every character in every movie and novel that did this very thing? Stupid, stupid, stupid. But something compelled her onward.

As she neared the woods, she heard a twig snap. She froze. "Bud, is that you?"

"Ellen?" a figure stepped from the trees. It was Bud.

Relief swept over her, but her back stiffened again when she saw the crazed look on his face.

"Bud, are you okay?"

"She's run off again." He panted as he walked toward her.

"Who? The ghost girl?"

"Yeah. Last time that son-of-a-bitch Clark threatened her, she was gone for weeks."

"Isn't that a good thing?" She studied his face now that he was standing in front of her.

He rested his hands on his knees and slumped over, like a broken man.

"Bud?" Ellen was confused. Why did he seem so torn up?

Bud stood up and moved closer. In a lower voice, he said, "I'm gonna tell you something, because I don't think I have a choice anymore, and because I think you might be able to help."

"Sure thing. Shoot." She regretted that last word in light of recent events.

"Millie doesn't know."

"Doesn't know what?"

"Could we meet somewhere to talk?"

"Why can't you tell me now?"

"It's such a long story. Why don't we meet for coffee over at Earl Abel's tomorrow afternoon, around three-o'clock?"

Earl Abel's was a nearby diner well-known for its coffee and pie. "Should I bring Sue and Tanya?"

"I've kept this to myself for many years, and it's gonna be hard to say. The fewer sets of eyes staring me down, the less difficult it'll be."

"Okay." Ellen looked at her phone. "I have somewhere to go in the morning, but I'll meet you at three-thirty. Is that all right?"

He nodded.

"Are you going to come get Millie now? She's covered in raw egg, poor thing."

"Can you see her home for me? I need to take care of something."

Was he serious? What did he have to take care of out here? Was he going after the ghost? "Of course."

Bud disappeared into the woods.

Chapter Sixteen: The State Hospital

At noon on Sunday, Sue pulled up to the curb in front of Ellen's house, where Ellen was anxiously waiting.

"Do you have the photo?" Sue asked when Ellen climbed into the backseat beside Tanya and behind Jan. She meant the photo of Cynthia Piers from the box they found in the attic.

"Yep. Let's go."

"Hello, Ellen. How are you today?" Jan asked from the passenger's seat.

"I'm doing pretty well. How are you?"

"Not looking forward to this trip, that's for sure."

"Mother said she doesn't mind helping us," Sue said. "But she hasn't stopped complaining since she stepped foot in this car."

"Now, let's not exaggerate," Jan said. "That's a form of dishonesty. Didn't I teach you anything?"

"Please don't feel like you have to do this," Ellen said to Jan. "We could try it on our own."

"I know you could, dear, but this will be so much faster. My friend Betty can get us in and out of there in a pinch, so you don't have to wait who knows how many days to speak with an administrator. They're pretty busy over there, as you can imagine."

"And you really think the long-lost cousin approach is better than the truth?" Ellen asked.

"Absolutely," Jan said. "They're wary of outsiders and investigators of any kind. It's better to pretend you're looking for a family member."

"We are looking for a family member," Sue said. "Just not one of our own."

"Follow my lead," Jan said. "If there's a patient named Cynthia who resembles the woman in that photo, I'll get you in."

"We'll have to treat you to dinner sometime," Tanya said.

"That would be nice," Jan said. "I'd certainly take you up on that."

A few minutes later, as they drove across town, Tanya turned to Ellen. "I'm worried about you going alone to meet Bud Forrester later. He and his wife seem nice enough, but you never know. There's something creepy about him. About both of them."

"Someone sounds paranoid," Sue said from behind the wheel.

"It doesn't hurt to be cautious," Tanya said. "I'm just sayin'."

"I would certainly agree with that statement," Jan offered. "But I've spoken to Millie on the phone several times since meeting her, and I think she's nice enough."

"That doesn't mean her husband is," Tanya said.

"We're just meeting for coffee," Ellen reminded them. "I'm not going anywhere alone with him. I want to hear his story."

"We do, too," Sue said. "Every word."

"Don't you think it's strange that he doesn't want us there?" Tanya asked.

"Not necessarily." Ellen tugged at the shoulder harness of her seatbelt. "Maybe it's hard enough to tell one person, let alone three."

"Maybe," Sue said. "Or maybe one person is easier to deceive."

"You don't trust him either?" Ellen was surprised. She'd thought Sue had come to like the Forresters, since her mother seemed to like them. Maybe she was just jealous that she hadn't been invited.

"Not completely. I don't think he and his wife are creepy, but I do think you should proceed with caution."

"So maybe I did teach you a thing or two," Jan said to her daughter.

"Well, I *will* proceed with caution," Ellen said. "I promise."

The front entrance to the state hospital resembled a military base. Sue had to show the guard her driver's license and tell the purpose of their visit before they were allowed in. Sue did what her mother had told her to do and said they were guests

181

of Betty Johnson. The guard—a tall, thin boy who looked too young to be employed—made a call and then let them though.

"What is this? A prison?" Tanya asked once they were past the gate.

"For some patients, I suppose it is," Jan replied.

Ellen thought the grounds resembled a middle school more than a prison: covered walkways, multiple buildings, a parking lot, and several benches all added to the feel of an institution with a lot of people under strict control but with an attempt to make visitors feel comfortable. They saw a chapel at the far left and a family resource center between the chapel and the main facility. Sue parked the car, and they all climbed out.

"This brings back so many hard memories," Jan said as she led them toward the front office. "This is not an easy place to work at, or even to visit. And poor Betty has been here all this time."

"I'm not sure if I can stomach this," Tanya said. "Is it really that bad?"

"It depends on which ward our Cynthia is in," Jan said.

When they reached the main office, Betty was already waiting there to greet Jan.

"It's so good to see you," the short, round, black woman said as she embraced Sue's mother.

"You haven't changed," Jan said. "How is that possible?"

"Oh, go on, girl. You know that ain't true. It's been, what, fifteen years?" Betty laughed.

"Sixteen," Jan said.

"You lookin' good, though," Betty added.

"How are you holding up?" Jan asked.

"Oh, they tryin' to kill me," Betty said.

Jan cocked her head to the side. "The patients or the management?"

"The patients can't help themselves. It's Linda. She has me over in Acute now."

"Oh, boy."

"Don't you know it? We've got Wall-Pisser, Poop-Thrower, Finger-Biter, Laugh-Till-She-Cries, and Ol' Yeller. They my best friends."

"Why did they move you from Chemical? You were always so good with the addicts."

"Who knows? Maybe it's 'cause I've been here the longest and Acute takes a seasoned pro."

"I'm sure that's it." Jan turned to Sue and pulled her closer. "Betty, have you ever met my daughter?"

"Oh, that's your daughter? She looks just like you. How do you do?"

"I'm fine. It's nice to meet you." Sue extended her hand.

Betty took it and said, "Likewise. I'm Betty."

"Sue. And these are my friends, Tanya and Ellen."

"It's so nice to meet you all," Betty said, shaking their hands. "So, what can I do for you today?"

Jan moved between Sue and Ellen and linked her arm in Ellen's. "This is one of my daughter's dearest friends. I'd do anything for this woman. So when she told me she was trying to find a cousin of hers who the family had lost track of, well, I decided to help. After doing a little investigating, we think she may be a patient here, probably in Extended, because she would have been admitted around 1994 or '95."

"What's the patient's name?" Betty asked.

Ellen handed her the photo. "Cynthia Piers, but her last name may be different."

"Oh, look how good she looks in this photo," Betty murmured.

Ellen's heart skipped a beat. "Does that mean you know her?"

"I sure do. I mean, I know her face. Cynthia doesn't talk, so I don't *know her* know her. I only recognize her because I got moved from Chemical Dependency to the Extended Care Unit about a year or two after you left, Jan, and I was there till they moved me to Acute last year."

"Would it be possible for us to see her?" Sue asked.

"I would need to get approval from her doctor," Betty said. "But honestly, I don't see why not. She hasn't had a single visitor in the twenty years she's been here that I'm aware of."

How sad, Ellen thought.

"Wait," Tanya said. "If Cynthia doesn't talk, how do you know her name?"

"That's a good question," Betty said. "I'll see if I can find the answer. Meanwhile, why don't you all have a seat over there in the lobby, and I'll let you know what the doctor says as soon as I can?" Betty pointed to a cluster of chairs just outside of the main office.

"Thank you, Betty," Jan said, shaking her friend's hand with both of hers. "I knew I could count on you."

When the four women were seated, Ellen asked them, "So if the patient here is the ghost's mother, how do we tell the ghost? Do we have to have another séance or something?"

Sue didn't hesitate. "Not a séance. A crossover ceremony."

A half hour later, Betty returned to the lobby and gave the good news. "Follow me to your cousin," Betty said to Ellen with a smile.

"Can we come, too?" Sue asked.

"The doctor is worried that Cynthia might be overwhelmed by too many visitors at once, so he only approved Ellen. We'll see how it goes today, okay?"

Ellen knew Sue hated being left out of the important moment and was probably wishing they'd said Cynthia was *her* cousin instead. Tanya was more patient. She wished Ellen good luck as Ellen followed Betty.

Ellen followed the nurse through a common area. A few patients sat together around one table playing Dominoes, and another sat on a sofa watching an old console television. From the common area, Ellen followed Betty past a big dining area where two employees were wiping down tables and tidying up chairs.

One man sat in a wheelchair further down the hall staring, like a sentinel, at all who passed by. As Ellen neared him, he clicked his tongue at her, reminding her of the days when she was young and construction workers used to make the same sound, taunting her as a sexual object. Where she was annoyed as a youngster, she was entertained as a middle-aged woman. She smiled at the man and winked as she passed him.

"Who are you?" he shouted after her, reminding Ellen of an angry version of the caterpillar from Alice's Wonderland. His face was even kind of round and insect-like. She imagined him smoking a hookah. "Who are you?"

She turned and waved but soon regretted having given him the attention. She could hear him shouting after her all the way down the hall.

Ellen followed Betty around a corner, where they reached a set of double doors. Betty entered a code into a keypad before the doors swung open.

"Welcome to Extended Care," Betty said. "This is where our long-term patients live."

Ellen followed Betty past a nurse's station and down a long hallway. All of the doors leading from the hallway were closed save one. Ellen glanced through the open door to see a man in a leather jacket sitting beside a woman, who was tucked under covers in a bed. Ellen thought a husband was probably visiting his wife or a brother his sister. She could tell by the way he looked at her—with sadness, despair, and affection—that he was related to her.

They came to room 12.

"This is Cynthia's room." Betty knocked on the door and said, "It's Nurse Betty. I'm coming in with a visitor today."

Ellen didn't know what to expect, but her heart pounded against her ribs as she followed the nurse inside Cynthia's room. The blinds were pulled up, and the afternoon sun shone into a very plain and sterile room, like most hospital rooms Ellen had visited and even stayed in throughout her life. Lying on the bed beneath a crumpled sheet with her eyes open and her face blank was a strikingly bright-eyed woman with pale blonde hair and a pale face—an older version of the woman in the photograph. Now that she saw the woman in person, Ellen could see a definite resemblance to the girl she had seen at the Gold House.

Cynthia didn't look at them as they entered.

"Your cousin Ellen is here," Betty said. "She's been looking for you."

This got the woman's attention. She furrowed her brows and turned what seemed to be horrified eyes toward Ellen.

Ellen stared back, speechless.

"Do you remember your cousin?" Betty asked the patient.

Cynthia looked Ellen up and down, from head to toe, studying her, but said nothing. She continued to frown and to furl her brows as though Ellen were repugnant to her. Clearly agitated, Cynthia lay back in her bed and pulled her sheet up to her chin. Then she stared off and ignored her visitors.

"Maybe I should go," Ellen said to Betty. "I didn't mean to upset her."

"She has never reacted to anything or anyone before," Betty said. "So this is actually progress. Go ahead and try to talk to her."

Ellen took a deep breath and let it out slowly as she moved a little closer to the bed. "Hello, Cynthia. I've been looking for you because, well because I was wondering if you could tell me if you once lived at the Gold House with Dr. Piers, and…"

Cynthia glared at her and her nostrils flared. Was this confirmation or just crazy behavior?

"Could you nod your head if you ever lived at the Gold House? Were you a patient of Dr. Piers?" Ellen asked.

Cynthia's eyes widened, but she did not move her head.

"And did you have a daughter?" Ellen asked.

At this, Cynthia jumped out of the bed and stepped within inches of Ellen. She stared Ellen down, like an enemy about to attack.

"I ain't never seen her act like this before," Betty whispered. "Let's back out of the room, nice and easy."

Chapter Seventeen: Bud's Story Begins

As Sue drove everyone home, Ellen told them about her encounter with Cynthia.

"I think she's the right Cynthia," Ellen said when she'd finished her story. "But I can't be sure. I'll try to visit her again tomorrow after work."

"I'll remind Betty to add you to the list of approved visitors," Jan said.

"But we're supposed to meet at Home Depot to pick out the exterior paint color tomorrow afternoon," Sue said. "Unless you want to trust Tanya and me with that."

As much as Ellen wanted to have some input in the color choice, she didn't want to ask them to wait on her. She knew they'd been looking forward to making a decision (she had been too) and that Ed's team would be ready to start on it at three o'clock tomorrow.

"Y'all go ahead," Ellen said. "I trust you."

Tanya reached over and touched Ellen's shoulder. "Are you sure you don't want us to wait in the car while you meet with Bud? Just in case he tries to pull something?"

"What could he pull in Earl Abel's?" Ellen asked. "I'll be fine. I promise."

A few hours later, Ellen sat across from Bud at the diner not far from the historic district. They had each ordered coffee and had made small-talk about—of all things—art, until their coffee arrived and they'd each taken a sip. Then Bud's face turned a shade paler.

"Thanks for meeting me," Bud said.

"It sounded pretty serious." She took another sip of the hot coffee.

"Indeed it is." He looked around the diner for the third time before adding, "You need to know this isn't easy for me, but I have no choice. I have to tell you…I need someone to know the truth, and I can't tell Millie. She can never know."

"Why not?"

"Just hear me all the way through before you judge. Can you do that for me?"

"I can try."

He lowered his voice again. "To give this a little context, there's something else you need to know," he said with a frown. He held an empty sugar packet and kept folding and unfolding it, never taking his eyes from it. "I'm in stage four, pancreatic cancer. The cancer has spread to my liver. The doctor won't give me a deadline but says that many patients survive two more years with the right treatment. That was two years ago."

Ellen covered her mouth. Her first thought was who would take care of his wife and mother-in-law. Would they be moved to a nursing home? They'd lived in that one house their whole lives, probably thinking they'd die there, too, and now that didn't look possible, unless they could afford to hire home care.

"So you can see, I'm living on borrowed time."

"I'm so sorry to hear this. Millie must be devastated."

"Millie doesn't know."

"What?"

"I refused treatment. The doctor told me the side effects included weakness, vomiting, and the list goes on. Who would take care of the girls?"

"You mean Millie and her mother?"

"That's right. There've only been a few times I've had to call someone in to help me, and the girls hated it. They made me promise not to let strangers in their business. It was humiliating, they said."

"But you can't do it alone. And," she hesitated, "what about when you're gone?"

"I'm going to keep my promise to them. After that, it's out of my hands." Then he added, "I never expected them to outlive me."

Ellen didn't know what to say. She took another sip of coffee.

"And now it's time to be practical. I have something I need to confess."

"I'm listening."

He fidgeted with the empty sugar packet again. "You need to let me explain some things before you get all offended and upset with me, okay?"

She was beginning to feel even more nervous and uncomfortable, not sure she could handle the enormous burden he seemed to want to unload on her. But what could she say? No thank you? I don't want to hear your story after all? "I'll do my best." Besides, she had no choice. She *had* to hear it.

"All right, then." He clasped his hands together on the table as sweat broke out on his forehead. "Amy isn't a ghost."

Ellen covered her mouth. She wasn't sure why she was shocked—hadn't she suspected this all along? So the girl was alive. And her name was Amy. Ellen clasped her hands together in her lap, holding on for dear life, as she waited for him to continue.

"At first, I thought she *was* a ghost, just like everyone else. She was so white and so thin. She was even smaller back then—and faster. Sometimes she seemed to disappear into thin air."

"When did you realize she wasn't a ghost?"

"Maybe six months after the first time I saw her. I had gone back to the dry creek bed to empty a pan of hot oil on a big mound of fire ants when I saw her watching me from a tree branch."

"She was up in a tree?"

"Yes she was. Just like a squirrel, eating a pecan."

193

"Did she say something to you?"

"Not at first, but I thought, why would a ghost need to eat? So I kept looking at her from the corner of my eye as I poured the oil. I don't think she knew I'd seen her. She was mashing pecans together in her hands and plucking out the meat like she hadn't eaten in days. That's when I realized she was a child who was alive and starving."

"So then what happened?" Ellen leaned forward and rested her elbows on the table, hugging the warm mug of coffee with both hands.

"Well, I'd just cut up and fried an entire chicken—way too much food for me and the girls—so, without looking up at her, I said, 'Do you want some fried chicken?'" He took a sip of his coffee. "She jumped from the tree and ran off, and I didn't see her again for another week or so."

"I wonder how she survived," Ellen said.

"There's a café on the other side of the green belt from my property. I later learned that she ate from the garbage cans behind that café."

"Poor thing."

"Yeah. She did that for almost a year before I finally got her to trust me."

"How did you manage that?"

"I found her nest one day in the attic, so I started taking food and leaving it for her on that old wooden table. She was probably nine or ten years old back then. She didn't know her age or her birthday, but that's our guess. This went on for months. You have to understand. She was wild, like a feral cat. She had no social skills and the language of maybe a second grader. I eventually taught her how to read."

"It's hard to imagine."

"From the time the house was abandoned to the time I got her to trust me—for that whole year—she was all alone. But she was actually better off on her own than she was when there were others living in that house."

Ellen furrowed her brows. "What do you mean?"

"I'm getting off track. I'll get to that."

"Why didn't you call the police, or Children's Protective Services? Why didn't you try to get her help?" Ellen couldn't stop herself from interrupting him.

"I did. I called them that very day I first saw her, but she ran away. The cops thought I was crazy. They couldn't find any evidence that anyone lived at the Gold House."

"Did they search the attic?"

"I don't know. I hadn't been in the attic yet, so I didn't think to ask."

"Why didn't you tell Millie?"

"At first, I didn't want to worry her. She had just had her third and final surgery and was coming to the realization that she would never walk again."

"I see. And later?"

"It's complicated."

Ellen narrowed her eyes.

"Look, I don't want to get too far ahead of myself."

Ellen nodded and sighed. "Please. Go on."

He took another sip of his coffee. "About three months after that day I first saw her, I took a bowl of chili over to the Gold House to leave on the old table, when this time, she was waiting for me."

Ellen gasped. "Did she speak to you?"

He nodded. "She said the same thing she said to Millie. She said, 'Where's my momma?' I told her I didn't know but she was probably dead."

Ellen jerked back her head. "How could you?"

"I believe in being straight with people."

"You could have fooled me. And she was a *little girl!*"

"She didn't believe me anyway. She started crying and said, 'You're wrong.' I asked her if she'd like to take a bath and get cleaned up. At first she said, 'No,' but when I told her I'd buy her new clothes, she agreed. She finished her chili and then followed me home."

"What about Millie?"

"At first, I wasn't going to hide her from Millie. It just so happened that Millie wasn't feeling well and was taking a nap, and I didn't want to disturb her. I took the girl upstairs and bathed her."

"*You* bathed her?" Ellen narrowed her eyes again.

"Don't look at me like that. It wasn't like that at all." Then he added. "Not then."

Ellen shivered and sat further back in her chair, wanting more distance between them.

"Just hear me out."

Ellen nodded without saying anything.

"I asked the girl if she'd like me to help her find a home, and she said she was waiting for her momma to come back for her—that if she left, her momma wouldn't know where to find her. I told her I'd tell her momma where she was, but then Amy ran away, and I couldn't find her for weeks."

"Sounds like she was scared to death. Did you ever look for her mother?"

"The mother is probably dead," he said. "Where else could she be? And why would she abandon her own daughter?"

"You should have done some research." Ellen decided to withhold her suspicions that Amy's mother might be alive and a patient at the state hospital. She needed to hear his story before she could determine how trustworthy he was.

"I did, but I wasn't lying when I said that house is haunted. Amy's no ghost, but there is something there, and it just might be her mother."

"Did you ever try to look for her mother, just in case?"

"Sure, but I had nothing to go on, and in those first months, dealing with Amy was like dealing with a wild animal. It took a long time for me to get her to trust me. Then, by the time I could get her to cooperate, well…" Tears formed in his eyes. He cleared his throat. "Well, I started to see her as the little girl I'd never had."

Ellen looked away, down at her mug of coffee. "But if that's the case, why didn't you tell Millie?"

Bud shook his head. "I don't know if you can understand this." Then he muttered. "Maybe this was a mistake."

"I'm listening. I'm trying to understand. Talk to me."

"When I met Millie back in the sixties, I was nothing. I had nobody. My parents were dead, and my older siblings had pretty much abandoned me. Hell, they had their own problems."

Ellen waited for him to continue as he wiped the tears that were flowing from his eyes.

"The only choice I had was to enlist. I served in Viet Nam and came back worse off than before I'd left. I was an alcoholic and would have succeeded in nothing but throwing my future away had Millie not come into my life. I'm telling you, she saved me from myself, and I'll be forever grateful."

That still didn't explain why he didn't tell her about Amy. Ellen took a deep breath and fought the urge to interrupt.

"But she and I hadn't been married long when the accident happened. From that moment on, my whole life became about taking care of her."

"That must have been hard."

"Like I said, she saved my life. So it was my turn to save her back."

"So why couldn't you tell her?" Ellen was trying to be patient, but she was failing.

"Because I didn't have anything of my own—never did. The house we live in belonged to Millie's family. And then my *life* belonged to her. Every waking moment became about taking care of her—and by then I was taking care of her mother, too. I just wanted *one thing* to be my own. This little girl needed someone. I could be the father she needed, the father I never had."

"I see."

"I liked having another life away from Millie. I know I was a selfish son-of-bitch not to tell her. And every day I would wake up and think this was the day I would tell her, but then I'd put it off, wanting to keep it to myself."

"I'm surprised Millie never suspected anything," Ellen said before taking another sip of her coffee. By now it was cold, so she waved to the waitress for a refill.

"The idea to dress Amy in the same kind of white dress all the time—that wasn't meant to trick Millie. That was meant to keep the neighbors from catching on, especially Mitchell Clark, who's been obsessed with the German gold for as long as I can remember."

"So you encouraged Amy to pretend to be a ghost?"

"Well, if she wouldn't let me find her a home, then we needed to protect the one she had."

"It's too bad you couldn't help her get psychiatric help."

"Oh, that was out of the question. The doctor is what got her all screwed up in the first place."

Ellen lifted her chin. "What do you mean?"

"I'll get to that part. Let me tell you this the way I need to tell you this. Okay?"

Ellen apologized.

"So, I took food over to the Gold House three times a day. Right after lunch, when Millie usually napped, I went over with books and read to Amy. That's how I taught her to read. Then every Sunday, I took her to my house so she could have her bath—always upstairs so we didn't disturb Millie."

Ellen knew he really meant, *so Millie didn't find out what I was up to.*

They sat in silence for a moment as the waitress topped off their mugs.

"After about three years of this sneaking around, I got tired of the lies. If I didn't clean the dishes right away, Millie noticed an extra dirty dish. Or she would search for our supper leftovers for a midnight snack and be surprised to find none. It didn't bother me at first, but over time, it took away some of the joy of it all. But then something happened that made it impossible for me to ever tell my wife. Something I've dreaded ever since."

Ellen felt the blood leave her face. Nausea crept up from her stomach to her throat.

Tears ran down Bud's cheeks. He glanced at his wristwatch. "Has it really been two hours?"

She looked up at a clock on the wall across the diner. It was a quarter to six.

Bud stood from his chair. "I need to get home to give my mother-in-law her next dose of medicine. And I need to get supper on the stove."

"You've got to be kidding me," Ellen said softly. "You can't stop now."

"Meet me here tomorrow at the same time?" His eyes beseeched hers. "Please?"

"I'll be here," she said, but she wasn't so sure he would.

Chapter Eighteen: Revelations

Paul was not at home when Ellen arrived that evening. Wondering where he was, she took her phone from her purse to call him. It was dead.

Great. She and Paul had gotten rid of their landline a few years ago, which meant she couldn't call him without plugging her cell phone in to a charger. It had been his idea to let the landline go. She hadn't liked it, preferring the old-fashioned phone to her cell. She could never remember to charge it. Only lately had she gotten better at it, but that didn't mean she didn't occasionally let it die.

She plugged it in and gave it a few minutes to get a charge while she went to the bathroom and changed clothes. She supposed there was plenty of leftover barbecue, so she didn't need to cook. Maybe Paul had gone to the store to pick something up to go with it. When she finally returned to her phone, she found eight missed calls—seven from Paul and one from her brother, Jody. Adrenaline pumped through her body at the realization that something must have happened. She tried Paul's number but got no answer. Before dialing her brother, she decided to listen to her voicemail.

The first one was from her brother:

Hi, Ellen. It's Jody. I hope you're doing well. Anyway, I'm calling because Mom didn't answer the phone this afternoon. We talk every Sunday at the same time, and this is the first time in years that she didn't pick up. (This surprised Ellen. She didn't know that about Jody and her mother.) *I've tried every hour for four hours and still nothing. Would you mind going over there and checking on her?*

The next message was from Paul:

Your brother called. He's trying to get ahold of your mother. Call me as soon as you can.

Then another from Paul:

I'm with your mother in the hospital at Brook Army Medical Center. They think she may have had a stroke. Please head over here when you get this message.

Ellen stuffed her phone back into her purse and rushed to her room to change again. As fast as she could, she raced to her car, and, as she headed to the hospital, she tried to call Paul over the speaker phone.

Still no answer.

A terrible thought ran through her mind, that perhaps she and Tanya now belonged to the motherless club. Even though Ellen had never been close to her mother, it was still a strange and frightening feeling to imagine herself without one. It made her loneliness more profound, as if she was a small vessel at sea without an anchor. Her mother had been a kind of anchor, even if she'd been little else. Her mother's existence had made Ellen feel grounded. Ellen had a past and a sense of home and of roots when she thought of her mother. The thought of Ima being gone made Ellen feel like she was untethered.

She listened to the rest of her messages—updates from Paul about her mother's condition. The most recent one said that she'd been moved from the ICU into room 231B. Ellen felt a wave of relief. She tried to call Paul again but got no answer.

***

The following morning, Ellen cancelled her classes from the hospital and called Sue and Tanya and told them about her mother's stroke. The doctors expected a full recovery but it might take several days, and they wanted to keep her mother at least until the end of the week.

Paul was still asleep when Ellen arrived home around 9:00 a.m. The buzz-saw sound of his snoring alerted her before she reached the bedroom door. Although she wanted to change clothes, she decided not to disturb him. She stripped down and fell into her son's old bed. It occurred to her that she still called it her *son's* old bed, even though she'd been sleeping in it for five years. Wasn't it about time she admitted to herself that this was *her* bed?

She'd hoped to fall asleep, but she had too many thoughts raging through her mind. The ghost girl wasn't a ghost. Her name was Amy. Amy's mother might be alive at the state hospital—if *that* Cynthia was indeed *Amy's* Cynthia. Bud's bizarre relationship with Amy had yet to be revealed. And Ellen's mother had nearly died.

Tears formed in Ellen's eyes. Her mother had nearly died. She hadn't died. But almost. Shouldn't Ellen take advantage of this second chance to right things with Ima Frost? Where to begin?

At some point, Ellen must have fallen asleep, because it was just after two o'clock when she next opened her eyes. She had missed her opportunity to go see Cynthia, for there wasn't enough time to drive to the state hospital now and get to Earl Abel's by three-thirty to meet Bud.

She went to shower and discovered that Paul was already gone. He must have decided to go into work. She'd thanked him again and again at the hospital for helping her mother, but he'd been so exhausted, that he'd left not long after she'd arrived.

Ships passing. That's what they'd become.

As she drove toward the diner, Ellen had the panicky feeling that Bud wouldn't be there, making her decision to skip the state hospital visit an unnecessary sacrifice. He'd been so shaky and pale and sweaty the previous afternoon that he'd likely be unable to muster up the courage to endure the whole ordeal a second time. If she didn't find him at the diner, she would go to his house and force the confession out of him. He had dragged her too far into his story to quit it now.

She entered the diner and held her breath as she scoured the room. Within seconds, she saw him already seated at a table in the back. She had worried for nothing. Of course he was here. He needed to tell his story as much as she needed to hear it.

"They were kept in the attic," Bud said before she had even sat down. Then he added, "I'm sorry. You want a cup of coffee?"

He waved to a waitress as she asked, "Who were kept in the attic?"

He glanced around the diner before lowering his voice. "The children."

The waitress approached their table. She wasn't the same pretty waitress from the previous evening. She was an old bag of bones with the wrinkled skin of a lifetime smoker. "Can I get you something?" she asked Ellen.

"Coffee, please."

"Would you like pie with that?"

"No thanks."

Once the waitress had left again, Bud said, "Millie told you what the doctor did to his patients, right? She told you about *organ stimulation*?" He whispered those last two words.

Ellen nodded.

"As you can imagine, this sometimes resulted in pregnancy. Those babies were kept in the attic. It was a nursery."

"All those awful instruments weren't up there when it was a nursery, right?"

Bud shrugged. "I only know what I've been able to piece together from what Barbara told my mother-in-law and from what I got out of Amy. Amy lived her whole life—from the time she was born to the time her mother disappeared—in the attic."

"She never went to school?"

Bud shook his head as he folded a white paper napkin into a tiny square. The he unfolded it and began again. "The children never left the attic."

"But there isn't a bathroom up there."

"A nurse took care of them. They used bed pans and old chamber pots."

Ellen shuddered. "How could Barbara allow that to happen? Why didn't she report the doctor?"

"I don't know. I guess she believed in what the doctor was doing."

The waitress brought Ellen her coffee. "Here you go, dear. Let me know if I can get you anything else."

"Thank you," Ellen said.

Once the waitress had left again, Bud said, "And that isn't all the nurse did."

Ellen took a sip of her coffee, overwhelmed with dread. She closed her eyes and opened them. "What else?"

"She was ordered by the doctor to practice preventive measures." Bud clenched his jaw.

"What preventive measures?"

He whispered, "Force feeding, massage therapy, straight-jacket therapy, and *organ stimulation*."

Ellen gasped. "The nurse…?"

Bud nodded. "Not Barbara. Another nurse. She eventually quit, but she confessed everything to Barbara before she left."

"Oh my God."

"Dr. Piers trained his son to use the same methods," Bud continued. "I guess Johnny was brainwashed. That's the only way I can see it."

"So Johnny…" Ellen couldn't complete the sentence.

"From the time Amy was born, Johnny *treated* her."

Tears flooded Ellen's eyes. How could any doctor believe this was good for people?

"Amy was molested until Johnny died," Bud said.

"So that's why you said she was better off after…"

"Exactly. At least no one was abusing her."

Until you came along, Ellen thought. Wasn't that Bud's big confession? Hadn't he taken over where Johnny had left off? Why else wouldn't he tell Millie?

Ellen's phone rang. It was Paul.

"I'm sorry. I need to answer this," she said.

Bud nodded his understanding.

Paul told Ellen he had gone to check on her mother and that she'd taken a turn for the worse. Ellen needed to come to the hospital right away.

"I've got to go," she told Bud. "It's my mother. She's in the hospital. Something's wrong."

"I'm so sorry. I hope everything's okay."

Ellen fished through her wallet and laid a five on the table.

"Keep it. I'll get the coffee."

She left the five. "Can I call you? Maybe we can meet later tonight or tomorrow?"

"I can't tonight. Let's shoot for tomorrow at this same time—unless something happens…"

Ellen found a pen from her purse. "I don't have your phone number. If you give it to me, I can text you."

"I don't have a cell phone."

Ellen jotted her number down on a napkin. "Call me tomorrow before you head over here, just in case." Then, as she pushed in her chair beneath the table, she asked, "Where's Amy *now*?"

"She's still missing—since Halloween."

When Ellen reached the nurse's station at the Brook Army Medical Center Hospital, Paul was already there waiting for her.

"The doctor was just here," he said. "Come with me for minute. There's a waiting room down the hall."

As they took their seats, Ellen said, "I don't understand why this is happening. The doctor said Mom would make a full recovery."

"When I brought her in yesterday, she was unconscious. The doctor needed permission to give her tPA—the stroke medication. I couldn't get ahold of you, so we called Jody, and he said to give it to her."

"I'm sorry I wasn't here."

"It wouldn't have mattered. Right? You would have said the same thing."

"Probably. Yes."

"The doctor told me that this afternoon, your mom asked to sign a Do Not Resuscitate Order. Apparently, she wasn't happy with the decision to give her treatment."

"But she could have been permanently disabled."

"I know."

"It's one thing to not want to live. I get that. But a stroke could have left her more miserable than she already was."

"I totally agree. But she signed the form. The doctor noticed some tremoring in her hand and ordered another test. They found an aneurysm in her brain. The medicine had caused it to rupture."

"Oh, no!"

"Jody is grabbing the first flight available."

Ellen's lungs emptied of air and she couldn't speak. She opened her mouth to say something, but nothing came out.

Paul put an arm around her, and she collapsed against him.

"She doesn't have much time," Paul said as he held her close. "You might want to go and see her while you still have the chance."

"Mom?" Ellen opened the door to her mother's hospital room and stepped inside.

Ima Frost looked dead.

Ellen lost her footing and fell to her knees.

Her mother opened her eyes. "What are you doing down there on the floor?"

Tears burst from Ellen's eyes. It took a minute to pull herself together. When she could, she climbed to her feet and said, "How do you feel?"

"Dizzy."

Ellen pulled a chair up to the bed and sat down beside her mother. "Can I get you anything?"

"Jody. Is he…?"

"On his way."

"He might not make it in time."

Ellen bit her lip. "Let's hope for the best."

Her mother rolled her eyes and sighed. "Hope. What's that ever gotten me?"

Ellen wiped her eyes. Her poor, miserable mother.

"Don't cry, Ellen," her mother said after a few minutes. "I don't like to see you so upset."

Ellen looked up from her clenched hands to her mother's face. "I'm sorry."

"Don't apologize. I'm the one who should apologize."

"Oh, Mom, you don't have anything to apologize for." The tears streamed down Ellen's cheeks.

"Everything is my fault," Ima said. "All of it. Your father wanted to be doctor. Did you know that?"

Ellen nodded. He'd talked about it his whole life—his dream deferred.

"He was gonna go away to college," Ima said. "I didn't want to lose him. I was afraid to lose him. So a few months before we graduated high school, I...I, I tricked him into marrying me. I seduced him and got pregnant with you."

"It takes two to tango, Mom."

"I told myself that for the longest time, but I can own it now. That was on me."

Ellen didn't know what to say. She took her mother's frail hand and gave it a gentle squeeze.

"Your father did the honorable thing and married me. Went into the service to support us. He returned from basic to his brand new baby girl. And you were the apple of his eye. For years, you were. Did you know that?"

Ellen hadn't known that. More tears flooded her eyes, and she sniffed.

"Those were the happiest days of my life," Ima said.

Ellen used her blouse to wipe her tears. They were out of control.

"When you started school, your father got restless. You see, he never really loved me the way I loved him. So I did the same thing. I got pregnant with Jody. And that worked for a while, too."

Her mother's eyes opened real wide and she cried out, "Ahhhh!"

"Mom? Mom! What is it?"

"My head hurts. The nurse gave me something for pain, but God does it hurt."

"Do you want me to call her?"

Her mom shook her head. "I want to be awake and looking at your sweet face when I go."

Uncontrollable sobs shook Ellen all over her body.

"Please don't cry," her mother said again.

Ellen fought the tears, tried to gain control. "I'm sorry."

"Jody. Please tell him that my final thoughts were of the two of you, and how much I've always loved you. I was a terrible mother, but I did love you."

"You weren't a terrible mother," Ellen lied.

"I was a scared, desperate, insecure woman who only thought of herself. Self-awareness is a good thing. At least I finally stopped lying to myself."

"I love you, Mom," Ellen said. "I love you so much."

It was her mother's turn to cry. "That makes me so happy to hear."

Chapter Nineteen: Who Are You?

When Jody finally arrived, it was too late. Their mother was gone.

He stayed with Ellen for two days. The first day, he went with her to say goodbye to Ima's body. They'd decided to have her cremated without a service, since she had no friends and so few family members. Jody wanted the ashes, and Ellen agreed to let him take them. It seemed only fair. Ellen had gotten their mother's final moments; he should have something, too.

Both nights, they stayed up talking in the front room long after Paul had gone to sleep. Being with her brother made Ellen happy. She realized how much she missed him.

Jody had the blonder, wispier hair of their father and the dark brown eyes of their mother. When he smiled, his sweet face presented the onlooker with a pair of deep dimples that came from their grandmother. Those dimples made Ellen's heart sing.

"Will you still come for Thanksgiving?" Ellen asked the second night. It was only two weeks away. "I'd sure like to see your family and to spend more time with you."

He gave her a smile, and those amazing dimples made another appearance. "I'd like that. I guess we need to decide what to do with the house."

"Let's have it there," Ellen said. "It can be our goodbye."

"Our last Thanksgiving at home."

"Exactly."

Ellen drove Jody to the airport on Wednesday evening. She'd decided to teach the next morning, and she planned to go to the state hospital afterward to see Cynthia.

On the way, she drove by the Gold House. Along with their condolences, Sue and Tanya had been sending photos to her and texting her about their progress. The exterior paint job was complete. She pulled up to the curb and nearly lost her breath. The house looked exactly like the vision she'd had weeks ago.

They'd resurrected the house. Now they needed to resurrect the people who lived there.

Sue and Tanya noticed her car and came out to say hello. They'd both come by with cards and flowers the day before. Today, they focused on happier things.

"Doesn't it look amazing?" Sue asked.

"That it does," Ellen agreed.

"Ed says we'll be done on the inside in three more weeks," Tanya added. "Can you believe it?"

"No." Ellen folded her arms in the chilly afternoon air. "Look. There's something I need to tell you. Something that Bud told me. I haven't had a chance to talk to you about this before now."

She told them what she knew about Amy.

"Oh my God," Sue said.

"That is too bizarre." Tanya pressed her palms to her cheeks. "I can't believe it. I honestly cannot believe it."

Ellen looked first at Sue and then at Tanya. "I want you two to know that, even though she's not a ghost, you have made a believer out of me."

"We don't need you to make us feel better," Tanya said. "We know what we know."

"I'm not trying to make you feel better. And I'm not saying I believe they are spirits or souls or what have you. But there is definitely an energy—some kind of impression in the universe—that gets left behind by the living. I've felt it. Even Bud says there's a ghost in there. Not Amy, but someone else."

She didn't tell them that she thought her mother's energy had visited her the two nights Jody was at her house. Ellen had sensed Ima standing over her as she was falling asleep.

"When do you see Bud again?" Sue asked. "To hear the rest of his story?"

"Tomorrow," Ellen said. "Right now, I'm on my way to see Cynthia. I'm going to tell her that if she's the Cynthia Piers from the Gold House, then her daughter's alive."

When Ellen arrived at the gate to the San Antonio State Hospital, she showed her driver's license to the guard and told him she was going to visit Cynthia Piers. He checked his database (for approved visitors, she supposed) and then waved her inside.

Betty wasn't on duty at this time, so Ellen felt a little less confident as a different nurse escorted her down the winding halls to the double doors with the electronic keypad. This nurse was less talkative and less friendly. She entered the code and said, "Go on down to room twelve."

"You aren't coming with me?" Ellen asked, surprised.

"Do you need me to?" the nurse asked impatiently.

"No. I guess not."

The nurse waited for Ellen to enter the double doors. Ellen stopped and looked back, wondering if she should really be doing this alone. Last time, Cynthia had become quite agitated. It had been frightening when the woman who hadn't spoken in twenty years had jumped out of her bed and had glared at Ellen. Through the windows in the double doors, Ellen could see the nurse walking away.

The Extended Care Unit had a different odor than the front part of the building. Whereas the front office and common areas had smelled like a school cafeteria, this ward reminded Ellen of a nursing home, even though she'd been told there was a separate geriatric unit.

She made her way down the hall to Cynthia's room. When she reached the door, she recalled the way Betty had knocked before entering.

Ellen tapped on the door and said, "You have a visitor." Then she took a deep breath and opened the door.

The woman was sitting in a chair near the window. She wore a loose nightgown and was barefooted, her hair uncombed. She gave Ellen the impression of a woman waiting to die. It reminded her of her mother. A chill slid up her back and made her twitch. As she entered the room, Cynthia never turned her gaze from the window.

"Hello, Cynthia," Ellen said.

Cynthia still did not look at her.

Ellen's patience vanished. Although she felt sorry for this woman who'd been institutionalized for her fifty-something years, Ellen was tired and frustrated and grieving the death of her mother, and she couldn't handle this. Why hadn't the nurse come with her? Ellen pinched her hands together, walked nervously in a circle at the end of the bed, and then groaned.

The groan, it seems, got Cynthia's attention.

"So you *can* hear me," Ellen said.

The woman began to turn away again toward the window, so Ellen quickly added, "So, I'm not really your cousin. And I don't even know if you can understand what I'm saying, but I've just bought a house in the historic district that was once owned by Dr. Jonathon Piers. He turned the house into an asylum, and I'm doing research on his past patients. It's important that others know what he did. It was wrong. And if you were one of his patients, I'm so sorry. But there's this girl. Her name is Amy. And she's looking for her mother."

The woman flinched and emitted an audible gasp.

Ellen waited for the woman to turn to her and miraculously speak, but that did not happen. Instead, the patient rocked forward and backward in her chair (it wasn't a rocking chair). She folded her arms across her chest, clasping each upper arm with the opposite hand, and vigorously rocked her body.

This was beyond the scope of Ellen's understanding. "I didn't mean to upset you. I just, it's just that if you're the Cynthia Piers who once lived at the Gold House, I thought you should know that your daughter is alive and searching for you. She hasn't left the attic all these years. She refuses to go on with her life. If you are her mother, I would like to know, so I can tell her where you are."

The woman continued to rock even more violently than before. Ellen was at a loss as to what to do. She stood there, dumbfounded, wondering if she should call a nurse. Then a strange idea came to her. The patient couldn't speak, but maybe she could write.

Ellen took her purse from her shoulder and dug through it for a pen and a scrap of paper. She found an old grocery list. The back of it was blank and would do. Then, hesitantly, like one would approach a stray dog, Ellen crossed the room toward the rocking woman and offered her the pen and paper.

"Do you think you could write down what you want to say to me?" Ellen asked gently.

To Ellen's great surprise, the woman slowed her rocking and snatched first the pen and then the paper from Ellen's hands.

At first, Ellen worried she would try to stab Ellen in the eye or perform some other violent act, and she wondered if she had been smart to give the patient a weapon that could be turned against her. But then she was relieved and perfectly stunned when the woman stopped rocking and flattened the paper on the table in front of her. The woman fitted the pen in her fist, and, with an unsteady hand and in the writing of a child, she wrote out, "Who are you?"

Ellen gaped for several seconds before she stammered, "Ellen Mohr."

The woman pointed the pen to the paper, as if to ask her question again.

Ellen recalled the angry caterpillar in the hall who had asked her, "Who are you?" He had shouted it again and again. Ellen clasped her hands together. "I'm an art instructor at a university here in San Antonio." *Who are you?* "I'm married—thirty years this year." *Who are you?* "I have two sons and a daughter—all in college. The oldest is in grad school." *Who are you?* "My mother just passed away two days ago." *Who are you?* "My father preceded her ten years ago. Heart failure." *Who are you?* "I have a brother, Jody, who lives with his family in Kentucky." *Who are you?* Ellen felt faint.

She had another surprise when the patient leaned over the table, put the pen to the paper, and scratched out, "Why?"

"Why what?" Ellen asked. "Why am I here? Why do I want to help you and Amy?"

221

The woman glared at her and pointed the pen to the last word she had written, again asking, "Why?"

Ellen wasn't sure what to say. She didn't know the answer herself. Why was she here? Why was she doing this? Who was she?

The woman pounded the point of the pen against the scrap of paper again and again until the pen burst and ink spilled across the table, smearing all over the patient's hand.

The patient screamed, as if she'd been mortally wounded. She leapt from the chair and rushed past Ellen to the bathroom. Ellen watched through the open door as the woman frantically scrubbed her hands and arm clean of the ink.

At that moment, a nurse walked in the room. "Is everything okay in here?"

Even though this was a much friendlier nurse than the woman who had escorted her previously, Ellen was so flustered, she couldn't speak.

"Cynthia?" the nurse called before noticing her at the bathroom sink. "Oh, there you are. Are you doing all right?"

The room began to spin. Ellen blinked and stumbled against the bed.

"Ma'am, are you okay?" the nurse asked.

Everything went dark

That evening, Ellen went to bed without eating. The nurse had speculated that Ellen had fainted because she had locked her knees, cutting off the blood flow to her brain. The nurse had given her a glass of water and then encouraged her to go home and take it easy. Ellen had left, frustrated.

Paul had picked up Chinese food on the way home from work, but Ellen had said she'd eat it for lunch the next day. She didn't tell him what she had learned from Bud about Amy or about what had happened at the state hospital. She was too drained. She went to her son's old room—*her* room, dammit!— and lay down.

Who was she? And why was she doing this?

Chapter Twenty: Creature of Habit

The next day, Ellen went by the Gold House after work to check on the progress of the reconstruction. Tanya was there, and Sue was on her way.

Tanya gave Ellen a tour of the completed kitchen. It looked amazing—solid stone counter tops, an old-fashioned apron sink, antique cupboards, and newly finished hardwood floors throughout the house.

"All the rooms are painted, too, except for the attic," Tanya said. "We'll have to move a lot of that stuff out if we want to paint the attic, too."

"I think we should do that," Ellen said. "It will force us to go through everything."

"Sue said the same thing. I guess I'm out-voted."

"You don't think we should paint it?"

"It's just a lot of work, going through all of that stuff. I'm still helping my father go through my mother's things. It's really taxing."

Ellen bit her lip. She hadn't even thought about cleaning out her mother's house. She put her hand to her head to steady herself. "I just think it would be throwing away useful square footage not to clean it up and paint it."

"You're right," Tanya said. "I know it's the right thing to do."

"We can hire someone to help us."

"No, we shouldn't. It's already adding up to be more than we expected, especially when we had to pay for all that new wiring." Tanya put her hands on her hips. "And we still have to pay to have that dead tree out front removed. Ed recommended someone, but it won't be cheap."

"We'll figure something out. Let's not worry about it right now."

"Okay."

When Sue arrived with coffee for all three of them, Ellen thanked her and told them about her encounter with Cynthia as they sat at the dining room table and drank up.

"How strange," Sue said when Ellen had finished her story.

"I'm not giving up on her," Ellen said. "I'm going again tomorrow. Today, I meet with Bud."

She saw him at one of the back tables slumped over a cup of coffee. His knee bounced beneath the table like a basketball. Part of her wanted to shrink away from this man, who must have done something really awful, something he wanted to unload on her; but, another part of her knew she could not go back. She could only move forward. She had gone too far.

When she sat across from him, he immediately waved to the waitress and asked her for another cup of coffee. Ellen was full from the one Sue had brought, but she went ahead and accepted the cup anyway.

"Thank you," she said to the waitress.

Once they were alone again, Bud said, "How are you holding up?"

"Fair," she said. "Not good, but okay. How are you?"

"The same. *Fair*'s the right word. I've been better, and I've been worse."

They both smiled.

Ellen found herself happy to have the warm mug between her hands. She held on for dear life as she anticipated the rest of his story.

"You have to understand something," Bud said, realizing how anxious she was for him to continue. "Like I said, Amy never left that attic. And although the first doctor had offed himself in—let me see—1972, I believe, Johnny had taken over the practice. I don't know if he had an actual medical degree, but they called him Dr. Piers, just like they had his father."

"He may not have had an actual degree? How could he practice medicine without a degree?"

"That's the thing," Bud said. "He wasn't really taking in any new patients. After the scandal surrounding his father, no one in their right mind would admit a loved one into that rest home again. But there were two or three patients that continued to live there, and based on what Amy has told me, I think Johnny *treated* them."

"Did Barbara continue to work there after the first doctor's death?"

"Oh, no. She left as soon as it all came out in the papers. She was lucky charges weren't ever brought up against her. If any of those patients had loved ones who actually cared about them, Barbara would have been in trouble. But it seems to me that the Gold House was a place where people dumped their unwanted women. If a girl got pregnant out of wedlock, she got sent to Dr. Piers. If a girl wanted to marry someone the family didn't approve of, she got sent to Dr. Piers. If a man fell out of love with his wife, he sent her to Dr. Piers."

"Oh my God."

"Based on what I've managed to piece together, I don't think the majority of those women were ever really sick. It's our society that was sick."

Ellen blinked. Just when she thought Bud belonged at the very bottom of the barrel, he said something truly profound. "I think you're right."

"But I think the doctor believed in what he was doing. He had trained underneath someone else who had practiced these techniques on Civil War veterans."

Ellen shuddered.

"That's why he committed suicide, I think," Bud continued. "Because he believed in what he was doing and couldn't handle the way the papers were portraying him."

"Sounds like the doctor was the one who was sick," Ellen said.

"Damn straight," Bud agreed. "And he passed on that sickness to all of his children—his bastard children. He was never married."

"So you think Johnny was sick, too?"

"Well, what do you think happened to the children in the attic once they were no longer children?"

"They became patients?" Ellen guessed.

"This is what I think," Bud said. "I think those two or three patients that were living with Johnny after his father's death were his half-sisters, probably each from a different woman."

Ellen's mouth dropped open. Was Bud saying what she thought he was saying? Was Johnny having sex with his own sisters?

"Enter Amy," he said.

"So you think Amy was the product of..." she couldn't say it.

"Yes, I do," he said. "And like I said before, she, too, was *treated* by the doctor, by her very own father."

Nausea swept up from Ellen's belly to her throat. She thought she was going to be sick. She put her hand to her head to steady the dizziness that was on the brink of overwhelming her.

"Are you okay?" Bud asked.

Ellen tried to breathe.

Bud acted fast. He grabbed a half-empty glass of water from a nearby vacant table, dipped a paper napkin into it, and then placed it on Ellen's forehead. The cool compress steadied the dizziness, and she was able to breathe. She took the napkin from him and held it against her own head. Then, she took a few deep breaths and let them out slowly.

"Thank you," she said after a moment.

"I know this is troubling," Bud said. "You tell me if this is too much for you. You're going through a lot right now, with your mother passing."

Ellen closed her eyes, shook her head, and then looked at him. "It's okay. Please go on."

"What I've been trying to help you to understand is that this child was raised in a *sexual* climate to be an active *sexual* being." He whispered the word "sexual" both times he said it.

Ellen clutched her mug of coffee, fearing his next words. So that's what he was leading to. He was looking to excuse his behavior.

"In those early days, after I'd finally gotten her to trust me," he said, "she asked me to...*touch her*." He whispered those last two words.

Ellen was horrified, dreading to hear any more.

"At first I got angry with her," he said. "I told her she was naughty." Tears came to his eyes. "I'm ashamed to admit this, but I even called her a little whore." He cleared his throat and wiped his eyes. "That was before I understood what had happened to her, what all she'd been through."

"So you didn't...?"

"No. Of course not." His face turned dark red. "And this went on—her demanding to be touched. This went on for many months. I became more patient as I got to know her. I taught her that private parts were private, that she had to wait until she was an adult and married. I read books to her with stories that might teach her the proper way to behave. I tried to help her understand about love."

"Did that work?"

"I thought so." He took a quick sip of his coffee before he continued. "Then one night, there was a terrible thunderstorm. I was sound asleep and hadn't felt her sneak into my bed. As you know, Millie and her mother sleep downstairs. Amy knew where to find me, because she bathed upstairs and she knew where my room was."

Ellen took the wet napkin and held it to her head again, trying to stave off the dizziness.

"I'm telling you, Ellen, I was asleep." He burst into tears—hard, heavy, and guttural. Spit flew from his mouth as he said, "I didn't realize what she was doing." He covered his eyes and shook. He shook the whole table. She had to steady their coffee mugs. "I thought I was dreaming. When I woke up, I was looking down at my little girl. Oh, god. And she was smiling."

Chapter Twenty-One: Cynthia Piers

Saturday morning, Ellen did something she hadn't done in years: she went out to the art studio in her backyard, opened all the shutters, dusted the shelves, washed her brushes, mixed some paints, and she painted.

Using the box of photos from the Gold House, she began with Marcia Gold.

After an initial sketch, she added her base colors. Then she started bringing some of the features to life—a little shading here, a little highlighting there. She had to work to get the mouth just right. She was vaguely aware when notifications chirped on her phone, but she couldn't be bothered. She had submerged into another realm altogether where she could be present and not be present, where she could find herself and lose herself at the same time.

When she next looked up, it was dusk.

Sunday afternoon, she took the painting of Marcia to the Gold House. She hadn't yet put it in a frame, but she couldn't wait another second. A force beyond her control seemed to compel her to march over to the mantle, to take down the painting of Inger Borhmann, which Ed or one of his contractors must have rehung after the paint job, and to replace it with Marcia Gold. When the new painting was in its rightful place, the whole house seemed to sigh. Yes. This was right and good.

As she stepped back to gaze at the portrait a moment longer, feeling very satisfied with the way it had turned out and thrilled that she had actually *painted* again, her phone rang. It was the San Antonio State Hospital.

"Hello?"

"Hello, Ellen," Betty's voice said over the phone. "You won't believe what happened this morning."

"What?"

"Cynthia spoke!" Betty cried cheerfully. "For the first time in twenty years! And she's asking for you!"

Ellen entered Cynthia's room with a mixture of hope and dread.

The patient was sitting by the window in a different nightgown than she had worn during their first encounter. Her hair was brushed, and she was wearing slippers. As Ellen neared her, the woman glared at her.

"He loved me," Cynthia said emphatically.

Ellen was afraid to sit in the chair across the table from the woman, so she remained standing near the bed. "Who?"

"Johnny."

"So you *are* the Cynthia Piers who lived at the Gold House?" Ellen asked.

The woman stared blankly at Ellen for a long moment before she nodded.

Ellen took off her coat and clutched it in her arms as if it were a newborn baby.

"He said it was natural for patients to fall in love with their doctors," Cynthia said. "But he loved me. He loved me back."

"I see." Ellen wondered if they'd been unaware that they shared the same father.

"He moved me downstairs with him. We watched television. And he let me go out with him. We ate at restaurants. We bought food for the others. He even took me to the movie theater once. I was no longer a patient when they brought me here. But they wouldn't believe me. No one would listen to me. So I told her to hide."

"You told who to hide?"

Tears filled Cynthia's eyes, and she barely squeaked out her answer. "Amy."

Ellen sucked in her lips and began pacing at the end of the bed, clutching her coat close to her.

"First the police came. Then the doctors. They took Johnny away."

"Took him away?" Ellen was confused. "I thought he had died."

"Yes. They came and took him."

Ellen covered her mouth and said nothing. How long had she held onto the body before someone had come for it?

"I knew they were coming back for me. And for Regina and Carmen. I could tell. So I told her to stay in the attic. She was such a good girl. I didn't want them to take her away, too." Then she added. "No one would listen to me. I was not a patient! I told them to take Regina and Carmen. They were patients, but I was not! I was Johnny's wife!"

"Did you get married? Have a wedding?"

After a few moments, Cynthia shook her head and hung it in shame.

"And Regina and Carmen? Are they still here? Still alive?"

Cynthia shook her head again. "I tried to tell them that I didn't belong here, but they wouldn't listen. So I stopped talking."

Ellen turned and met the woman's eyes. "I'm listening to you, Cynthia."

Cynthia looked up at Ellen, as if she was trying to decide if she could trust her. "Is Amy okay? Can I see her?"

Ellen froze in her tracks. At the moment, she didn't know the answer to those questions. She swallowed hard and did the only thing she could do. She lied.

Two hours later, Bud met Ellen out on his front porch. He didn't look her in the eye or give her the friendly greeting he'd given her in the past. She could tell he was embarrassed that she knew his deepest, darkest secret. And maybe she should be disgusted with him and not have anything to do with him, but the truth was that she just felt sorry for him. Not knowing for certain what really happened that night, she wasn't ready to exonerate him completely, but she wasn't ready to judge and condemn him, either.

"Let's take a walk," he said as he stepped down to the sidewalk.

She followed him.

When they reached the curb, she asked, "Any sign of Amy?"

"No."

"Has she ever been gone this long?"

"Sure, but not lately. I don't know where she's getting her meals."

"Are you worried?"

"Damn straight, I'm worried."

Ellen's gaze fell on the house next door—on the Gold House. It looked amazing in the late afternoon sun. "Should we check the attic?"

"Yes, if you don't mind."

They walked across the lawn to the empty house. Ed and his team had needed to take off this Saturday. Sue and Tanya weren't there, either. The last Ellen had heard, they were off picking out bathroom fixtures.

"Are you planning to do something about the old tree?" Bud asked her.

"We're having it removed."

"Good. It's a hazard having a dead tree of that size so close to the house. I've wanted to have it removed myself."

Ellen took out her key and unlocked the front door. Although the electrical had been completed recently, they were still waiting on City Public Service to turn the energy on for them. Luckily, the afternoon sun gave them enough light to make their way up the stairs.

"It looks really nice in here," Bud said.

"Thanks. I think so, too."

Ellen led the way to the attic stairs. There were no more locks on the doors, so she didn't have to worry about being locked out.

"We still need to sort through all the mess up here," she said as they reached the attic floor and looked around for some sign of Amy. "I don't see her here, Bud."

Bud crossed the room to a back corner. Ellen studied him. What was he doing? In another moment, he'd lifted a trap door.

"I didn't know that was there!" she said.

Ellen followed and looked over his shoulder. Beneath the trap door was a small niche about four feet long by four feet wide and only two feet deep. The niche was lined with a blanket and pillow.

Ellen covered her mouth. "Is that where she sleeps?"

"Only sometimes, when she needs to hide."

"I didn't even know that door was there," she repeated.

"It's a good hiding place. It's too bad she's not here."

"Where do you suppose she is?"

He closed the trap door. "I honestly don't know. Maybe she's in some kind of trouble."

Ellen crossed her arms. "Bud, I know you don't want to hear this, but I think we need to call the police."

He looked sharply down at her but didn't say anything for several seconds. "She'll turn up."

Bud led the way from the attic.

"There's something else I was wondering about," Ellen said as they took the steps down to the second floor.

"What's that?" Bud asked.

"Did Amy really kill Millie's dog?"

They reached the second floor and crossed the hall over to the next set of steps. "No. I don't know who did, but when Millie assumed the ghost did it, it helped her, I think. It gave her some closure, at least. Pedro may have even died of old age, but it helped my case to say the ghost did it."

"What about the neighbors' cats?"

"Amy would never kill an animal. Hell, she could make a *rat* her friend." He led the way down toward the bottom floor. "You have to remember that, except for me, she was all alone. She turned to animals for companionship. Any stray dog or cat or rat or mouse became Amy's new best friend."

Ellen wondered about the four dead rats she and Sue and Jan had found that first day in the attic.

Bud continued, "I just said those things about her because I needed everyone to be afraid of her, so they would leave her and this house alone."

"I see."

"But the person responsible for the deaths of those animals is probably Mitchell Clark."

"Why? I don't understand?"

They reached the bottom floor. "I don't know either, but that's what Amy says, and I believe her."

"Does she know where the gold is?" Ellen asked.

"There's no gold."

Ellen furrowed her brows. "Are you sure?"

"Don't you think someone would have found it by now?"

"Not necessarily."

"She doesn't know anything about it," Bud said.

Ellen wasn't sure she believed him. Then she asked, "What if Amy's mother is alive?"

"Then she's a terrible person for abandoning her daughter like that."

"But what if she couldn't help it?"

"How's that even possible?"

"There's something you need to know." Ellen bit the inside of her lower lip. This was not going to be easy. She wasn't sure if he'd be relieved or upset.

"Tell me."

"I took some samples from the attic and sent them to an online lab. They were able to find an 86 percent DNA match with a current patient at the San Antonio State Hospital."

"What you are saying?"

"I've found Amy's mother. And she's alive."

Chapter Twenty-Two: The Hunt for Amy

The Wednesday before Thanksgiving, Ellen, Tanya, and Sue took three homemade pies to the Extended Care Unit of the state hospital and visited Cynthia. Tanya and Sue were curious about seeing Cynthia in person, but they didn't want to risk frightening the patient back into silence, so they remained near the door. Ellen mentioned that they were her friends, that they'd each made a pie, and they'd come to wish Cynthia a happy Thanksgiving. Although not as talkative as she'd been during Ellen's last visit, Cynthia did ask about her daughter. Ellen didn't want to admit the truth—that she didn't know where Amy was—so she told the woman that she was waiting for the right moment to tell Amy.

"Amy doesn't know about me yet?" Cynthia asked.

"Not yet."

Cynthia folded her arms across her chest, clasping each upper arm with the opposite hand, and began to rock in her chair. Ellen glanced back at her friends, bewildered and unsure of what to do. Tanya shrugged. Sue shook her head. Then Tanya stepped out of the room, and Sue followed her.

After another long minute, Cynthia stopped rocking, turned her bright eyes on Ellen, and asked, "Why?"

"It's delicate," Ellen said. "I want to see you get better, and make sure you can handle this. Both of you. I'll keep you posted."

And, like a coward, Ellen fled the room.

The last Thanksgiving in her childhood home with Paul and her kids and Jody and his family was both a happy and sad event. Although she and Jody found it difficult to decide what to do about the house (he wanted a place to stay when he visited San Antonio and didn't want to sell it, whereas Ellen hoped to use her part of the proceeds to invest more in the Gold House), there was one thing Ellen did know for sure now that her mother had passed: ghosts were real. She'd already come to this conclusion the two nights she had felt her mother looking over her in the wake of her mother's death, but that Thanksgiving day, she could feel her mother all over the house. She'd been there celebrating with them.

The Saturday after Thanksgiving, after Jody and his wife and kids had got on the road and after all the leftovers were put away, Ellen made a quick call to Bud to see if he had any news about Amy.

"Let me call you back," he murmured.

A few minutes later, he called.

"Still no sign of her," he said. "She hasn't disappeared for this long in years. I don't know what to do. I even went over and paid a visit to Mitchell Clark, thinking maybe he'd been up to something."

"I was thinking the very same thing," Ellen said. "Did you learn anything?"

"He didn't let me in the door—not that he usually would. We've never been on friendly terms."

"How old do you think Amy is?" Ellen asked.

"Late twenties," he said. "Why?"

"Maybe it's time to call the police," Ellen said.

"Let's give her a few more days."

That night, Ellen convinced Sue and Tanya to go with her to spy on Mitchell Clark.

Sue offered to drive. She picked up Ellen and then Tanya and drove out to the historic district. As they drove, they planned their strategies.

"Keep us on speaker the entire time," Ellen told Sue. "Just in case."

"Don't worry. I'll only hang up if my mother calls," Sue said with a smile.

"You better not!" Tanya gave Sue a playful punch in the arm from the backseat.

"Don't worry, ladies," Sue said. "I've got you covered. I'll sit in front of the Gold House, and if you need me to drive up the road and pick you up, you just let me know. If you need an emergency latte and muffin, well I can get you those, too."

"Maybe we need code names," Ellen said. "I call Ziva."

"You can have her," Tanya said. "I call Agent Scully."

"Given your phobias," Sue said to Tanya, "I think your code name should be Mr. Monk."

"Ha-ha," Tanya said sarcastically.

It wasn't long before Sue pulled up to the curb in front of the Gold House. This was the first time Ellen had seen it completely restored at night. Tears filled her eyes. The house looked regal. They just needed to get rid of the dead tree that still loomed over the property with its sad and weary branches. Luckily, the tree removal service had been scheduled to come on Thursday.

Ellen bit her lip as she checked the torch app on her phone once more. "Are we ready, Agent Scully?"

Tanya gave her a nod. "But we stay together, okay? Promise me we won't split up."

"I promise," she said. "But I really want to hear you call me Ziva."

"Lead the way, Ziva David," Tanya said.

With a smile on her face and with her heart beating fast against her ribs, Ellen opened the car door and stepped out onto the street. It was after nine o'clock, and the moon was now a tiny crescent sliver. Clouds filled the chilly sky, and, except for the section of street in front of the Forrester's house where a lamppost illuminated about thirty square feet, the night was dark.

There were a few lights on at the Robertson's house, but the same could not be said of Mitchell Clark's Italianate-style home.

"Ready Agent Sully?" Ellen asked.

"I guess so, Ziva David."

Joking with Tanya and Sue had kept Ellen from being terrified over what she and her friends were attempting to do. What if this gold-digging stranger *had* abducted Amy? What if Tanya and Ellen were spotted by him and captured, too? Ellen had 9-1-1 on speed dial, and she wasn't afraid to use it.

After they'd passed Ida and Sam Robertson's Victorian, they left the street and took cover in the trees between the two houses as they made their way to Mitchell Clark's side windows. Ellen experienced a moment of déjà vu as she recalled the night of the séance and the image of Bud Forrester peeking into the dining room of the Gold House. The screens over the windows of Mitchell Clark's Italianate were full of dirt and cobwebs, making it difficult for Ellen and Tanya to see inside. As they inched their way around the back of the house, they kept Sue on their phones in conference-call mode. Like most of the houses in this area, there was no fence, so they had easy access to the back.

"We're at the back porch," Ellen whispered into her phone.

Both of the windows from the back porch were open a few inches. Ellen and Tanya exchanged glances before Ellen wrapped her fingers around the edge of one of the windows and lifted. It opened another ten inches and was now wide enough for her to fit through.

Tanya shook her head and pointed to the shed that was out toward the dry creek bed on the edge of the woods.

Ellen nodded and followed Tanya toward the shed. It made sense to check this first. Less risky.

The twelve by twelve metal building was about eight feet tall and faced the house. When Ellen tried the door, she found it locked. Tanya pointed around the side, where there was a small square window up high. Ellen followed her to it. Six-foot Tanya could easily see inside, but Ellen had to get on her tip-toes and crane her neck to get the slightest peek.

Something moved inside.

Ellen and Tanya both saw it at the same time. Ellen knew this because she heard Tanya suck in a surprised gulp of air. It was too dark to tell what it was that had moved, but, as the windows were closed, it couldn't have been caused by the wind.

Tanya turned on the torch app of her phone and shined it through the window.

Just then, Ellen heard Sue's voice come over her phone. "Abort! Abort! A truck is pulling into the driveway!"

Ellen turned in time to see two headlights shining toward her. She and Tanya ran for the woods.

Once they were scrambling behind the trees, Ellen said, "There's a café on the other side of the creek bed. Keep going."

Tanya led the way past the trees toward the creek, which was full of rocks and leaves and dirt. Even with both of their phones shining on the ground, navigation wasn't easy. It seemed to take forever to get down the hill of one side of the creek and up the other side. Ellen's heart was beating fast, and she felt a little delirious, giggling despite her fear. They hurried through another line of trees before they spotted pavement and the backs of buildings. But between them and the line of buildings was a chain-link fence.

"Just great," Ellen said.

"Come on." Tanya put her hands along the top rod of the fence. "We can do this." She pressed the toe of one sneaker against the chain-link and brought the other foot all the way up to the top, pushed off with her foot and hands, and made it to the other side.

Ellen felt abandoned. She laughed and cried at the same time. "I can't climb that stupid fence."

"Come on, Ziva David," Tanya said.

"I really don't think I can do it." Ellen put her hands on the fence the way Tanya had, but getting her feet high enough to leap over seemed impossible. "Maybe it doesn't go all the way down the block. Maybe there's an opening further up the way."

Tanya walked with her in the direction of the Gold House—Tanya on one side of the fence and Ellen on the other—when suddenly, behind them, they saw a beam of light heading toward them. Someone had followed them into the woods.

"Oh, shit!" Ellen whispered frantically.

"You can do it. I'll help you. But hurry!"

246

Ellen put her elbows on the top of the fence and leaned her body over it. She pulled up one leg as high as she could, but the only way over was to fall. She rolled over, head first, landing on hard pavement on the other side. Tanya did her best to help her, dragging Ellen's body over the fence, but Ellen took her down with her.

"Oh!" Ellen cried.

"You okay?" Tanya asked as she climbed to her feet and leaned over Ellen.

"Who's there?" came a voice from the woods.

It sounded like Mitchell Clark.

Tanya helped Ellen from the ground before they ran— pathetically, but as fast as they could—around the back of the building to the street on the other side.

"That was close!" Ellen said with a laugh of relief under the safety of the street light and near other people and cars. She was badly bruised on her elbow and knees and stinging from where the fence had scraped against her but was glad to be alive.

"Too close!" Tanya agreed, giggling.

Into her phone, Ellen said, "Sue, drive around the block. There's a Kwik Laundry, a gas station, and a little Italian café called Nona's. We'll be waiting inside the café."

Tanya and Ellen went inside and grabbed a booth. They ordered cups of coffee for themselves and for Sue, who arrived about five minutes later.

"There was something in the shed," Tanya said to Sue as she slid in the booth beside her.

"But we couldn't tell what it was," Ellen added.

"Well, as long as we're here, we may as well try the cheesecake," Sue said.

"I'll share one with you." Tanya took a sip of her coffee.

"No, I want my own," Sue said. "All this detective work has built up my appetite."

So they ordered three slices of cheesecake with their coffee, and then Sue, after hearing more about what they saw in the shed, said, "I have an idea."

Tuesday after work, Ellen met Tanya at the Gold House to carry out Sue's plan. Sue was in position at the meeting of the San Antonio Conservation Society. The purpose of the meeting was to discuss the plans for the Gold House. Sue had created a Power Point presentation about the hope of converting the building into a museum honoring the women who had suffered under the rest cure treatment originally created by Weir Mitchell and made even more horrific by Jonathon Piers. She'd included photos of their renovations, too. The real purpose of the meeting was to keep Mitchell Clark occupied for a couple of hours while Tanya and Ellen investigated his storage shed in the light of day.

First, Ellen and Tanya went inside the Gold House to talk with Ed and to check on the progress of the bathrooms. As anxious as they were to find Amy, they didn't want anyone on the construction crew wondering why their cars were parked in front of the house. So they did a quick run through first.

The energy had been turned on, and it felt amazing to flip a switch and have light.

"That light over the mantle really highlights your painting of Marcia," Tanya said.

"I still need to get a frame for it."

"It's beautiful. You did a nice job."

Ellen held back tears, feeling a little choked up over the fact that, even though she hadn't painted in years, she'd been able to pull off such an important piece. The painting was important to her, but it was also important to her friends, and—this was a *feeling*, but an undeniable one to Ellen—it was important to this house.

Ellen followed Tanya to each of the bathrooms to check out the installation of the new fixtures. It was fun to turn on and off the light in each room as they went. And Ellen turned on and off the faucets in each of the bathrooms to make sure they worked properly. The house was really close now to being complete.

All that was left to deal with was the attic and the dead tree.

They told Ed how happy they were. They would call him when they had the attic ready. Right now, they said, they were going for a walk to check out the rest of the neighborhood.

Ed shook each of their hands and said he would be out of the house within the hour. He just needed to clean up and pack his tools.

"We better get started," Tanya said to Ellen.

Ellen followed Tanya from the back door, down the back steps, and out into the woods. They followed the dry creek past the Robertson's Victorian toward Mitchell Clark's Italianate.

"What if she's dead?" Ellen hadn't meant to sound so pessimistic, but she was full of dread. "How in the hell can I go back to Cynthia and say, 'Oops. I made a mistake. Your daughter isn't really alive after all. Sorry.'"

"We can't think like that," Tanya said.

"I'm scared," Ellen said.

"Me, too."

"At the first sign of foul play, we call the cops. Agreed?"

Tanya nodded.

Mitchell's metal building came into view. Ellen and Tanya glanced nervously at one another as they made their way to the side window. Tanya looked through the pane first. Ellen pushed up on her tip-toes and craned her neck to see inside.

Ellen wasn't sure what she was seeing. Were those...

"Cats?" Tanya whispered. "Are those cats?"

"That's what it looks like. Maybe six or seven of them."

"Why do you think he has cats locked up in his storage shed?"

"That's a good question. Can you see anything else?"

"No sign of Amy."

"Should we check the house?" Ellen asked. As soon as she'd suggested it, adrenaline pumped through her body. She'd really believed she'd find Amy in the shed. Disappointment and fear coursed through her.

Tanya let out a deep breath. "I guess we should."

As they picked their way across the lawn to the back porch, Ellen said, "If nothing else, we need to call the humane society. I wonder if those cats have food and water."

"I couldn't tell."

When they reached the porch, they found the windows were closed, and there was nothing to grab onto on the outside to lift them open. Ellen tried pressing against the glass and lifting but had no luck.

"Oh, hell," Ellen moaned. "Now what do we do."

Tanya pulled open the back screen door and tried the knob on the old wooden door. It opened.

"That was easy," Ellen said.

"I don't think a kidnapper would keep his house unlocked," Tanya added.

"Well, he might not be keeping her here. But maybe we can find some clues. Let's go in."

Ellen led the way. They walked into a sunroom with a sofa and coffee table. Although the plaid sofa was old and worn, the room was surprisingly neat and tidy for a man obsessed with finding gold. Ellen had imagined muddy shovels and a careless attitude toward anything else.

They stepped up from the sunroom into the kitchen. There were a few bowls in the sink, but, otherwise, it was also neat—not immaculate by any means, but neat. From the kitchen, they could see into the dining room and living areas. The stairs to the second story were near the front door.

"I feel weird being in someone else's house," Tanya whispered. "What if a neighbor saw us come inside? What if we get caught?"

"Let's make it quick," Ellen said. Then she called out, "Amy? Amy, are you here?"

"What are you doing?" Tanya said in a panic. "Someone's going to hear you."

"*Who*'s going to hear me?"

"A neighbor out walking or something. I don't know. Just keep it down."

"All right, all right." Ellen grabbed the bannister. "I'm going upstairs. Coming?"

Ellen took the carpeted stairs to the second floor, where there were a series of closed doors along a hallway. The worn shaggy brown carpeting from the stairs continued up here. Ellen wondered if hardwood floors were preserved beneath it. The HGTV addict in her came out at the most inopportune moments.

The first door opened to the master bedroom.

"Wow. He makes his bed," Ellen whispered.

"This feels so wrong—being in this house. Hurry up."

"Amy?" Ellen called out, wondering if they should check the closet and beneath the bed.

"She's not in there, come on."

Ellen closed the door and opened the second door. It led to a spare bedroom with a twin bed, a gun cabinet, and a collection of hunting magazines. It was dusty but neat.

"I don't think she's here," Tanya said. "Let's get out of here."

"We're almost done," Ellen said. "Come on."

Ellen opened the door at the end of the hall. There was a big wooden desk in the middle of the room with bookshelves on one wall and a bulletin board on another. Stretched out over the expanse of the big desk was a huge hand-drawn map. Ellen had only to study the old parchment paper for a moment to recognize the Gold House and its surrounding property. A one-inch grid had been penciled over the map with penciled x's filling nearly every one.

"This is a map of our property," Tanya said.

"It's his record, I bet," Ellen said. "His way of keeping track of all the places he's already searched for the gold."

"It looks like he's searched every possible square inch."

"It sure does," Ellen agreed. "Maybe the gold isn't there anymore. Maybe Marcia did something with it."

"Maybe so."

"This is so sad," Ellen whispered. "He's spent so much time and energy searching for something that isn't there. I wonder why he's so obsessed."

"Who knows?" Tanya said. "We should go now."

"What the hell's going on in here?"

Ellen and Tanya turned to find Mitchell Clark in the doorway pointing a revolver directly at them.

"What are you doing in my house?" he demanded.

Chapter Twenty-Three: The Ghost of Marcia Gold

With his free hand, Mitchell Clark pulled a cell phone from his trouser pocket. "I'm calling the police. You two don't move, and I won't shoot."

"Fine," Ellen said boldly. "I wanted to call them myself, to tell them about all those cats you've got locked up in your shed."

Mitchell stopped dialing and returned his phone to his pocket. "You've been snooping around back there, have you?"

"Please don't shoot us." Tanya put her hands in the air. "We're sorry."

"We're just trying to find Amy," Ellen explained, lifting her hands, too. She may have even peed a little.

"Who's Amy?" He continued to point the revolver at them.

"The ghost girl," Tanya said. "At the Gold House."

"She's dead, isn't she?" Ellen accused as hopelessness washed over her.

"Of course the ghost is dead," he said. "She's been dead for over a hundred years."

Ellen and Tanya exchanged glances.

"I don't think we're talking about the same person," Tanya said.

"I'm talking about the ghost of Marcia Gold," Mitchell said. "My great-grandmother."

"Your great-grandmother?" Tanya repeated.

"You're a descendant of Marcia Gold?" Ellen asked with surprise.

"Not that it's helped me claim her house over the years," he complained. "About ten years ago, I fought for it in the courts and lost."

"Then why didn't you just buy it?" Tanya asked.

"Why should I buy something that's rightfully mine?"

"Look, could you just lower your gun and talk to us?" Ellen said. "I'm sure we can work something out."

"You two need to get off my property," he demanded angrily. "You won the battle over the Gold House, but this place is mine. And if I ever find the gold, that's mine, too!"

"What makes you think it's still there?" Ellen's heart was about to burst from her chest. Why on earth did she think she could be so brave?

"Because that damn ghost won't let me rest until I find it," he said. "I would have given up years ago if she didn't torment me in my dreams. Now you two get out of here."

"Okay," Tanya started to leave, but Ellen pulled her back.

"What the heck, Ellen?" Tanya whispered. "Let's get out of here."

"Wait a minute." Ellen was confused. "The ghost isn't really a ghost. Her name is Amy. We think she's a descendant of Marcia's, too."

"I think I know a ghost when I see one," he said. "Now, do I need to put a bullet through your head to get you out of here?"

"Nope," Tanya dashed from the room and down the stairs.

Ellen stood there with her hands in the air, totally conflicted. The need to understand the truth was greater than her fear. "Shoot me if you want," she said. "But I have a diary you might be interested in. It was written by Marcia Gold in the summer of 1881. And in it, she talks about the gold."

Mitchell's mouth dropped open. "Where is it? Where did you find it? Give it to me, now!" He put the gun a few inches from her face.

She may have peed a little more.

"I don't have it on me. And if you want it, you better lower that gun and talk to me like a normal human being."

He lowered the gun. "How can I trust you'll give it to me? And how do I know you aren't bluffing?" He raised the gun again.

"I'm not bluffing. I swear there's a diary. Marcia wrote about her love for Joseph Clark in it. Was that your great-grandfather?"

Mitchell lowered the gun. "Yes."

"She wrote fondly of him. You should read it, since they're you're ancestors."

"Ellen?" Tanya called from downstairs.

"I'm okay!" Ellen called back. Then to Mitchell, she said, "So, can we go downstairs and talk like civilized people?"

He stuffed his gun in the back of his waistband and stepped away from the door. "After you."

Ellen led the way down the stairs, where Tanya was waiting by the front door.

"Ellen, let's get out of here," Tanya said.

"I told Mitchell about the diary," Ellen said. "I told him I'd give it to him, but I have a few conditions."

"What conditions?" Mitchell asked as they reached the ground level.

Tanya opened the front door. "Why don't we discuss this outside?"

Ellen followed Tanya through the door. Mitchell was right behind her.

A few houses away, Sue was parked in front of the Gold House. When she saw them coming out of Mitchell's Italianate, she drove her car in front of it and rolled down her window.

"Everything okay over there?" Sue called out.

"I'm not sure," Tanya called back from the front porch as she stepped down onto the sidewalk.

"Where's the diary?" Mitchell asked again. "I'm not fooling around with you ladies all evening."

Evening? Ellen looked up to the sky. From where the sun was positioned, she imagined it must be around four o'clock. Time had gone by quickly this afternoon. She glanced over at

Tanya, who stood on the curb next to Sue's car, probably telling Sue what they had found and what had happened.

"Are you going to tell me or not?" Mitchell demanded.

"I'm not telling you where it is until you answer a few questions," Ellen said to Mitchell. "First of all, the girl that you shot at on Halloween night…"

"You mean the ghost?" he interrupted.

"She's not a ghost," Ellen said. "Her name is Amy. Bud Forrester has been taking care of her all these years. It's a long story, but the short of it is that she's missing. You know anything about that?"

Mitchell gawked at her. "Are you bullshitting me?"

"I promise I'm not," Ellen said.

He fell onto a rocking chair and put his hand to his mouth. She could see the wheels spinning in his head as he processed what he'd just been told. "Are you saying that ghost in the white dress isn't a ghost? That isn't the same Marcia Gold that haunts me in my dreams?"

"She's a living breathing young woman, and her name is Amy. Bud found her years ago and has tried to help her, but she refuses to leave the house because she thinks her mother's coming back for her."

"I'll be damned," he muttered.

"So Bud helped her keep up the pretense of being a ghost to protect both her and the property from outsiders."

"How old is she?" Mitchell asked.

259

"Bud said late twenties."

"I've been casting spells against her all these years," he said. "No wonder they never worked. The spells are meant for evil spirits."

"Okay, so you can't tell me where she is, I guess," Ellen muttered. "But what about the cats? Why do you have six or seven cats locked up in your storage shed?"

"Those are strays," he said. "And none of your damn business."

"Do they have food and water? And a litter box that gets changed regularly?"

"Yes, they do. Look, no one wants those damn cats. I'm doing the neighborhood a favor."

"Keeping them locked up like that? Why not take them to a shelter where they can be adopted by people who want them?"

"Look, you don't know what kind of hell I live in, so you just keep that judgmental tone to yourself."

"Tell me about it. I'm listening."

Ellen noticed Sue climb out of her car and head up the sidewalk, with Tanya behind her.

"What are y'all doing up there?" Sue asked.

"Negotiating," Ellen replied. "I told him he could have Marcia's diary if he answered a few questions."

"Well, why don't we all go over to the Gold House and talk?" Sue suggested. "That's where the diary is, anyway, and more chairs to sit on. Plus, I found a pizzeria around the block that delivers. Can I order us a pizza?"

"I would agree to that as long as Mr. Clark leaves his gun behind," Tanya said.

"Are we seriously ordering a pizza?" Ellen asked.

"I just gave a two-hour Power Point presentation, and they didn't have any refreshments," Sue said. "I'm tired and hungry, and I want to sit down. But I also want to hear what Mr. Clark has to say."

As soon as they entered the Gold House, Mitchell Clark stood before the newly painted portrait of Marcia Gold and froze.

In the next instant, he took a pouch from his jacket pocket and, with his other hand, sprinkled powder from the pouch onto the floor in front of him.

"What are you doing?" Ellen shouted. "You're making a mess!"

Mitchell returned the pouch to his pocket and spun on his heels to look at Ellen and her friends. "This is goofer dust. It keeps the bad spirits away. And this woman," he pointed to the portrait of Marcia, "she's the worst of them all."

"Now, Mr. Clark," Sue began, "I want to know why you think Marcia Gold is a bad spirit, but I want to sit down first. Can we please all sit at the table? Our pizza should be here soon."

Once they were seated, Mitchell took out his pouch and sprinkled more of the powder near his feet.

"Please don't pour anymore of that dirt on our beautiful hardwood floors," Sue said. "We already had the house cleansed with a smudge stick ceremony. There are no more bad spirits here."

"Look, my great-grandmother has been haunting my family for over a hundred years, so please excuse me if I seem a little paranoid."

"Do you know why?" Ellen asked.

"She wants us to find her father's gold," he said. "My father tried, his father tried. She won't let us rest."

"At least we know she married Joseph after all," Tanya said. "I'm glad."

"They didn't marry," Mitchell said. "Joseph's parents wouldn't allow it. She gave birth to my grandfather out of wedlock, and then Joseph's parents took the baby away. Joseph died shortly after. My grandfather was raised by my great-great grandparents. They said Marcia was a witch. She's a witch who won't let any of us rest until we find the gold."

"What do you mean she won't let you rest?" Sue asked.

"She comes to me in my dreams," he said. "Or should I say nightmares? Lord knows I've tried. Over the years, I've dug up every place possible on this property."

"Why do you think she wants you to find the gold?" Ellen asked.

Mitchell sat back on the wooden chair and crossed one leg over the other. "Bring me the diary, and I'll tell you."

Ellen glanced first at Sue and then at Tanya. They both nodded. Ellen got up and went to the trunk they'd been storing in the master bedroom. When she returned, she handed it over to Mitchell.

The pizza arrived. Ellen was surprised that Mitchell didn't try to leave with the diary. Instead he scoured the pages right then and there and even ate a couple of slices of pizza. They had a stash of Styrofoam cups in the kitchen, which Tanya filled with water from the kitchen sink for each of them.

The three women watched Mitchell's reactions to the diary as he read. Ellen wasn't sure, but she thought she saw a tear escape one of his eyes. As he reached the end, his hands began to tremble.

"Are you okay?" Ellen asked.

He cleared his throat. "She sounds different in her diary."

"Maybe she wasn't the witch your great-great grandparents made her out to be," Sue suggested.

Aloud, he read, *"He recorded the location of the gold in permanent ink in several places beneath the wallpaper."* He looked up at Ellen. "Did you find anything written on the walls?"

"Just a bunch of algebra," Sue said.

"No map," Tanya added.

"What kind of algebra?" Mitchell asked. "And where?" He jumped up from the table.

"We've already painted over it," Ellen said.

"I've got some paint stripper in my shed."

"No!" Tanya cried. "Throwing dirt on our floors is enough for one day."

"Wait, I took photos, remember?" Sue said.

"Where are they?" Mitchell demanded.

"I don't have my camera with me, but I included some of the photos in my Power Point presentation. If you would have stayed for the whole thing, you would have seen them."

Mitchell frowned. "Where's that presentation? On a computer?"

"I've got my laptop out in the car. Just a minute, and I'll go get it."

Mitchell walked with Sue. Tanya began clearing off the table. Ellen's heart was beating fast.

Sue returned with her laptop. She set it on the table and opened it, powered it up. The four of them stood around the table waiting as Sue pulled up her Power Point presentation and skipped through her slides.

"Not that one." She clicked on the next slide. "Wait for it." She clicked. "Wait for it." She clicked again. "There it is. Can you see those algebraic equations? We assumed they had something to do with the building dimensions, but we did think it might be some kind of code."

Mitchell leaned in to get a better view of the screen. "That's not algebra...or code," he said, suddenly very excited. "Well, I'll be damned."

"What?" the three women said at once.

"Those are coordinates. Very precise coordinates in latitude and longitude." He pulled out his phone. "I have an app that can tell us the exact location of those coordinates."

Ellen held her breath as he entered the numbers into his phone.

"This app will tell me when I'm standing in the right location." He took a few steps one way, and then another, the whole while staring down at his phone.

He headed toward the back door and then stopped. "That's not right. Wait a minute." He turned and headed toward the front door.

Ellen, Sue, and Tanya followed him outside. He stepped from the porch onto the sidewalk. He took a few steps to his right, toward the Forrester's Victorian, and then stopped. He pivoted. He took a few steps toward the Robertson's Victorian, still staring down at his phone. Then he turned toward the street and halted right before the dead tree.

He looked up at them, his face full of astonishment. "It's pointing here, beneath this goddamn tree."

Chapter Twenty-Four: Clues in the Attic

"I'll be right back with my tools," Mitchell Clark, full of excitement, said, as he stuffed his phone in his pocket.

Sue put her hands on her hips. "You realize this is our land, don't you Mr. Clark?"

Mitchell gritted his teeth and narrowed his eyes. "That gold belongs to my family. You wouldn't have found it if it weren't for me."

"That goes both ways," Tanya said.

"Now hold on," Ellen said. "We don't even know if it's still there."

"Well, we're about to find out," Mitchell said. "I'll get this tree down with my chainsaw and then dig up the roots. I'll find it before sundown!"

"You will do nothing of the kind," Sue insisted. "We already have a tree removal service coming on Thursday. If you touch that tree, I'll call the cops. You're trespassing on our property."

"*Who*'s trespassing on *who*'s property?" He gave Ellen and Tanya an angry glare.

"Listen to me," Ellen said. "Both of you listen. If there's gold under that tree, we should split it three ways: Mr. Clark gets one third, Amy gets one third, and we get one-third, to be divided evenly among the three of us." She motioned to Sue, Tanya, and herself.

Mitchell started to object, but Ellen continued, "You won't have a leg to stand on in court, Mr. Clark. You have no proof that Marcia Gold is your ancestor other than stories your family has passed down to you and a few bad dreams. And we believe Amy is also Marcia's descendant, and she needs the money more than any of us. And since the three of us own this land, we have the best legal claim to it of anyone. So before anybody starts digging, I think we need to agree—right here, right now—that that's the way it's going to be."

That night, Ellen told Paul all that had been happening at the Gold House. She had expected him to be concerned about Amy, moved by the fact that they'd found her mother, and excited about the possibility of gold; but, instead, he was angry.

"Why would anyone break into the house of a suspect?" he asked. "You should have let the police do the investigating. You could have been killed."

"But I wasn't."

"You're lucky. It was really stupid, Ellen. I thought you were smarter than that."

He shuffled away from the den toward their bedroom— *his* bedroom.

Tuesday after work, Ellen met Tanya and Sue at the Gold House where they were determined to make progress on the attic. As soon as she reached the top of the stairs and saw her two friends sitting on folded metal chairs with papers in their hands, she could tell something was up.

"What's going on?" she asked.

The bins they had marked as "donations," "trash," and "keep," were mostly empty.

"We found something," Tanya said. "And it's really strange. Come here."

Ellen crossed the room and looked over Tanya's shoulder.

"They're letters," Sue said. "Some are written by Joseph Clark. They were scattered all over the place."

"That's not the strange part," Tanya said. "Look at this. This letter is addressed to Marcia and is signed 'Joseph Clark.' But this letter is almost an exact copy and it's addressed to someone named Jason."

"Let me see those." Ellen took the letters from Tanya and held one in each hand. One page was yellowed but neatly creased with three folds. The other page was a piece of white wide-ruled notebook paper with the standard three holes punched in the left-hand margin. The yellowed letter, dated November 8, 1882, was written in Joseph's neat handwriting:

My Dearest Marcia,

Without my family's support, I will need to put our future on hold until I find employment.

But do not allow this wrinkle to dishearten you or to make you doubt my love for you. Our love is like a solid rock. It is thick and hard and cannot break, even under pressure. Water and soil wash away. Animals and plants grow old and die. But the rock of our love grows bigger and more solid with the layers of time. When everything else passes, the rock of our love is still there.

I was unsuccessful at finding work in Dallas, but do not despair. Tomorrow, I leave for Houston, where I am told the opportunities are overflowing.

Yours Always,
Joseph Clark

Ellen compared that letter to the other, which was written as if by a child in cruder form:

My Dearest Jason,

Do not allow this wrinkle to dishearten you or to make you doubt my love for you. Our love is like a solid rock. It is thick and hard and cannot break, even under pressure. Water and soil wash away. Animals and plants grow old and die. But the rock of our love grows bigger and more solid with the layers of time. When everything else passes, the rock of our love is still there.

I was unsuccessful at meeting with you last night, but if you come again tonight, I will be here.

There was an additional line that followed, but it was scratched out beyond recognition.

"I don't understand," Ellen said after she'd read and compared the letters.

"This one is signed 'Amy,'" Sue said. "Come take a look. I think Amy has been using Joseph's letters to Marcia to help her compose her own letters to someone named Jason."

"The letters by Amy aren't dated, though," Tanya said. "So we don't know how old they are."

Ellen took the two letters from Sue's hands and read the first, dated January 3, 1882, from Joseph:

My Dearest Marcia,

I cannot wait to introduce you to my family. I have told them much about you, and, as anyone would expect, they are impressed that, at such a young age, you are already a successful teacher at a reputable school for girls. They have invited us for a visit so they can meet the girl of my dreams in person. I hope you won't mind.

I am more nervous about your impression of them than I am about their impression of you. You are like an exquisite crystal—pure, beautiful, strong, and clear. All who gaze upon you cannot help but be transfixed. I have no doubt they will covet you as they would a high-quality diamond.

But your impression of them is not as easy for me to guess. They are a strict pair, set in their ways, and not very tolerant of those who think differently than they. I hope you can bear to be around them for my sake if you cannot love them as I do.

I will write as soon as they have settled on a date. Until then, be safe, my love.

Yours Always,
Joseph Clark

Ellen compared that letter to the second, which read:

My Dearest Jason,

You are like an exquisite crystal—pure, beautiful, strong, and clear. All who gaze upon you cannot help but be transfixed.

The lines following it were scratched out with thick ink and the paper was crumpled.

"And here's one more match I was able to make from the pile." Sue handed two more pages to Ellen.

271

Ellen glanced at each and then read the one dated August 10, 1882 and signed by Joseph:

My Dearest Marcia,

While I agree that my parents' expectations are old-fashioned and unfair, I'd rather hoped your love for me would be greater than your need to stand on principle. You must know that it's true what they say about teaching old dogs new tricks. My parents are old dogs who believe a wife and mother should forego her own ambitions and put her family above all else.

You are not malleable gypsum, my love. No, you are crystalline in your convictions, like granite and gneiss. I love you for it, though it may be the death of me.

Yours Always,
Joseph Clark

In Ellen's other hand was the crumpled copy by Amy:

My Dearest Jason,

I'd rather hoped your love for me would be greater than your need to stand on principle. You are not malleable gypsum, my love. No, you are crystalline in your convictions, like granite and gneiss. I love you for it, though it may be the death of me.

Yours Always,
Amy

No lines were scratched out, but the multiple creases in the paper suggested that the page had been crumpled like a piece of trash.

"Who do you suppose this Jason is?" Ellen asked Sue.

"I think that's a question you should ask Bud," Sue replied.

"Maybe Amy hasn't been abducted," Tanya added. "Maybe she's run off with Jason."

Ellen took out her cell phone and dialed the Forresters' number. Bud usually picked up after one or two rings, but by the tenth ring, Ellen had been about to hang up when Millie answered.

"Hi, Millie. This is Ellen. I'm sorry to bother you. Is Bud not at home?"

"No, he's here," she said in between fast and heavy breaths.

Ellen felt awful. Millie must have had a hard time getting to the phone. "Oh. May I speak with him?"

Millie's voice cracked with her next words. "I'm afraid he's under the weather today. I'd hate to disturb him."

Ellen immediately thought of the cancer. "I'm sorry to hear that, Millie. Is there anything I can do? Can I bring you anything?"

"I don't want to be a burden. I have enough food here to last me a few days. I just took my mother a bowl of mac-n-cheese. I can also empty our bags and this and that on my own. We'll be alright. The only thing I can't do by myself is get in and out of my chair. If worse comes to worst, I'll call Sam Robertson."

"How long has Bud been ill?"

"This just started yesterday."

"Did you have to sleep in your chair last night?"

"Yes, but it wasn't too bad. I have a head rest that I can adjust myself."

Ellen wondered about bed sores. "Can I please come and check on you all? I'm really worried. I'm calling from the Gold House and could be there in a few minutes."

"I'd be too embarrassed for anyone to see me under these conditions," Millie said. "I haven't had a shower or been able to change my clothes and this and that."

"I don't care. It won't bother me."

"But it will bother me."

"How does Bud look? Is he breathing okay?"

"He's upstairs in his room, so I can't check on him."

Ellen's heartrate increased. She clutched the phone in both hands and asked, "When was the last time you spoke to him?"

"A few hours ago. I asked him if he wanted to come down and eat, but he said he didn't want anything."

Ellen breathed a sigh of relief. "Please let me run upstairs and check on him. What if he needs a doctor but is too stubborn to tell you?"

Millie didn't answer right away. Then she said, "I suppose I could leave the back door unlocked and hide in my room while you're here."

"Thank you! I'll be right over."

"Give me about fifteen minutes."

"Will do." Ellen hung up and said, "I wish he'd tell Millie about the cancer. Do you think I should say something to her?"

Sue shook her head. "I don't think so. That has to be his choice."

"It could save his life, though," Ellen said. "Or, at least prolong it. If Millie knew, she'd insist that he get treatment."

"But that's not what he wants," Tanya said. "I think you have to respect his wishes."

"I'm also thinking about Amy," Ellen said. "What if we don't find her in time to say goodbye to him?"

Fifteen minutes later, Ellen made her way across the lawn from the Gold House to the Forresters' Victorian. She envied their back yard because it was full of trees—pecan and oak. She wished there were as many trees at the Gold House, but there was just the one, and it was dead.

She supposed if they discovered that the tree really had been protecting German gold all these years, then the Forresters could keep their wooded lawn.

Ellen turned the knob on the back door and found it unlocked, just as Millie had said it would be. Ellen pushed the door open and stepped inside. The kitchen sink was full of dishes, and there was food and crumbs on the counter, along with half-empty mugs of coffee. She resisted the urge to tidy it for Millie and continued toward the front of the house to the stairwell.

As she took the stairs, she imagined all the times Amy had snuck up to bathe. Every Sunday, the ghost girl would take this very path. At the top of the landing, the first door to the left was a bathroom—probably *the* bathroom. Across the hall, another door was ajar. Bud's room?

"Bud? Are you awake?" Ellen said gently from the hallway. She wanted to give him a moment to make himself decent if he wasn't already. "It's Ellen. I've come to check on you."

"Oh, lord," she heard him murmur.

"Is that okay? Can I come in?" She waited outside his door, full of uncertainty.

"You won't like what you see, but go ahead and come on in."

She pushed the door all the way open and stepped inside. Bud was on a double bed beneath a navy blue comforter. Although only his face was visible, it was yellowish-orange.

She crossed the room and bent over him, moving the white bangs away from his forehead. The whites of his eyes were yellow, too. "Oh, my God, Bud. You're jaundiced. You need to see a doctor as soon as possible."

He closed his eyes and spoke slowly. "I've already told you how this is going down."

Ellen linked her fingers together as if in prayer. "But this could be an easy fix. I understand rejecting chemotherapy and other treatments that weaken you. I get that. But this may be something the doctors can fix without treating the cancer. You've got to give them a chance. For Millie and for Millie's mother. And for Amy."

Bud looked up at her. The hope in his eyes broke her heart. "You've seen Amy?"

Ellen shook her head. "Not yet. But we'll find her. Have you ever heard her speak of someone named Jason?"

"No. Why?"

"Do you know of a Jason in the area?"

"One of the twins down the street goes by 'Jay,'" he said. "I don't know if that's his full name. He and his brother mow my lawn. Why?"

"It's just a theory. If you let me take you to the emergency room, I'll tell you about it on the way."

Chapter Twenty-Five: Near Misses

Wednesday morning, Ellen turned in her grades electronically and said goodbye to another semester. She had decided not to give her classes a final exam project in light of all she was going through. The students had not complained.

Ellen then went by Panera and picked up both potato and broccoli cheese soup, along with bread and cookies, for Millie and her mother. Millie had agreed to unlock the back door but had refused to be seen again, so Ellen left everything out on the kitchen counter. Then Ellen met Tanya and Sue at the Gold House to continue their work in the attic.

As they sorted and organized, Ellen told her friends the latest news about Bud. His bile duct bypass surgery had been a success. This would buy him a little more time. The doctor hadn't seemed very optimistic about how much more time, but at least it would make Bud more comfortable. The hospital would release him by the end of the week.

Tanya had made a batch of brownies for them to snack on, and Sue had brought coffee, which made their work more tolerable.

Sue stopped organizing for a moment to have a brownie and said, "Oh, I almost forgot to tell you something I discovered last night. It's really shocking. I can't believe I forgot to tell you."

"About Amy?" Tanya asked.

"No. About Mitchell."

"What?" Ellen asked.

"Well, I was curious about that dust he sprinkled on the floors downstairs," Sue said. "So I Googled it."

"Oh my gosh, I should have thought of that," Tanya said. "He called it goofer or something like that, right?"

"Yes, goofer dust," Sue said. "It's an old African American powder made from graveyard dirt, snake skin, and powdered bones."

Ellen shuddered. "That's so gross."

"Powdered bones?" Tanya asked. "What kind of powdered bones?"

"The most commonly used bone is cat," Sue said.

Tanya's eye widened. "Cat bones?" Tanya glanced at Ellen.

Ellen covered her mouth. "Do you think that's what he does with all those stray cats he's got locked in the shed? Do you think he kills them and turns them to powder for his spells?"

"That's exactly what I think," Sue said.

"We need to call the humane society," Tanya said. "We can't let him keep doing that."

"I agree we should do something," Sue said. "But I think we should wait until the tree is removed and we find out whatever there is to find out. We need his cooperation."

Ellen thought that was sound advice. "But after that, we have to do something."

A few hours later, Ellen, Tanya, and Sue took a break from organizing the attic to lunch at the café they had discovered around the block. Apparently, Nona's was a popular place, because it was still crowded at two o'clock when they arrived. Luckily, they didn't have to wait long for a table.

Once they were seated and were handed menus, Sue said, "I have an idea."

"What is it?" Tanya asked.

"Why don't we tell Mitchell Clark that the only way he can have his share of the gold is if he promises to take the cats to the humane society and to never kill another one again?"

"That's brilliant!" Ellen said. "Good thinking, Sue."

"Maybe we should make sure he does it before the tree service comes tomorrow," Tanya said. "We could even offer to take the cats there ourselves."

"Good idea, Tanya," Ellen said. "Maybe we should stop by later today to pay him a visit."

"What does he do, anyway?" Tanya wondered. "Is he retired? He's the same age as we are."

"Bud said his family was in the oil industry," Ellen said. "Mitchell lives off oil money."

"I wonder how he's dealing with being made to wait for our tree people," Sue said. "I bet it's eating him up."

"Do you guys really think there's gold beneath that tree?" Tanya asked doubtfully.

"I hope so!" Sue said.

"I'm not sure," Ellen admitted. "I suppose it's possible, but I'm trying not to get too excited."

Their conversation ended when their waiter approached their table. "Can I get you ladies something to drink?"

They all wanted water, so he left to get that for them, and after, Tanya said, "Did you see his nametag?"

"No," Ellen said. "Why?"

"Our waiter's name is Jason."

Ellen and Sue gawked at one another.

"Jason is a popular name," Sue said. "It's probably a coincidence."

"You're probably right," Ellen said. "But Bud did say that Amy used to eat from the cans in back. Maybe she's been inside to eat since then. And maybe that's how they met."

"Why don't you ask him?" Tanya said. "It couldn't hurt."

Sue lowered her voice. "How do you ask someone if they know a girl who pretends to be a ghost?"

Tanya giggled. "Good point. But you should say something."

"Why me?" Sue asked.

"Because of the three of us, you're the bravest one with people," Ellen said.

"That's right," Tanya said. "Besides, we did all the work sneaking into Mitchell's house—even had a gun pulled on us."

"That two-hour Power Point presentation was no easy task," Sue said defensively.

Jason appeared with their water. "Are you ladies ready to order?"

Sue glanced around the café. "Um, yes. But first I have a question for you."

"Sure. Do you want to hear about today's specials?"

"As a matter of fact, I do," Sue said. "But that wasn't my question." She cleared her throat. "We're looking for a young woman about your age named Amy Piers. Do you know her?"

The young man frowned. "No. Why?"

"We're worried about her," Ellen said. "We haven't seen her for many weeks."

"Sorry to hear that. I hope you find her soon. Would you like to hear about the specials now?"

When they'd finished their lunch and were heading around the block in Sue's car back to the Gold House, they were shocked to see Mitchell Clark in their front lawn demolishing the tree with his chainsaw.

"Oh, shit!" Ellen cried.

"I guess it really was eating him up inside," Tanya said as they pulled up to the curb.

As soon as Sue had parked, they climbed out of the car and charged toward him. Sue had one fist on her hip and was shaking a finger at him before he even turned and noticed them.

He shut off the chainsaw and gave them an angry glare.

Ellen lifted both palms up and shook her head. "What in the world are you doing?"

"We had a deal!" Sue shouted, wagging her finger. "Are you trying to get the jump on us, or what?"

"You vandalize my property, I vandalize yours!" he shouted back.

"What the hell are you talking about?" Ellen asked.

"Don't act like you don't know!" he said as he brought the chainsaw back to life and turned again to the tree.

Ellen marched right up to him—didn't even care if he accidentally chopped off one of her own limbs. There was no way she was going to let him think he was in charge of this show. If they let him dismantle and remove the tree, he might think he had a claim to all the gold. She tapped him on the shoulder and screamed, "If you don't stop, I'm calling the police."

"Go right ahead!" he hollered back. "I'll show them the damage you did to my storage shed."

Ellen narrowed her eyes. "Your storage shed? We didn't touch it!"

He turned off the chainsaw again. "I came home from running errands to find the shed door wide open, the lock busted, and all the cats gone. Who else would do that?"

Ellen glanced at her friends. Who else would?

"Well, we sure as heck didn't," Sue said taking out her phone. "I'm calling 9-1-1 if you don't leave immediately."

"Fine. I'll leave," he said. "But I'll be back tomorrow."

"Fine!" Sue shouted as he stomped away.

Once he was down the street, the three women recovered from the shock and headed back to their work in the attic.

"That man is a lunatic," Tanya said on the way up the stairs.

"But he sure is attractive, isn't he?" Sue said.

"Sue!" Tanya chastised.

"But who else knew about the cats?" Ellen asked.

When they reached the attic, they were surprised to find that things weren't exactly as they had left them. The most obvious change was the empty pan of brownies.

"Do you think Mitchell Clark finished off our brownies before attacking the tree?" Tanya wondered out loud.

"The letters from Joseph Clark and the copycats written by Amy are missing, too," Sue said. "Why would he want those?"

"I don't think he took the letters," Ellen said as a strange thought occurred to her. "I don't think he took the brownies, either." She walked over to the corner and lifted the trap door. The pillow and blanket were still there, but they weren't in the same position in which she had last seen them. She stooped over the niche to get a closer look. Lying across the pillow was a brand new long white hair. She lifted it between her thumb and index finger and held it up in the light. It was an exact match to the one she'd sent to the lab. "Amy was here. She must have overheard us earlier talking about the cats. *She* set them free."

Tanya pressed her palms to her face. "Amy was hiding here all morning?"

"That gives me chills," Sue said.

Ellen closed the trap door and let the single strand of hair fall from her fingers. "At least we know she's alive. I wonder where she is now."

Chapter Twenty-Six: The Search Continues

While the tree removal service cut down the dead tree in front of the Gold House, Ellen walked down the street toward the house of the twins who helped Bud with his lawn. Tanya and Sue stayed behind to keep an eye on the progress with the workers and to prevent Mitchell Clark from finding the gold without them.

Ellen knew it was a longshot that the one twin who went by "Jay" might be the "Jason" in Amy's letters, but she didn't have any other leads, and she was desperate to find Amy. She couldn't help but suspect that Bud's sudden turn for the worse was due to his worry. Maybe if Amy could be found, Bud's strength would return.

And then there was Cynthia. Ellen hadn't been back to see Cynthia since the Wednesday before Thanksgiving—over a week ago. She imagined the poor woman must be anxious for some news. It must be torture, in fact, for a mother who hadn't seen her daughter in twenty years to be told she could see her, but not yet. To make her wait was cruel.

Ellen turned up the sidewalk of the other Greek revival on their block. It wasn't in as good of shape as most of the houses on Alta Vista Street. Bud had said that the twins' mother was a single parent who worked long hours as a teacher. Her sons had been in and out of trouble with the law over the years, but Bud didn't think they were bad to the core—just restless and undisciplined. They'd dropped out of high school several years ago and worked odd and end jobs around the neighborhood.

Ellen knocked on the door, expecting one of the boys to answer, since it was the morning of a school day, but a woman came to the door.

"Hello," Ellen said. "My name is Ellen Mohr. I'm one of the new owners of the Gold House."

"Hello," the woman said. "How can I help you?"

"Bud Forrester mentioned that your sons are sometimes available for yard work?" Ellen said. "I was hoping to talk to them about helping me with some of my landscaping. Would that be okay?"

"Oh, of course," the woman said. "Let me call Nick." The woman turned toward the foyer behind her and hollered up the stairs, "Nick? Can you come to the door, please?"

A young man called from the top of the stairs, "Mom, you're supposed to be in bed. What are you doing?"

The woman smiled at Ellen. "I'm not feeling well today. My son's taking care of me."

"I'm so sorry to disturb you," Ellen said. "Should I come at another time?"

"It's okay," the woman said. "I'll let you two talk. I'm going back to bed."

The woman left the threshold and was replaced by a handsome young man, in his mid-twenties. "Hi. What's up?"

"Hi, Nick. I'm Ellen Mohr. Bud told me you and Jason sometimes help him with his yard work."

"That's right."

When he didn't correct her use of the name "Jason," she filled with hope and excitement and asked, "It is *Jason*, right? Or is it *Jay*?"

"Jay."

"Is that short for *Jason*?"

"No. It's just *Jay*."

"Oh, I'm sorry." Her heart sank.

"No, worries."

"I might have some work for you and your brother at the Gold House. Interested?"

"Yes, ma'am. Just let me know what you need and when you need it, and we'll be there."

"You're not worried about the ghost?" she asked, fishing.

"Nah. I don't believe in that stuff."

"But a lot of people around here seem to," she said.

He shrugged.

"Can I let you in on a little secret?"

His face lost its color and she suddenly realized he knew something. "A secret?"

"There's a girl who's been living in the attic, but she isn't a ghost. But you already knew that, didn't you?"

"What? That's crazy. How would I know that?"

289

She wasn't buying it. "You're not a very good liar, Nick."

He glanced behind him before stepping out onto the porch and closing the door behind him. "She's an orphan. She don't ever hurt nobody. And now you and your friends are making her homeless."

"She's been missing. Do you know where she is?"

"Maybe the Forresters'."

Ellen folded her arms at her chest. "Bud hasn't seen her in many weeks. He's worried, and he's sick. He might not have a lot of time left."

"If I see her, I'll tell her. But listen, my mom...she don't know about Amy. Amy made us promise not to tell."

"When was the last time you saw her?"

"I let her stay with us Thanksgiving night, like when we were younger. She used to come and stay with me and my brother, especially when it got cold. My mom never knew. We snuck her food, too. She's not a criminal or anything. She just don't have nobody looking out for her."

"Do you know anyone named Jason?" Ellen asked.

"I think that's the dude who got her pregnant."

Ellen gasped. "How do you know she's pregnant?"

"Dang!" He smacked a palm against his forehead. "I wasn't supposed to say nothing."

"Now it's more important than ever that I find her." Ellen took a pen and piece of paper from her purse and wrote her phone number down. "If you see her, please have her call me." She handed him the paper.

He stuffed it in the front pocket of his jeans. "I doubt she will, ma'am. She thinks you want to take away her baby."

"Me?" Ellen pressed her hand to her chest and pulled in her chin. Surely he was mistaken. Amy had seemed to understand that Ellen and her friends were trying to help her find her mother. She'd defended them on Halloween from the egg bombers. "No. I didn't even know about the baby. Listen to me, Nick. I've found Amy's mother. I want to take Amy to see her."

Nick narrowed his eyes. "She'll think it's a trick. She won't believe you. She won't go nowhere with you."

"Do you have any idea where I can find Jason?" Ellen asked.

"Nah. Sorry. Now I gotta go check on my mom."

Ellen watched the young man return indoors. She stood there on his porch, wondering.

Then her phone buzzed. It was Sue.

"Hey," Ellen answered.

"We've found something!" Sue cried into the phone.

Ellen half-ran down Alta Vista Street from the twins' house toward her Greek revival, where a huge truck and trailer were pulling away with the dismembered old tree. As she reached the front lawn, she found Mitchell Clark and Tanya each holding an end of a wooden chest about two and a half feet long, two feet wide, and one foot high.

Her heart hammered against her ribs, and it wasn't *just* from the running.

"Put it down on the porch," Sue was saying. "Don't take that dirty thing in the house."

Ellen met them on the porch where Mitchell was trying to wedge a crowbar beneath the lid of the chest.

"Did you find out anything about Amy?" Tanya asked.

Sue kicked a clump of dirt off the porch. "Was the twin named Jason?"

"The twin isn't Jason," Ellen said, "but they do know Amy. They just saw her last week. Apparently they've helped her throughout their lives without their mother knowing."

"You talking about Nick and Jay Aresco?" Mitchell asked as he continued to work the crowbar.

"The twins who live down the street," Ellen said. "Yes." She hadn't known their last name, but she assumed she and Mitchell were referring to the same twins.

"Did the twins know a *Jason*?" Sue asked.

"Nick couldn't give me any information about Jason's whereabouts, but he had heard of him."

"Maybe he knows more than he's letting on," Tanya suggested.

"Well, there's something else," Ellen said as her friends waited for an explanation. "According to Nick, she's pregnant with Jason's baby."

"Oh, no!" Tanya said.

"She thinks we want to take her baby away," Ellen said. "Just like she was taken from her mother."

Sue shook her head. "We have to find her."

Ellen folded her hands together as a feeling of helplessness washed over her. "Cynthia Piers has got to be wondering why I haven't brought Amy to see her."

Mitchell suddenly stopped trying to pry open the chest. He looked from one woman to the other before asking, "Cynthia Piers? Did you say Cynthia Piers?"

"Yes," Ellen said. "Why?"

He dropped the crowbar on the porch at his feet and brought a hand to his chest. "Cynthia's alive?"

Ellen exchanged glances with Sue and Tanya. "Yes. She's a patient in the San Antonio State Hospital," Ellen said.

Tears filled Mitchell's eyes. "Those bastards! I should have known!"

"Mr. Clark, what happened?" Sue asked. "How do you know Cynthia?"

"She was Johnny's girl," he said as he stared off into space. "Johnny and I used to run around together. Sometimes the three of us went out together. She was Johnny's girl, but I was in love with her."

Ellen tried to hide her surprise, but if the expressions on Sue and Tanya's faces were any indication of her own, she was failing. Mitchell Clark had been in love with Cynthia Piers?

"Amy's her daughter," Ellen said. "Cynthia told Amy to hide when the doctors and the police came to shut down the asylum. They took Cynthia to the state hospital, and she hasn't seen Amy since."

"And now Amy's missing," Tanya said. "We haven't been able to find her."

"And she's pregnant," Sue added.

"All these years, I've been trying to get her to leave," Mitchell said. "Casting spells with my goofer dust. And I guess now I need to help you find her. For Cindy. There's a spell for that, too."

"No animals can be harmed," Ellen said.

"They were strays," Mitchell said defensively. "The shelters don't ever have enough room for them, and only a few have no-kill policies. They were going to be destroyed anyway."

"Please promise us," Tanya said. "We can't accept your help to find Amy if it means animals are going to die. We don't agree with that."

"The cat powder is only used in casting against evil spirits," he said. "I was desperate. Marcia's ghost…"

"Marcia isn't an evil spirit," Ellen said. "We found letters in the attic written by your great grandfather, Joseph. His parents wanted her to give up her teaching career. She refused."

"They didn't agree with her decision," Sue added. "That's why they took her baby away."

"If she's been haunting you, it's been to help you." Tanya pointed to the chest. "She helped you find this."

"So why don't you open it?" Sue prompted.

He took up the crowbar and thrust it beneath the lid. After another few minutes of rattling the bar back and forth against the old wood, he finally pried the chest open.

They leaned over and peered inside, where they found three rows of ten gold bars stacked at least three bars high.

Ellen plucked one from the chest with trembling hands. Embossed were the words *Degussa* and *Feingold*, along with a set of numbers. There was also an interesting seal at the top—a diamond shape with a sun on one side and the moon on the other.

Ellen held her breath and rubbed her eyes. She wanted to pinch herself.

Mitchell pulled out a leather pouch that had been wedged between the rows of gold. He opened it and found documents folded inside. Although written in German, the name Friedrich Ernst Roessler and the date 1843 were easily recognizable.

"I think we hit the mother lode," Mitchell said beneath his breath.

Chapter Twenty-Seven: Last-Chance Meetings

Ellen drove her vehicle up to the gated entrance of the state hospital with Mitchell Clark in her passenger's seat. She could tell during the drive over—since he'd spoken in an uncharacteristically animated voice about what their attorneys were reporting back to them about the gold—that he was nervous.

It had been two weeks since they'd removed the dead tree and pulled the wooden chest from the ground in front of the Gold House. During that time, both of their attorneys had confirmed that the bars had been sold to Theodore Gold in 1843. The attorneys also had the bars valued at $30,000 each. With 90 bars in total, the chest of gold was worth 2.7 million. After considering the income tax, their attorneys had estimated that Mitchell and Amy would receive $500,000 each and Sue, Tanya, and Ellen would receive $170,000 each. That wouldn't buy Ellen a vacation home and houses for her children, but it would mean that they wouldn't have to sell the Gold House. They could fulfill their dream of turning it into a museum, where all the women in the shoebox of photos would be visible.

In fact, over the past two weeks, Ellen's art studio had seen a lot of action. Each morning, she painted for at least three hours, losing herself and finding herself in the process, and when she met Tanya and Sue at the Gold House each afternoon to continue their work in the attic, she often had a new painting to show them of another of the women who'd once been invisible—Hilary Turner, Victoria Schmidt, and Regina Piers. Seeing their faces prominently displayed in the very house that had once imprisoned them somehow gave Ellen and her friends hope that Amy would be found and reunited with her mother.

Ellen's attorney also helped them to set up a trust fund for Amy. It was set up so that if Cynthia were ever discharged from the state hospital, she would be entitled to half the fund.

As Ellen parked her car in front of the main building, she said to Mitchell, "Keep in mind that she's hardly spoken in twenty years. She's not the same woman you knew back in the late 80's and early 90's."

He gave her a curt nod and followed her to the entrance.

After checking her and Mitchell in at the front office, a nurse escorted them through the building to the Extended Care Unit. Ellen glanced around the ward for a sign of Betty Johnson, but Jan's old friend didn't seem to be on duty today. Then she remembered that Betty didn't work in Extended; she was stationed in Acute Care.

The nurse tapped on Cynthia's door and said, "You have visitors today, Cynthia."

Cynthia was in her bed. Her pale hair was mussed and the covers pulled up to her waist. When her bright eyes turned to her visitors, her mouth fell open, and she covered her head with her blanket.

Ellen hadn't expected that reaction. She stood, stunned, near the door, as Mitchell crossed the room toward the bed.

"Cindy?" Mitchell said. "Is it really you?"

"No!" the woman cried. "It's not!"

Mitchell pulled one of the chairs to the bedside and said, "Can I please have a look at you?"

Ellen was surprised by the change in his voice. He was actually capable of being gentle?

"I look awful right now! I don't want to be seen!" Cynthia cried from beneath her covers.

"You could never look awful," Mitchell said. "Besides, I've already seen you. I know it's you. I just can't believe it, but I know it's true. And I am so damned happy to see you."

Tears flooded Mitchell's eyes and rolled down his cheeks. His voice was even choked by them.

Slowly, Cynthia slid the blanket away from her head. Her eyes were also full of tears. Mitchell was right: the woman could never look awful. Her bright eyes and pale hair and smooth features would be beautiful under any circumstances.

Mitchell leaned forward and took both her hands in his. He couldn't stop staring at her as the tears continued to fall.

And then something else unexpected happened that shocked Ellen to her core: Cynthia smiled and said, "I'm so damned happy to see you, too, Mitch."

Sue's mother, Jan, had struck up a real friendship with Millie, and so she'd asked Sue if she and Tanya and Ellen would join her for a little Christmas gathering at the Forresters a week before Christmas. According to Jan, the Forresters didn't have a tree or anything festive in their house, and she thought it would be fun to do a little decorating for them. Tanya had a small, table-top tree in her attic, so she brought it along. Jan had some ornaments and garland. Sue had made a beautiful wreath for their door. And Ellen had baked some breads and pies. Sue had also made her famous dip and brought along a box of crackers. Tanya had made eggnog.

Although Bud could get around, he was dramatically altered. Since his surgery, he hadn't regained his pink complexion or his full strength and endurance. He was thinner, frailer, less jovial. He did smile, though, and he thanked them for bringing them some Christmas cheer.

Two days later, however, Bud took another turn. Ellen found out about Bud from Jan, who now spoke with Millie daily. Jan said that Millie had called for an ambulance after Bud had passed out on the sofa and wouldn't wake up.

Kidney failure. That's what would kill Bud Forrester. But it would happen in his home. He'd refused to go to the hospital, and Millie had respected his wishes.

The day before Bud died, two days before Christmas, Ellen went to visit him, hoping to reassure him that she would find Amy. She would never give up the search, no matter how long it took.

He was lying on a sheet on the sofa in the back of the house in a sunroom that resembled the one in Mitchell Clark's Italianate. Although floral, the sofa even appeared to be from the same era as Mitchell's. Bud's head was propped up on two pillows, and a light wool blanket covered him from his chest to his toes. Sue and Tanya had come along, but they remained in the front of the house with Millie, because they knew what Ellen wanted to say to Bud, and Millie wasn't to hear it.

"I will find her," Ellen said in a low tone. "I promise you, Bud."

"She came to see me," he said through ragged breaths. "Last night."

"What?" Ellen wondered if he'd imagined it. Millie had said he'd been in and out of consciousness.

"At first, I thought she was an angel," he said. His voice was scratchy and harder to understand than usual. "Wearing one of her white dresses, she looked just like an angel."

"Did you tell her about her mother? About the gold?"

Bud shook his head. "I didn't have a chance. She was too quick."

Now Ellen really did think he'd probably imagined it, but that was okay. It was good for a dying man to have his illusions.

"She thanked me for all I'd done for her over the years. She kissed my cheek and told me I was the best father a girl could hope for." A tear slipped from the corner of Bud's eyes and ran toward his ear.

"I'm so happy to hear that," Ellen said.

"Do you think our lord God will forgive me for my transgression?" he asked.

Ellen bit her lip and nodded. "I believe he already has."

"She told me she wanted to give me something to take with me, to hold close to me," he said. He struggled for a moment to breathe before he continued, "A long time ago, we picked a day to make her birthday, and every year, I gave her a little gift. One of the first gifts I ever gave her was a gold-plated necklace with her name on it."

"That was so kind of you," Ellen said.

"This morning, when I woke up, I thought I'd probably dreamt it all up, or imagined it." He met Ellen's eyes and gave her a smile. "You probably think the same thing."

Ellen smiled back but didn't say one way or the other.

"But look what I found clutched in my hand."

He opened his hand, which was resting on his chest. Ellen peered over him to get a closer look. In the folds of his wrinkled palm was a dainty gold chain, and on the chain, in gold-plated script, was the name *Amy*.

Ellen sucked in a gulp of air. Amy *had* been there. Bud hadn't imagined it.

"Remember to keep our secret from Millie," Bud said. "She doesn't know how to keep them, but you do, don't you?"

Ellen nodded as she held back tears. "Of course."

A few minutes later, when Sue and Tanya had gone to say their goodbyes to Bud, Ellen sat in the front living room with Millie, making small talk. Millie had asked how she would be spending her Christmas, and Ellen told her about having her brother and his family on Christmas day.

Then, Millie gave Ellen a peculiar look and said, "I want you to know something, Ellen."

"Sure. What is it?"

"I *am* good at keeping secrets," Millie said. "I've kept Bud's for twenty years."

Ellen's brows flew up in shock. "You know?"

"Of course I know. I know my Bud, and he was trying too hard, with all the ghost stories. Plus, she's been in this house too many times for the charade to have lasted."

"Why didn't you tell him?"

Tears formed in Millie's eyes. "If he'd wanted me to know, he would have told me. There was a reason he needed to keep her for himself. And after all he's done for me and my mother, I couldn't take that away from him."

"She was the daughter he always wanted," Ellen quickly added, lest Millie suspect something else.

Millie nodded as the tears fell. "Yes, I know."

Chapter Twenty-Eight: The Cranberry Sauce

It was Ellen's first Christmas without a mother. Tanya's, too. The feeling of being untethered quickly, faded, however, when Ellen began her preparations for her holiday feast. The preparations weren't different from any other year, really. She'd been in charge of making the turkey for as long as she could remember. The only thing her mother had contributed was the can of cranberry sauce.

Cranberry sauce! Ellen had almost forgotten. She didn't care for it herself, and neither did Paul or the kids, but it was Jody's favorite. He had even once said that it wouldn't be Christmas without it. And now, here it was, Christmas Eve night, and she didn't have a can of cranberry sauce!

Paul was already snoring in his recliner. She didn't have the heart to wake him and beg him to go out in the weather. It rarely ever snowed in San Antonio, but tonight it was sleeting and the weatherman had said there was a possibility of snow by morning. The icy roads were the very reason her children had decided to wait and drive over tomorrow.

Maybe she should wait and run out for the cranberry sauce in the morning. The traffic on Christmas Eve night would be a nightmare—all those other people were out getting the things they'd forgotten, too. How many other people had just remembered the cranberry sauce?

But would anything be open on Christmas day? And if she did find someplace—maybe a Walgreen's or an E-Z Mart—would they have a can of cranberry sauce? She couldn't take the chance. She had to go out tonight.

First she called Sue and Tanya to see if either had a can to spare. Sue was planning to make homemade cranberry sauce and offered to bring some to Ellen in the morning, but Jody only liked the canned stuff. Ellen had made some for him once, and he hadn't liked it. Ellen had wondered if he'd only said so to make their mother feel better about her annual contribution. Ellen hadn't meant to "show up" her mother, but maybe that's how her brother had taken it, and, as always, he'd come to their mother's rescue.

"There's just something special about that canned stuff," he had said. "This is good, Ellen, but it's just not the same."

Tanya didn't have any cranberry sauce, so Ellen put on her shoes and her coat and headed out in the cold sleet and busy roads.

The grocery store was packed. Ellen got lucky and found a parking spot close to the front. She clutched her coat tightly around her and marched through the sleet and the wind to the double glass doors.

The heat felt good inside, but she still wanted to get in and out as quickly as possible. She weaved around shoppers and their full baskets as she made her way to the canned goods aisle, the whole way praying there would be at least one can left.

And there was! She snatched it from the shelf, the last can of cranberry sauce. She felt victorious! Christmas had been saved! Jody's first Christmas without their mother wouldn't be spoiled now that there would be canned cranberry sauce. It was even the same brand that their mother had always bought.

She made her way to the lines and sighed. This was going to take a long time. Even though eight registers were open, the lines were ten to twelve people deep, and the self-serve lines were even longer. All of this waiting around for one can of cranberry sauce. No, it was more than that. She was waiting around to save her brother's Christmas.

As she stood there with her shoulders slumped, she occupied herself by watching people.

And that's when she saw her at the front of the line two registers away.

Amy!

Ellen studied her for a moment to be sure. Without her usual white dress, the young woman looked different. The pale hair and bright eyes looked less, well, ghostly, on a woman wearing a red sweater and black jeans. And her white hair, usually long and straight, was up in a ponytail tonight.

Amy wasn't alone. The waiter from Nona's stood beside her! Ellen couldn't believe he had lied to them. That had been *the Jason* after all!

Oh, no no no no no! Amy and Jason were paying for their groceries and leaving the store. What should Ellen do? She still had seven people in front of her. By the time she'd finish checking out, Amy would be long gone. And if she left the can of cranberry sauce for later, it might not be here when she returned.

What was more important? Her brother's Christmas or Cynthia's peace of mind?

Ellen stepped out of the line and started to take the can back, but before reaching the aisle, slipped the can into her coat pocket. Then she left the store in search of Amy and Jason.

Ellen had never ever stolen a single thing in her life—not even a pen from the faculty workroom—so taking the can of cranberry sauce was no easy decision. Her heart pounded against her ribs as she imagined being detained, questioned, and fined. Would she be held in a cell overnight? She had no idea what the punishment was for shoplifting, but she supposed if she was going to be caught, it would happen now, and it wasn't. She reached her car and climbed in as she scanned the lot for signs of Amy and Jason. Then she saw them, running across the asphalt and laughing in the sleet toward the very back of the lot. It was the white ponytail waving in the wind that gave them away, though they had no idea someone was watching them. Its translucence caught Ellen's attention, and she would not look away from it.

The young couple climbed into a red Honda Civic. Luckily for Ellen, the red color was easy to spot as she weaved her way through the crowded lot after them.

Then Ellen broke the law a second time by calling Sue on her cell phone while driving. She had only to press one number to call her on speed dial, and she put Sue on speaker to be hand's free, but it was still illegal, as far as Ellen knew.

"Hello?" Sue answered.

"You won't believe this," Ellen said as she weaved through the lot, trying to catch up to the red Honda Civic before it disappeared in the busy streets of San Antonio.

"What?"

"I saw Amy!"

"Oh my God! Where?"

"At H.E.B. I had to steal a can of cranberry sauce to do it, but I'm in the car now, following her."

"You stole a can of cranberry sauce?"

"Let's not focus on that right now, Sue. Okay? I just said I'm in the car, following her."

"Be careful. We wouldn't want you to kill yourself trying to catch up with her," Sue warned. "The roads are slick tonight."

"I'm just a few cars behind her," Ellen said. "We're still stuck in the parking lot. Can you get Tanya on a conference call? She'll want to hear about this, too."

"Sure. Let me put you on hold."

A family with two small children crossed in front of Ellen, forcing her to wait as the red Honda turned down another row in the lot.

"Shit, shit, shit," Ellen muttered, not realizing Tanya and Sue were back on the line.

"What's happening?" Tanya asked.

"Oh, I'm losing her in the parking lot," Ellen said. "No, wait. I see her car again."

"Where are you?" Tanya said. "I'm at H.E.B., too."

"Oh my gosh! Is that you coming out of the store now?" Ellen asked.

Tanya waved. "Yes. It's me. Can I climb in with you?"

As soon as Ellen could, she pulled up in front of Tanya.

"I needed flour for my gravy tomorrow," Tanya said as she put her small bag on the floorboard and buckled in.

"I could have given you some," Sue said over the phone. "Why didn't you call? I know how you hate to drive."

"Especially at night in the sleet," Ellen added. Then she said, "You see that red Honda Civic right there? That's them."

"Them?" Tanya and Sue said at the same time.

"Jason is with her," Ellen said. "And it's *our* Jason from Nona's!"

"No way!" Tanya said.

"I knew it!" Sue cried. "I had a feeling he was lying to us."

Ellen rolled her eyes, and Tanya saw her and giggled.

"I'm telling you, I have the gift," Sue reiterated. "I sense things."

Ellen shook her head. Good ol' Sue. Maybe she really did have the gift.

The red Honda Civic turned from the parking lot onto the main road. Ellen was still three cars behind them.

"Watch them for me," Ellen said to Tanya. "Help me see which way they turn."

"Don't hit that lady!" Tanya hollered.

Ellen slammed on her brakes. "There's a crosswalk, woman," Ellen muttered, even though she often crossed here, too.

"Be careful!" Sue said over the phone.

"There they go!" Tanya said. "They turned right, toward downtown."

After Ellen turned onto the main road, she inched her way to the right lane and, as soon as she could, she turned right.

"Do you see them yet?" Ellen asked as she scanned the cars in front of her.

"Not yet. Oh, there! Left-hand lane!"

"Oh, gosh. Are they turning?"

"Looks like it."

Ellen put on her left blinker and hoped these cars beside her would have mercy on her.

"These people aren't going to let me in," Ellen said.

"Roll down your window and wave to them," Sue suggested. "It's harder for them to ignore you that way."

"But it's freezing out there," Ellen protested.

"Do you want to catch her?" Sue asked.

Ellen rolled down her window and shivered with the freezing air that rushed into her vehicle. She waved to the car beside her, shouting, "Please?"

The car beside her slowed down and let her in.

"Okay, now once more," Tanya said.

Ellen waved and begged.

The car beside her ignored her.

"Damn you," Ellen cursed beneath her breath.

"Just slow down until someone lets you over," Tanya said.

"But no one can get around me."

"They'll have to wait. Come on. Wave to that car, like Sue said."

Ellen waved and was full of relief when the white Camry let her in.

"Thank you!" Ellen shouted into the cold night, even though the couple had their windows up and surely could not hear her.

Ellen rolled her window up, too, and turned up the heater. "Can you still see them?" she asked Tanya.

"They just made the left turn right up here."

By the time Ellen was able to make the same turn, the red car was out of sight. They had entered a residential area not far from theirs. "What now?"

"Keep driving down this street," Tanya said. "I'll look down all the roads on the right, and you try to look down all the roads on the left."

The vehicle hydroplaned when Ellen took her eyes off the road, and it sent her heart pounding. "Shit!"

"Are y'all okay?" Sue asked.

"Yes. We're okay," Ellen said.

"You just watch the road," Tanya said to Ellen. "I'll glance both ways. Just slow down a little."

They drove past six streets. Nausea coated Ellen's belly. She couldn't believe they had come this far only to lose them. She'd stolen a canned good from the store, for crying out loud. She'd become a criminal for this! "No. We can't lose them. We can't!"

"Look!" Tanya pointed to an apartment complex straight ahead. "Isn't that them? They're carrying groceries up to the second floor."

"Do you see their red Civic?" Ellen asked.

Tanya glanced all around the parking lot. "No."

"Then how do we know for sure? I can't see them from this distance. Can you? Can you see her white hair?"

"Just pull in and park," Tanya said. "Unless you have a better idea."

"Where are you guys?" Sue asked.

"The Emerald Forest Apartments." Ellen turned into the apartment complex. "Did you see what unit they went into?"

"That one." Tanya pointed. "I can't see the number though."

There were no available parking places near the unit Tanya had indicated, so Ellen drove around the building. "Oh, my God. Look!"

Parked in the very first spot around the corner was a red Honda Civic.

"That can't be just a coincidence," Tanya said.

"What?" Sue asked. "Do you see their car?"

"Yes!" Ellen said. "Let's park and go knock on the door."

As they took the stairs to the second floor, Ellen's heart was beating out of control. First, she was worried that they'd already lost Amy and that the people they had seen carrying the groceries were not Amy and Jason. Second, she worried that even if they had found Amy, that Amy wouldn't trust them, just as Nick had said.

"What should I say?" Ellen asked Tanya as they neared the unit.

"Just say we found your mother," Tanya said.

Ellen stopped a few yards away from the door. "Listen." She put a hand on Tanya's shoulder. "Don't you think it's kind of neat that we lost our mothers, but we're helping Amy to find hers?"

Tears rushed to Tanya's eyes. "We didn't lose our mothers."

Ellen nodded. "You're right."

Then she knocked on the door.

The curtain at the front window moved, but no one came to the door. Ellen knocked again.

"Leave us alone!" Jason's voice carried through the door.

Ellen and Tanya exchanged glances.

"Please!" Ellen said. "We want to help Amy. We've found her mother."

"Why should I believe you?' Amy shouted through the door. "I saw you cooperating with that evil man, the one who threatened to shoot me on Halloween! The one who's killed every animal I've ever loved! You should have freed those cats as soon as you discovered them! Why should I believe a word you say? Now leave us alone. My boyfriend has a gun!"

Tanya grabbed Ellen's arm and pulled her away from the door, but Ellen resisted.

"We can't just give up," Ellen whispered.

"I don't want us to get killed either," Tanya said.

"Are you still there, Sue?" Ellen said into the phone.

"Yeah. I heard her. And I have an idea."

"We're listening," Tanya said.

"Leave her a note with how she can find her mother. Put her mother's name, the San Antonio State Hospital, Extended Care Ward, and the address and phone number on a piece of paper and put it in an envelope and tape it to the door. Her curiosity is bound to get the best of her."

"That's a great idea, Sue," Tanya said, "except that we don't have paper, an envelope, or any tape."

"And with all this sleet, I'm not sure the tape will hold anyway," Ellen said. "The envelope might be gone by morning."

"Could you slide it under the door?" Sue asked. "Or is there a doormat?"

"No. That won't work either," Tanya said. "What can we do?"

"I know!" Ellen said, as an idea hit her. "I just finished my painting of Cynthia Piers. Sue, could you please go over to my house and get it from my studio in back—it's not locked— and bring it along with paper and an envelope and maybe a plastic bag to protect the painting?"

"Like a garbage bag?" Sue asked.

"That would work," Ellen said.

"Why don't we just go get that stuff so Sue doesn't have to get out in this mess?" Tanya asked.

"I'm afraid they'll run away," Ellen said. "Then Amy will be lost again."

"Let me just get dressed," Sue said. "I'll be there as soon as I can."

Chapter Twenty-Nine: Christmas Day

Ellen was tired Christmas morning, but as soon as Lane and Alison walked through the door with their overnight bags, her world instantly improved. Nolan wasn't far behind them, and within the hour, Jody and his family arrived as well.

They were all together under one roof. No amount of fatigue could prevent Ellen from being happy.

As she was transferring her dressing from a pan to a serving dish and Lane was at the stove mashing the potatoes, Paul came in to see if there was anything more he should do. He'd put the ice chest full of ice over by the drinks, he said, and Alison had set the table. Nolan had the turkey all cut up and out on a platter. What else did she need?

She looked up at Paul and smiled, thinking that she had everything she could possibly need.

He returned her smile and leaned a little closer and said, "You look absolutely breathtaking today."

After her initial shock, she laughed and pecked his cheek, and then turned away to hide the tears that had filled her eyes.

If only every day could be like this.

The cranberry sauce! She couldn't believe she'd almost forgotten after all she'd gone through to get it. She whipped out her can-opener and then poured the sauce onto a serving dish. At that very moment, Jody came into the kitchen to snatch a sweet pickle from a relish tray on the bar, and he smiled at her.

"You got the cranberry sauce!" he said.

She smiled. "The canned stuff. The kind you like."

He kissed her cheek. "I miss her so much today."

"She'll be there tonight when you go home." Jody and his family would be staying the night at their mother's house across town.

He wrinkled his brow. "You really think so?"

"I know so," she said. "I could sense her all around us at Thanksgiving."

"I didn't think you believed in that kind of thing."

She winked and said, "Let's keep it our little secret."

"Speaking of secrets," he said. "I have one of my own."

"Oh?"

"I've never really liked cranberry sauce."

They spent a lovely day enjoying the meal she had made, the desserts Jody and his wife, June, had baked, and the games of dominoes and rummy and pinochle they all played at various times in between. Jody's little boys ran around the house like two wild pups, chasing Lane until Lane collapsed on the rug with exhaustion.

Then Alison called everyone to the window at the front room. "Hurry! Come see!"

They all gathered around in awe at the very unusual sight of a white Christmas in San Antonio. At least four inches of soft snow covered the ground, some of it even sticking to the branches of trees. It was still falling, too, coating the street out front so that it was difficult to tell where the yard ended and the street began.

The kids clamored for their coats and gloves and scurried out to play in it, and the clean lines were instantly ravaged by their footprints. Paul threw on his boots and joined in the fun, starting a snowball fight with their sons.

The ringing of Ellen's cell phone brought her from the window and back into the kitchen, where she'd left it on the bar. She didn't recognize the number, but who would be calling on Christmas day? It wouldn't be a sales call.

"Hello?" she said.

"Hello, Mrs. Mohr. It's Mitchell Clark."

He was probably the last person on Earth she would have guessed.

"I'm sorry to bother you on Christmas day," he said. "And I also apologize for getting your number from the Conservation Society and using it for personal reasons."

"That's all right," Ellen said. "Has something happened?"

"Yes," he said. "It certainly has. And I have you and your friends to thank for it. And I'm not talking about the gold,

317

even though that's part of it. My great-grandmother hasn't visited my dreams since the day we found it."

"If you're not talking about the gold, do you mean finding Cynthia?"

He cleared his throat, and she could tell that he was struggling to keep his voice from breaking up. "I thought she was gone. My whole life, well…let's just say it's amazing to me that your life can be one kind of thing, and then one day, it can all change, and your life can be an entirely different thing."

So he wasn't the most articulate man. "I understand."

"Amy came to see her today," he said.

"What?" Ellen felt a surge of adrenaline course through her body. Tears, which had already formed in her eyes, spilled down her cheeks. "What happened?"

"I was there at the hospital, spending Christmas with her. I've been to see her every day since that day we went together. And I'm working with her doctor to get her released, possibly as soon as late January."

"That's wonderful news!" Ellen said, bringing her hand to her cheek. "And what about Amy?"

"Cindy and I were sitting together by the window in her room talking, just like we always do. We have a lot of catching up to do. Then we heard a knock and the nurse said she had visitors. My first thought was that it would be you and your friends, but it was Amy and her boyfriend, Jason."

"What did Amy say when she saw you there?"

"She didn't recognize me at first," he said. "I shaved my beard and was wearing a suit and tie—not my usual attire. And as soon as she saw her mother, she didn't see anyone else in the room."

"I wish I could have been there," she said.

"There wasn't a dry eye in the joint," he said. "Even the nurses were crying, once they'd heard about it."

"I'm so happy to hear that. Thanks so much for calling and letting me know. I wasn't sure if Amy would find our note."

"She brought the painting with her. She read us your letter. We all had another cry after that."

Ellen struggled with her own tears. "Thank you."

"No, thank you. You have literally made my life. When Cindy's released, she's moving in with me. Amy and Jason are getting married, now that they can afford it because of the trust fund. Their baby is due in May. I'm going to help them find a house nearby so we can all be together. Things will probably be a little rough between me and Amy for a while—she hasn't forgiven me for what I did to her cats, but at least she sees my point of view and understands why I did what I did."

"She'll forgive you, in time."

"I wouldn't have believed that before, but now I believe anything's possible. And I owe it all to you."

"You don't owe me anything, Mr. Clark."

"God bless you, Mrs. Mohr. Merry Christmas."

Chapter Thirty: The Gold House Museum

"**I** think we've made my mother the happiest woman on the planet," Sue said as she handed Ellen the "Now Open" sign to put in the yard at the Gold House. "She's so excited to be all settled in. I'm actually jealous. Her bathroom is nicer than mine."

Ellen took the sign and hammered it into the ground. "Well, she's the best person for the job. She already knows so much about all the old equipment. And when Amy and Jason passed on our offer, your mother was the next best option."

"And being right next-door to Millie will come in handy. They've become such good friends."

"An answer to one of your prayers, I know." Ellen said.

"I think the handsome male nurse my mom found for her sealed their friendship, don't you think?" Sue said with a laugh.

"I bet so. I still can't believe Millie agreed to that, though."

Tanya stepped down from the porch and joined them on the front lawn. "Looks good," she said of the sign. "I've got the lemonade poured and the cookies on platters. I think we're all set."

Ellen glanced at the time on her cell phone. "With ten minutes to spare. Shall we go inside?"

As they headed back toward the house, Sue asked Tanya, "Did the guys finish hanging all the paintings?"

"Dave said they got all that were in the back of Paul's van," Tanya said. "Was that all of them?"

"Those were the last of them," Ellen said.

Tanya led the way up the front steps.

The big pots of wisteria beside each column added a nice touch to the front porch, even though the flowers wouldn't bloom for another few months. The wreath Sue had made of silk orchids for the front door was also welcoming. But to Ellen, it wasn't until you were all the way inside the house and appreciating all the details at once that the enormity of what they'd accomplished actually hit you.

"Your paintings are amazing," Tanya said beside her. "Especially now that they're all framed and hung on the walls."

Paul was straightening the final painting on the living room wall. He climbed down from the ladder, noticed Ellen across the room, and winked.

"Look at all those faces," Sue said. "All these women are finally visible after being hidden away in these walls for decades."

"Bravo," Penelope Williams said from the front foyer. The president of the Conservation Society was the first member to arrive to their special grand opening. "That's all I can say. Bravo."

"Wait till you see the rest of it," Sue said. "We have the rooms upstairs fitted out with all the equipment, looking exactly as they would have in the asylum."

"People will finally get to see firsthand how these women were treated," Ellen said.

"And maybe seeing it will prevent something like this from ever happening again," Tanya said.

The End

Please enjoy the first chapter of the next book in the series, *The Case of the Abandoned Warehouse:*

Chapter One: La Quinta Tulsa

"What in the world is that?" Sue asked as she entered Ellen and Tanya's hotel room. Her full figure filled the entryway, where she pointed at the floor.

Ellen thought Sue looked surprisingly perky and refreshed, given what she'd been through the day before.

"Tanya's butterflies," Ellen said.

"Not butterflies." Tanya pushed her blonde hair behind her ears before she picked up the three-foot by three-foot dome-shaped net that sat on the carpet near the door. About two dozen tiny green cocoons clung to the underside of it. "Chrysalises. I didn't want to leave them behind, just in case they hatched."

"You brought them on the *train*?" Sue's brown hair brushed her shoulders as she bobbed her head in disbelief. "*Dave* couldn't let them out?"

"He's flying to D.C. tomorrow," Tanya said. "I couldn't have them trapped if they hatched while we were gone." Then she added. "And I really didn't want to miss it."

"I think it's pretty cool." Ellen hadn't thought so at first, especially after all the looks she'd had to endure from the other passengers on the train from San Antonio; but, she found herself bonding with the little chrysalises over the past few days, as if they were newborn puppies or kittens. And it had been...surprising.

"Well, then you better not pay too much attention to the windshield on your rental car," Sue said as she sat on the end of one of the double beds. "Tulsa has been swarmed with butterflies lately, and many of them have met an untimely death."

"Oh, stop." Tanya moved the net to the other side of the room, near the sliding glass doors to the balcony, which overlooked their spectacular view of the parking lot.

"Don't be crass, Sue," Ellen whispered.

It seemed to Ellen that Tanya looked thinner than usual and more fragile. It had been just over a year since Tanya's mother passed last September, and Tanya hadn't been able to shake off her depression. Ellen had begun taking antidepressants after her own mother had died last November, and she felt they were helping; but, Tanya wanted to avoid medication and was trying things like hatching butterflies and taking vitamins and drinking herbal tea.

In fact, Ellen had been worried Tanya would bail on her at the last minute and not attend Sue's daughter's wedding.

"What made you decide to hatch butterflies anyway, Tanya?" Sue asked.

"I was looking for something new to try, something fun."

"I could have saved you some trouble and taken you to that new Mexican food restaurant near our neighborhood. I hear they serve delicious margaritas," Sue said with a giggle.

Ellen frowned. She doubted Sue could understand the depth of Tanya's despair. Sue didn't belong to the Motherless Club. Sue didn't understand the loneliness that tugged at the heart of a motherless adult child.

"I'm surprised you're here early." Ellen slipped on her shoes and searched around the room for her purse. "Aren't you exhausted after the wedding?"

"Yes, but I'm also starving, and my hunger won out." Then she pointed at Ellen's black capris and emerald green top. "We could be twins today. We must be on the same wavelength."

"I guess so." Ellen laughed. Tanya was wearing a baby blue top with blue jeans.

"The wedding was beautiful, by the way." Tanya sat in the small chair near the desk to buckle on her sandals. "We didn't get a chance to talk to you much last night, but we enjoyed it."

"Yes. It was nicely done," Ellen said. "Is Tom flying back today?"

Sue shifted on the bed. "Yeah. He offered to fly with my mom so she wouldn't have to travel alone. I'm sure they've landed by now. And Lexi and Stephen are probably landing in Vancouver within the hour. Lexi called from the airport this morning to thank me for all I did."

"That was nice." Ellen found her purse and pulled the strap across her shoulder. "Especially considering how hard it was on you—having the wedding here in the groom's hometown instead of back home in San Antonio."

"Well, like I said before, her college friends are here," Sue said. "And my mother is our only family back in San Antonio. Tom's mother and brother live in Stillwater. It just made sense to have it here." Then Sue added, "It means a lot to me that you girls made the trip to be there."

"We wouldn't have missed it," Ellen said.

"Of course not." Tanya stood up and checked her reflection in the mirror over the desk.

"It's too bad Nolan couldn't make it," Sue said of Ellen's oldest son, in medical school at OSU in Oklahoma City.

"He wanted to, but he's an intern now, and his hours are crazy."

"You must be so proud of him," Sue said.

"And you must be so happy for Lexi," Ellen said.

"Yes, I am. But right now, I'm anxious for lunch. Are y'all ready to go?"

"Ready," Tanya said. "And after we hit the casino, Ellen has something interesting in mind for us."

Sue climbed to her feet. "Oh? What?"

"It's a surprise," Ellen said. "And don't worry. There will be plenty of margaritas to be had where we're going."

Thanks again for supporting me and my work. Your comments and reviews mean so much to me, and your reviews are especially important in advancing my career.

You can find free ebooks, and frequent giveaways, along with the next book in *The Mystery House Series*, on my website at http://www.evapohler.com.

Here's a list of all my books:

The Gatekeeper's Sons (#1)

The Gatekeeper's Challenge (#2)

The Gatekeeper's Daughter (#3)

The Gatekeeper's House (#4)

The Gatekeeper's Secret (#5)

The Gatekeeper's Promise (#6)

The Gatekeeper's Bride (#0)

Hypnos: A Gatekeeper's Spin-Off Series (#1)

32362965R00202

Made in the USA
San Bernardino, CA
13 April 2019